# Into Our Viewscreen Rose a Dazzling Ship . . . Lights Glowed Red, Blue, Yellow, White . . . *Star Empire!*

"What is the purpose of your mission?" Kirk demanded.

"That will be revealed only to your boarding party."

"We will not comply with terrorists," our captain said.

The young face on the viewscreen, a face whose nuances I thought I knew, paused for response. "We must speak in person, *Enterprise*. Please comply."

Captain Kirk gazed into that face as though the young man had just walked up and tweaked his nose. "Mr. Spock?" he invited.

Spock tilted his head. "Security. Place Lieutenant Piper under arrest. Charge: conspiracy with terrorists."

"Sir—no!"

Security yanked me away. . . .

# Look for STAR TREK Fiction from Pocket Books

# DREADNOUGHT!

## DIANE CAREY

# A STAR TREK®
## —NOVEL—

**POCKET BOOKS**

New York    London    Toronto    Sydney    Tokyo

An *Original* Publication of POCKET BOOKS

POCKET BOOKS, a division of Simon & Schuster Inc.
1230 Avenue of the Americas, New York, NY 10020

This book is published by Pocket Books, a division of
Simon & Schuster Inc., under exclusive license from
Paramount Pictures Corporation.

ISBN: 0-671-66500-6

First Pocket Books printing May 1986

15  14  13  12  11  10  9  8  7

POCKET and colophon are trademarks of
Simon & Schuster Inc.

STAR TREK is a Registered Trademark of
Paramount Pictures Corporation.

Printed in the U.S.A.

# AUTHOR'S NOTE

With thousands of words comprising various novels (published and not) under my belt, I finally had to admit I was destined to write a Star Trek® Novel. As a first-generation Trekker, I am one of the lucky ones who discovered Trek early on and have enjoyed it the longest. As with many primary disciples and new inductees alike, I'm reveling in its resurrection. It's like getting the last word, or the biggest we-told-you-so in recent history.

I thank my closest friends—Deb, Robin, Barb, Val, Mary Ann, Nicole, Brian, Mike, David—for support through many nonpublished years and for help on this particularly thrilling project. They've lent new meaning to the old phrase "I couldn't have done it without you." The Tycho fighter and Arco attack sled were designed by Brian Thomas, and other hardware are a recognizable amalgam of past Trek details which I enjoyed restructuring to my own purposes. The biggest thank-you of all, as usual, must go to my husband, Gregory Brodeur, who works with me on plotting, characterization, and anything else in the book-writing process, who edits everything before it ever gets out of the house, and who helps me form idea-seeds into beautiful, full-bodied books.

Don't look for me in church; I'm off studying Kolinahr. In case you hadn't noticed, Star Trek® is making us in its own image.

Come with me now to Star Fleet Academy and let's go through it all again, together. May I say, before we begin, that anything appearing familiar is purely intentional.

Diane Carey

# DREADNOUGHT!

# Chapter One

"ENEMY CRUISERS DEAD ahead!"

"How many, Lieutenant Broxon?"

"Four, Captain. Four."

"Communications, advise them of our situation."

"Aye. Captain Piper, they refuse to receive. Subspace hailing frequencies on reverse scramb—"

"Two more ships, ma'am, bearing point-zero-zero-five and point-zero-fifty. Entering spherical envelope . . . Captain, they're firing!"

"Raise shields!"

I already knew it was too late. The critical tactical error resulted in my being hurled backward into my command chair—not a place I felt worthy of. Only my better-than-average height kept me from sprawling onto the deck. Staggering up, I barked out the first order I could think of: "Fire at will! Helm, evasive action!"

Illya Galina turned to look at me, his faced limned with panic beneath a cap of sweat-caked blond hair. "Helm doesn't respond. Direct . . . direct hit in—"

Our main viewscreen glittered with a new blast. A

9

thought later, impact came, taking out the entire port side of the bridge and six bridge personnel with it. My hands shook as I dived forward to the mangled helm, running my fingers over deadened switches, desperate to find even one that would tell me my ship was still with me. The screen dimmed again as the blast dissipated, leaving only the crackling vista of Romulan starships maneuvering for the kill. "Dispatch mayday! Divert helm to auxiliary control."

"Aye—ma'am, auxiliary cont—" Communications Officer Page choked, and it was the first time I realized there was smoke billowing from the upper space sensor platform. He recovered and gasped, "Auxiliary cannot connect. Can't override damage to main circuitry."

"Engineering! Damage report." I managed to brush my hair out of my face and vowed it would be the last time I went without a haircut before a voyage. Something within me didn't allow the thought to penetrate that this might be my last voyage. It very well might be, but they were *not* taking my ship.

The intercom crackled with the comfortingly deep voice of Chief Engineer Silayna. *"Impulse drive down. One warp drive nacelle severely damaged, but marginally operable. Shields fading. Forward shields gone entirely. Took two direct hits to main engine room and we're trying to—"*

"Do I have phasers?"

*"—disengage primary pow—"* The transmission snapped and died.

"Silayna! Brian, I need phasers!" I grasped at controls that were hot and sparking, vaulting over the fallen bodies of my bridge crew, and with a stab of horror came the realization that I was alone, alone on the bridge of a starship. My crew was dead or dying. My ship was much the same. I hurdled the forms of people I needed badly now, begging and cajoling the instruments to resurrect themselves enough to save the ship. None would. Even if the main computer was still working, most of the connections had been severed, rendering useless any order I might think of. I shoved Illya's body away, hammering at the subspace frequency override. "Mayday! Mayday! This is Captain Piper, Federation Starship *Liberty*. We are surrounded by Romulan vessels. Engaging self-destruct mode; repeat, engaging self-destruct—"

My voice jammed in my throat. As I had bumped the empty chair at the navigational console, I felt the bulge of a communicator at my hip. Evidently I had forgotten to turn it over to the clerk after the last landing party excursion. Funny . . . that wasn't like me. I didn't like anything that marred my freedom of movement. Pausing only a moment, feeling the smoke sting my eyes when I failed to blink, I caught at the communicator until it fell into my hands and desperately tuned it to computer override, thanking providence that I had bothered to study the nuances of direct tie-in. It was a radical, almost terroristic procedure, frowned upon to a point where hardly anyone knew about it. My own awareness came only from a latent addiction to the short stories of Nal Eiili of Proxima II, which were a series of computer crime mysteries for teenagers. Certainly I had no idea whether such a fictional marriage between auxiliary computer and hand communicator would actually work, and certainly I was going to die trying it.

"Computer! Override tie-in, command authorization code T-Rescue. Emergency!" I waited. There was a muted percussion of clicks beneath the demolished library console. "Implement override. Emergency." My voice cracked.

Another blast took out the defense subsystems monitor. Beyond the mangled station I could see the wing of a Romulan bird of prey gliding past our starboard. I was thrown to my side on the upper walkway, but I managed to keep hold of the communicator and some of my wits. Smoke blinded me now and I was choking. There was no response from the computer. My ploy was failing. Still, possibly to stave off the inevitability of mental collapse, I continued to gasp the override directive. "Code T-Rescue, command authorization, emer—"

*"Working. Specify."*

Damn! At least something was going to happen. "Computer, link auxiliary warp drive controls. Critical adversity catalog number eight-eight-one, tape deck C-one-A. Evasive action. Implement!"

*"Working. Sensors indicate enemy vessels at all vector points."*

"Acknowledged. Do we have phasers?"

*"Affirmative. One-half potency on secondary batteries."*

"Bleed off impulse power batteries and divert to phasers. Pinpoint nearest enemy vessel's engineering section, aim, and fire!" Ridiculous. Yelling at the computer wasn't going to help. "Implement evasive action one-four-zero degrees declination plane." I felt the commands shudder through the crippled equipment, jumping damaged connections, inventing frequencies, shortcutting schematics that were popping on and off the last three viewing screens still providing information. Shredded circuitry was knitting wherever it could find power, threading together and tapping other computers to draw power back to *Liberty*.

*Other computers* . . . a distant signal flickered in my mind. *Other* . . .

I shook off the temptation to think, feeling in my veins the pulsing blood of my remaining crew below-decks, separated from me, their life force joining with mine in a surge of survival instinct. *They were not taking my ship*.

"You're not taking this ship!" I shouted at the fizzing shape of another Romulan vessel as it veered in and fired. The blast shook the bridge. I could feel the entire primary hull of *Liberty* shifting away from the engineering hull, feel the nacelles cutting loose, the shields finally falling as the last of the power was tapped by my loyal computer as it struggled to implement my last order.

My last order.

The very last.

The hull shuddered under me and myriad voices began to penetrate the bulkheads.

Suddenly everything stopped. Everything. The noises all went away—the hum of machinery and computer circuits ceased. Only the voices remained.

"What the hell—" someone said, like a ghost calling from another dimension.

I closed my eyes. The voices began to solidify behind the walls. "Overload! Access lights, go to emergency power. Goddamn insane cadet!"

"Auxiliary power, where's the juice?"

"Whole main simulator's down."

"That's not possible."

"It's a junction overload. She made the system try to fight itself."

13

"Harrison, what's taking so long? Oh—'scuse me, Captain."

"Tech crew, report to simulator A on the double."

"Where's Lieutenant Selok? Maybe he can talk to it."

The universe began to subdivide. Slowly I remembered: I was no different from anybody else. They'd done it to me, just as I'd heard they would. Not only had I failed, but I'd destroyed the simulator in the process. I had never heard of that happening before. So why did it have to happen to me?

Voices buzzed. They were talking about me. I heard my name spinning like a dervish through the corridor.

"All right. That's enough. Quite enough."

There was a whirling sensation that nearly threw me flat. The hum of ventilators rose. The smoke began to clear. I lay on my side, blinking into a maze of lights and humanoid shapes. I felt violated.

"Quite enough, Mister Piper. Please relax."

Swallowing was an effort, but I did manage to get to my feet from my kneeling position on the upper deck before Commander Josephson approached me. Behind him, foggy forms of Star Fleet upper-echelon personnel stood soberly watching me. To my left, Illya Galina was crawling out from beneath part of his control panel, staring at me with something that might have been astonishment. Outside the simulation chamber, technicians were scrambling to disengage the simulation computer from all the other computers in the immediate area. Only then did I realize what I had done.

"Rather a unique display, Lieutenant," the Commander grumbled, his black eyes and swarthy complexion obscured by the clearing smoke. He stopped in his advance to let two "dead" members of the bridge crew rise and step aside. There were coughs and sneezes all around, and a general feeling of discomfort. "Tell me . . . at which point did you decide there was no *Kobayashi Maru?*"

I cleared my throat and packed back my hair in a gesture that was too feminine, suddenly aware that my nonregulation backcombs had failed to keep the layered, honey-brown strands out of my face. "It had to be a trap. There was no other possibility."

"At which *point*."

"When the second contingent of enemy vessels appeared, sir. At that point it became clear there were too many of them for a simple border patrol. So many ships would not have allowed a distress call to penetrate the neutral zone."

"Your estimation of your performance?" Josephson repressed the quirkish grin he was known for.

"Inadequate, sir."

"Why?"

"I raised shields too late. I failed to order weapons armed upon entry into the neutral zone. I also should have dispatched a communiqué to Star Fleet Command that I was about to breach the Organian accord by attempting rescue of *Kobayashi Maru*. By failing to do so, I prevented any possibility of *Liberty*'s being rescued if it was indeed a trap."

He had a habit of tilting his head to favor his nearly deaf left ear. "All true. Final score?"

"Grade B midrange." I winced at giving myself such a high score. New shame engulfed me.

He raised his head, looking out into the main training depot beyond the shattered walls of the simulation chamber. "Are those systems clearing yet?"

"Getting there, Commander," a technician called. "It's a mess."

Josephson turned to me. "You caused quite a hullabaloo with the base computers."

I remained silent. There was nothing I could say.

"Lieutenant," he began slowly, "do you realize you have just come closer than any command-line cadet to actually checkmating the no-win scenario?"

Not knowing if it was a reprimand or a compliment, I gulped, "No, sir."

"Report to debriefing at two hundred hours. And Lieutenant . . . your assignment has just been changed. You won't be reporting to the *Magellan*."

"Sir?" I had turned away, but this stopped me. Not report to Captain Flynn? The sweat that had collected on my forehead seeped into the furrows of a confused expression. Had I done so badly that they would prevent my serving on a Galaxy-class ship? "Commander?"

He hadn't intended to tell me, yet it seemed he was itching to. I couldn't imagine Commander Josephson capable of petty arrogance, but all it took was this small prodding to make him turn back to me. "I've had a direct request, just now. You're to report to Docking Bay 12 at eight hundred thirty hours. You've been assigned to Captain Kirk."

I stared at him, my eyes stinging. This time, there was no smoke.

*Enterprise!*

# Chapter Two

BRIAN SILAYNA FOUND me in my quarters, staring at the wall. When I saw him, still wearing his standard Engineering Division jumpsuit in the familiar red of Star Fleet services, I stumbled into his arms and held him more tightly than I ever had, even at more intimate times. Together we hid in the threshold's shadow.

"They reassigned you," he said, not moving.

"Brian, they put me on *Enterprise!* They said I was asked for."

"Are you happy about it?"

I pulled away, knowing what he was really asking. I was nearly as tall as he was, tall enough to look straight into his dark eyes. "Yes."

His expression twitched. We'd been lovers for over a year. He knew what the answer meant.

I went on. "But I don't understand it."

"What do you mean?"

"I failed. I made tactical errors every step of the way. I lost the ship."

"Piper, everybody loses the ship. That's the purpose behind the *Kobayashi Maru* test. Even if you made the right decisions, the people around you are obligated to make sure every alternative fails. It was the same when I took the test. Except . . ." He put space between us, pensively fingering the mementos on my dresser and the open duffel bag I had been distractedly packing.

"Except?"

"Except that I didn't turn the whole starbase on its ear like you did."

Humiliated, I dropped onto my bed and put my back to him. "You're exaggerating."

"The hell I am. You set a record. There's only been one person ever to beat the no-win test, and he cheated."

"Who?"

"The same person who was in the observation room with Josephson. The same man who asked to put you on Star Fleet's sweetheart."

"Captain . . ."

"Kirk. Yes."

He sat next to me, a warm magnetic presence against my arm, evidently giving up trying to convince me that I had done something good. "I have to report to Captain Flynn at nine hundred hours. It won't be easy to go alone."

Clasping my hands between my knees, I waited until the knot in my throat dissolved before trying to speak. Brian was alluding, with his tone, to plans we'd made together, dreams we'd built, possible futures. "We've been lovers, Brian, and I do love you. Even more significantly, we've been friends. I cherish that. But if I learned anything from that test, I learned not to love too dearly anyone on my ship." With a shuddering breath I went on. "I can't tell you how strong the impulse was to leave the bridge and run to find you when I thought the engineering section had been hit. My mind was with you, with us, when the Romulans fired on *Liberty*. It curtailed my deductive reasoning. I had to force myself to think clearly, and I can't afford that. It's fatal to give in to love. I understand now why the Vulcans are so efficient, and why they survive. *Enterprise* will be better for me than serving on *Magellan* with a person I love."

Silence fell in my cabin, descending like a crystal-cloud I saw once on Proxima Beta. It felt just that heavy. "I don't mean to hurt you."

He sighed. "I would be hurt if anyone else told me this. You really intend to command, don't you, Piper?"

"If I'm good enough," I said. "But only if I'm good enough."

"You're always too hard on yourself."

"No I'm not."

"Yes you are."

"Command has to be." I stopped with that sharp remark, realizing I was on the verge of insulting him. He would make a fine assistant engineer on *Magellan*, and someday Brian would make an excellent chief engineer—I had no doubt of it. If he was lacking in any skill, his steadiness of character would make up for it. But he would never make an officer of the line. He didn't have the drive.

Yet, who was I to say? I compared myself to everyone and everyone to myself, always fighting to be an iota better, faster, that extra dimension more worthy than anyone around me. I didn't care what I had done to the computer system. I could deal with the whispers and rumors and the nicknames. I couldn't deal with having lost my ship.

Secretly I was angry with Brian for not telling me what to expect during *Kobayashi Maru,* though the secrecy in which the test was shrouded wasn't his fault. It might have been a streak of vindication or sniggering cruelty that kept upperclassmen from divulging the horrors of no-win, even secreting away the name of the ship that would make the fake distress call, but it was Star Fleet Academy tradition never to tip anyone's hand. I now understood that going into the test cold was the only way.

Brian put his arms around me. In friendship, but refusing love, I returned the embrace. "I'll miss you," he whispered simply. *"Enterprise*'s gain is my loss. I guess it's better than losing out to some smooth-talking midshipman. I love you, Piper."

My fingers found his hair. "We're too close," I warned. "We'll always be friends . . . that's good love too."

The soft beep of my intercom alarm seemed loud as a red alert klaxon. Dazedly I ordered it off.

"Eight hundred hours."

"Yes."

"Docking Bay 12 is waiting."

"Yes."

I had never been to Earth before graduating into command school. It was a nice enough planet, very blue and watery, and its atmosphere had a propensity for cumulus clouds, but it wasn't as consistently beautiful as Proxima Beta. But then, home is always more beautiful to those who leave with the idea of seldom returning. I kept a photoslide tape of Proxima's lush mossy landscape and dripping lepidodendron trees— moss was our most tenacious perennial—and in times of mental turmoil I would scan the collection, drugging myself with the bathed greens of the humid emerald planet that had spawned me. Meeting more and more Terrans now, here on our ancestral rocks, I often wondered how we had adapted to so many varieties of climate. Earth had more kinds of air than any place I knew of, and humans could breath them all. Being descended from humans who had colonized and adapted to Proxima made most of Earth uncomfortable for me. Though the heat of coastal California was easier to deal with than most localities on the planet, I couldn't get used to the wind. Every time I opened my mouth to breathe, some capricious little gust would steal my breath and leave me gasping. And I could never, *never* get used to that garish yellow sun.

I was quivering with anticipation as the shuttle arched out over the shimmer of Puget Sound, baring to me and the other passengers the volcanic topography that gave the area its flavor. Character. Like Brian.

I vowed that would be my last thought of him, and turned my mind to sifting out all the tidbits of near-legend that had come my way about the majestic *Enterprise* and her daring who's-who of officers. No ship had explored as far, encountered as much, endured as much as this starship, and no crew had survived so long under such a roster of impossible situations. Oh, yes, we'd heard plenty about these people. I'd heard and marveled at the stories like every other plebe, but, never expecting to find myself

21

serving on board her, I'd eventually discarded these bits of information. Now I had to gather them once again, force my mind to remember. It was my duty.

There she was. The buttresses of the docking bay opened before us as the shuttle maneuvered for final approach to *Enterprise*. Everyone in the shuttle was flashing looks at each other, trying to figure out which of us was to board the starship. Not me, though. I knew who it was.

I was looking at *her*.

She didn't look like a ship that had been from hell to Klingon and back, several times. She gleamed and glowed in the eternal night like a star instead of a starship. Her newly painted Fleet insignia and call letters stood out as though they had substance, her warp engine nacelles fanning out across the universe as though they knew its secrets. Vast, it was vast . . . shockingly bigger than I ever guessed a starship could be. Amazement shunted through me that mankind, any race, could engineer and actually build such a thing of power and grace. And I was going to board her. I was going to serve her. More than anything else, she appeared as a giant constellation of a winged horse, reared and prancing, refusing to look into the eyes of weak beings who had merely created her; life belonged to *Enterprise,* and she was in command of it.

When I arrived at the cabin assigned to me by the duty officer, I found precious few clues as to the habits of my suitemates. There were two cabins joined by a common head; my cabin had three bunks in typically austere Star Fleet style, and in deference to the unknowns who already called this home I found a noncommittal place to dump my gear. It was quiet and dim in here compared to the bustle going on all over the ship. Every transporter was busily rematerializing crewpeople from the surface. Not knowing whether the rush to board was usual, I took it as such and minded my own business. There was, though, a distended air of excitement. Probably just me. After all . . . *Enterprise*.

I stood in the middle of the cabin, feeling out of place and seeking out signals about those I was living with. Boldness took over when I spied a sealed canister on one of the vanities. That quarter had a few personal items around it: a 3-D of grinning people, all blond, obviously related to each other, was perched next to a discarded hand towel and a hairbrush. The lid of the canister came off easily—

And went right back on. We had insect life on Proxima, and pets too, but nothing like the writhing crayfishy half-snakes in there. I shuddered. To each its own.

The canister clunked back onto the vanity to the sibilance of the door opening. I turned, and it took every discipline I knew to bury the spontaneous gasp in my throat.

The Gorn was tall, much taller than I and too tall for the cabin portal, so she was stooping to come in, curving her reptilian spine and dipping the massive headful of undeniably carnivorous teeth. Her tyrannosauric appearance and glittering sapphire eyes gave her an aura of attack stance. Her skin was crimson, evidently to imitate the color of Star Fleet issue. She was wearing a Gorn tunic emblazoned with Fleet insignia and the cobra crest of Cestus System. I smiled. It couldn't hurt.

"I'm Piper. We're roommates, I guess."

The Gorn hissed, moved into the room, stood to full

height, and began touching me. I thought I was being searched, but soon it became evident she was introducing herself to me. Clawed pads rippled up and down my legs, and I raised my arms to let her explore.

Another voice sounded from the door, obviously human and very welcome. "Oh, y'all're here. Good." A sloppy young second lieutenant strode in with a medical officer directly behind him. He was blessed with a perpetually friendly face, a nose slightly crooked from a break long-healed, average height and hair, and nice eyes. His companion might or might not have been of Earth. "You must be Piper. I'm Judd Sandage, Starship services. I'm in charge of the officers' mess, so watch out what you eat. Y'all can call me Scanner. Everbody does, 'cuz I got some great dream of working in the sensory. Too bad about triple bunkin', ain't it? They got decks five and eight closed down for bulkhead repairs, so even the officers are sharing." He squinted as though he'd just thought of something. "Y'know, I hope you speak English."

I laughed. "Yes, I do, Scanner."

"Good," he drawled. "And you don't mind the unisex setup."

"I asked for it."

"Glad to hear it. It don't pay to be shy on a starship." He waved a hand. "This here is Dr. Merete AndrusTaurus, and the one checkin' you out is Telosirizharcrede of Cestus Eliar. We know it as Wren's Planet. You know . . . Cestus Seven?"

"Oh!" I blurted, and frightened Telosirizharcrede with my enthusiasm. She jolted away, hissing, but I snatched her paw and smiled away both our embarrassments. "Is she one of the first?"

"*The* first. They just started bilingual training for

24

Eliarn cadets. Osira is the Gorn ambassador's daughter."

"Ah, so diplomatic immunity."

"Yeah, she sideswiped a shipload of red tape."

I was still holding Osira's hand—paw—and with a look I hoped was as friendly on Wren's Planet as it was on Proxima, I replaced her pads on my leg and she continued scouring me.

"Where are you from?" the medical officer asked. She was a stocky woman, plantinum haired and with slightly upturned eyes that hinted at alien cells in Terran bloodlines.

"Proxima Beta."

"That's why you're tall."

"I thought I was, till I met Osira."

. Dr. AndrusTaurus said, "We're system-mates. I'm from Earth Outpost Walter Twelve. I did biomorphology training on Proxima Alpha. What section are you assigned to?"

"A nice quiet place in Environmental Control. They tell me it's temporary. I'm a captaincy candidate, so they'll be moving me around a lot."

"One of *them,*" Scanner whistled, rolling his eyes. "Probably chompin' to get to the bridge."

"Not too soon. I'm still reeling from finding myself on this ship instead of *Magellan.*"

"Know anything about her?" Merete asked.

"I know about the officers," I said shrugging, "and the usual tall tales. Same as everybody."

Scanner gestured to an empty bunk. "All yours. You'd best stay belowdecks till you get used to everything."

I sat down, testing the mattress for comfort. There wasn't much. They deliberately made them that way to keep us from sleeping too much, I had always thought. "I intend to. Sure, I want bridge duty, but not till I warm up to the ship and get to know her."

"Good sense." Scanner leaned against the vanity and pocketed his hands. I got a mental vision of a plow reposing next to him. His demeanor defied the stiff military line of his uniform, making it seem more like grubby overalls. He was the kind of person that couldn't be decorated at any cost. "What's your first name?"

"Piper." The look on his face made me explain. "Proxima was just colonized four generations ago, so we're all one family. We have no use for clan identification, so we each have one name."

"You don't have another one, like the Vulcans?"

"Just Piper."

"Hey, I'm country. I can live with it. You'll have to get squared away later. Something's up and we're supposed to report to stations in forty minutes, prepared for battlestations."

"Battlestations? A drill?"

"Nope, no drill. Right, Merete?"

She shook her head. "We don't know what it is. Usually, with Captain Kirk, that means he doesn't know the whole story either. He's pretty good about letting the crew know what's going on. He figures we should, since we risk our lives here."

"When are we leaving?"

"Leaving?" Scanner blasted. "Girl, we warped out of the Sol System twenty minutes ago!"

"What? I didn't feel anything!"

"That's *Enterprise*. Smo-o-o-th."

Merete got up from where she had been lounging on

her bunk. "They received a special dispatch from Star Fleet Command about an hour and a half ago. I was in Sickbay when the Captain buzzed Dr. McCoy about it. He called a senior officers' meeting, and ten minutes later the whole shore leave roster was cancelled and here we are."

"I had to bump up dinner a half hour. We'll have to hustle if we want to get some grub," Scanner said.

Osira hissed something, drawing attention back to herself, and Scanner nodded an answer. On an inspiration he said, "Sound, Osira. Let her hear your voice."

Telosirizharcrede parted her maw, but her voice never reached the necessary decibels for me to hear it.

The door opened. Glowing corridor lights eclipsed a narrow form and enhanced the dimness where we were standing. We all looked but no one moved, held by the coronaed shape in the doorway. Then Scanner ordered the lighting to intensify. We blinked, and the entity at the door sharpened into full color. He was wearing a standard gold and black uniform with lieutenant's bars, yet he wore it more like a ceremonial tunic than military issue. He moved gracefully, more so than most Vulcans, his youthful features already cultivating the lionic grandeur typical of older Vulcans, yet it was plateaus deeper with resentment and distance. He was fairer than most Vulcans I knew, with lighter eyes and hair like burnished brass.

He came into the room. His amber eyes refused all but the most fleeting contact with us. Probably it was only bureaucratic error that quartered a Vulcan with others, but it was telling on him. He went straight to his area, pausing only when he saw me. We exchanged a bald glare; his dry lips parted, then sealed without a sound. His expression changed, if only to become more recessed, but the civilized eyes narrowed a thought.

Scanner looked at me, then at the Vulcan. "I'm plain croakin' for lack of sustenance. Come on with me, 'sira. How 'bout you, Piper?"

"I'll go," Merete injected, and I nodded to her in thanks, though not accepting. "But I want to wash up first," she continued without a break. She started toward the head, following Scanner and Osira as they went through to their own cabin, Scanner yapping away in his Kentucky drawl about something delightfully insignificant.

When the portals between the cabins closed, I was alone with the Vulcan. I might as well have just been alone.

He was sitting at his desk, facing away from me. His shoulders were squared. He was not meditating. I went toward him.

"Sarda," I began, fully planning to come up with more to say.

His voice was a cutting edge. "There is no reason for us to intermingle. We have a propensity for mutual abrasion."

"And I'm tired of it." I forced myself into his periphery. "Is it so against *Kolinahr* to forgive?"

He turned to me—a surprise—and stood up, allowing me to read the control in his eyes. "Our history is an unfortunate one. However, nothing has changed. Forgiveness is a social enigma which does not alter circumstances."

"You deny forgiveness, yet you cower to bitterness. If emotion is foreign to you, how can you hate me so?" *I can wield logic too.*

28

It hit home. The flaw in his Vulcan façade flickered. After a moment he regained control. "I . . . do not hate you, Piper," he said, but he was using my name as a title, a rank, not as a name. The sound of it that way was galling. "I simply see no advantage to our speaking."

This was the first time in nearly an Earth-standard year that Sarda had spoken to me at all. I began to prefer the silence.

The lids dropped over my eyes, shutting out the sight of a man whose reputation my ignorance had spoiled, shutting in the knife-edged pain of knowing I had caused him to be ostracized by others of his kind at Star Fleet. To top it all off, he had to bear the degradation of bunking with me, especially when a Vulcan's most prized possessions are his solitude and privacy.

"As you wish," I said, forcing a strength I didn't feel.

Sarda walked away, directionless, silent.

"Remember," I added, "you do yourself and Star Fleet a disservice by denying your talent. I never meant to hurt you, Sarda. I thought you wanted—"

"There is no profit in repeating that which we both recall. Your interference was understandable, yet not within your right."

"And it cost you dearly, I realize that. I can't mend it. I can only apologize."

"Apology, like forgiveness, is peculiar to races enslaved by emotion. Vulcans are not among them. Since the error in lodging will be rectified soon, it will be mutually beneficial for you and me to avoid any excess contact. This is a large ship. I shall attempt to keep most of it between us."

"Sarda . . ."

"Good afternoon."


There was a little scratch on the door, and Scanner leaned in.

"Come," I offered limply.

"All clear?" He led the others in. Sarda had gone.

I nodded. "Thanks for doing that."

"You an' Sarda got a past, eh?"

"Not a nice one. Well . . . it *was* nice, once. But that's done with and can't be helped."

"Hm. Sorry to hear it." I was grateful to him for letting the matter drop. "Ready to go eat?"

"I suppose."

"It'll do you good," Merete decided. "Everybody needs time to get acclimated. Even captaincy candidates."

The ache behind my eyes got dull and throbbed. "All I want right now is to get lost in anonymity for a while. A crowded ship's mess hall sounds perfect."

We headed toward the door, but never made it. The intercom signals shattered our peace.

*"Lieutenant Piper to the bridge, immediately; Lieutenant Piper report to the bridge!"*

# Chapter Three

THE DOORS OF the bridge access turbolift slid open before me. My hair was tied up, my uniform pleat-perfect, my spine reed straight, and nothing but dignity glowed on my face as I strode confidently onto the bridge of the *Enterprise,* surrounded by my impressed superiors.

Well, that was a nice dream. Too bad it didn't happen that way.

Fact was, I stumbled out of the lift, hair flying in a wavy mass of light brown, my breath ragged from running the corridors, my mind clattering with questions and phobias. Only when I was hit full in the face by their uniforms did I remember I was still wearing my black zip-front jumpsuit. The hooded one with the flared legs and short wing sleeves. The one that *wasn't* regulation. The one that showed off too much of my figure, not enough of my efficiency, and nothing of my rank.

Momentum propelled me into the handrail. Hadn't even seen it.

"Oh . . . sorry," I murmured, rudely staring at the

arresting presence opposite me on the walkway. I thought of Sarda as I stared.

This wasn't Sarda.

I knew several Vulcans, but he was the most renowned. Even more grand than the rare holos I'd seen of him, his face was a catalog of experiences, even of emotions. The elegiac calm behind his lack of expression told of great hidden learning, nothing like the hauteur of other Vulcans. His eyes, like polished nitaglase, held a warmth equal to the restraint and staggering intellect. The smugness of my Vulcan fellowclassmen was strikingly absent in him. I didn't miss it.

*Commander Spock. I wonder if he'll ever speak to me.*

Everyone on the bridge seemed tall as I stood panting in front of them. It was a cruel illusion, since I was used to looking straight across or down at most people. The shortest person was Captain Kirk, but it took me awhile to notice that, because it was he who was the nucleus of the bridge. If I hadn't known better, I'd have guessed he was half Vulcan. He had the pride, the sturdiness, the same penetrating gaze as his companion, but he was also a little casual, a little cocky as he scanned me.

He gestured and said, "Down here, Lieutenant."

I blinked. Was that his voice? It was so soft!

Numb, I moved toward him. *Damn it, I'm trembling.*

I noticed the bridge crew, but only subliminally. They were an impressive collection of high-rankers, each with a reputation of his or her own, but I was dull to their legendary impact as I stiffly lowered myself down the access steps, concentrating only on not falling flat on my face.

"Lieutenant," the Captain began, hazel eyes clasping mine, "What do you know about the *Star Empire?*"

I did my best not to shrug. "Nothing, sir. Should I?"

He turned his head, still looking at me, and paced a few steps. "I asked you first."

A swallow did nothing for the dryness in my throat. "Sir, I . . . don't understand what you want. I've never heard of a starship called *Star Empire*. There isn't one."

"There is." Mr. Spock glided into motion, joining us near the command chair. "The ship is a prototype, the only one of her kind. Construction was recently completed at Star Fleet Headquarters. It is a thoroughly military machine, devoid of any luxuries typical of a patrol starship, with a usual complement of five hundred crewpersons."

Silence dropped on the bridge.

*Five* hundred . . .

"Lieutenant," Kirk prodded.

I jolted out of the hypnotism of Spock's voice. "How can that be? I just spent a year at Command Central. You can't hide an entire starship."

"You underestimate Command Intelligence, Lieutenant," Spock droned.

"But why? What purpose?"

"Exactly my question," Kirk said. "You almost destroyed the simulation computers with your communicator. Very innovative, but where did you learn such a ploy?"

Great. All I needed was to have to tell him I got it from reading children's stories. This time I did shrug. "Just happened to have read about the theory behind it, sir."

"Do you just happen to be aware of that technique's use by terrorists?"

"Yes, sir." Sure. Of course I was. It never occurred to me to lie.

A strange intimacy overtook our conversation as I locked eyes with him, seeking symbiosis that would help us understand one another. I lowered my voice as though he and I were alone. "What's it all about? And why am I here?"

"I was hoping you could tell me what your biocode is doing on an advance signal from *Star Empire*."

*"My* code? It has to be a mistake."

He paused for a leisurely sigh. "Uhura, please verify the coding."

The stunning black woman danced large hands over her board. "Biocode transmission, identify." She listened, then recited, "Code blood type O-positive, bone marrow D-hypercore, EEG catalog Z-four-twenty, indices ten and eleven. That's . . ." Her glance melted me. "Definitely Lieutenant Piper, sir."

"You're the only one who can clear that message when we receive it," Kirk fired, deliberately stealing my time to think. "I want to know why."

Breath came and went in a lump. I started to say something, stopped, squeezed my fists tight, then started again. "A message from a new starship," I muttered. I felt my eyes narrowing, a habit I had when I was trying to knit together a puzzle without enough pieces. "Why . . . don't we go back to Command Central and ask them?"

"They don't know."

"Who does know?"

"Only the insurgents who stole *Star Empire*."

"Stole it! A starship?"

"The only starship of its kind. We've been ordered to effect pursuit and dispatch the thieves. The confusing part is this advance biocode, telling us where *Star Empire* will be waiting for us. Why would they tip their hand, and why to you?"

"Evidently," Spock interrupted, "they wish to talk, and evidently they want the Lieutenant to do the listening."

"I can't imagine why," I said. "Sir, I don't know what to tell you. Believe me, Captain, if I knew . . ."

"That's exactly what you're going to do. You're going to *know*. Spock, summon my officers to the briefing room. Lieutenant Piper, come with me."

"*Star Empire* is a prototype MK-X Class One Federation dreadnought. As you can see on your monitors, it is a massive ship, roughly thirty percent heavier in deadweight tonnage than standard starships. There are three warp drive nacelles, the third mounted high on the rear on the primary hull. That hull is fifteen decks thick. Its construction was ordered by the Admiralty two solar years ago, during a peak uprising and series of border skirmishes with the Klingons during which the Klingon hierarchy was undergoing a purge. The ship was only recently completed, under the supervision of Vice-Admiral Vaughan Rittenhouse, who has guarded the project since its inception. *Star Empire* is capable of attaining a maximum burst speed three warp factors faster than *Enterprise,* carries five dual-mount phaser banks, four banks of photon torpedoes, triple shielding, and a full battery of state-of-the-art weaponry. We are severely outclassed."

Mr. Spock's final punctuation added gravity to his

monologue. I looked around, shyly moving only my eyes, trying to see the reactions around me. The briefing room was brimming with flag officers—most of the bridge crew was here, as were Dr. McCoy, saucily lounging in his seat and scraping the table with his fingernails, and Chief Engineer Scott, whose texts I'd heard Brian quote so often. Montgomery Scott wasn't at all the person I'd expected. First of all, he spoke with this fabulous trill I'd never heard before and I couldn't begin to guess which planet he hailed from. His dark hair had threads of silver, accented by a charcoaly moustache and a twinkle in a pair of hematite eyes. He watched the explanation and the interaction of his colleagues with a recessed scrutiny, as though he was delighted to be out of the limelight but quite ready to jump under it if necessary. Engineering, judging by the way he watched *Star Empire*'s complex schematics 3-D their way across the viewscreens, was less a career to him than it was pure religion.

And Sarda—he was here too. His wish to keep most of the ship between us was dead aborning. He stood behind his superior officer and never looked at me once. Apparently he had been promoted to the position of second officer of weapons engineering and design. I groaned mentally, remembering our past.

"Give the details of today's events, please, Mr. Spock," the Captain requested.

"Very well, sir. At fifteen hundred hours this afternoon, the *Star Empire* was piloted out of spacedock by persons of unknown identity, who apparently gained clearance through some form of high-style intelligence espionage. It was an exceptional accomplishment, considering the security cloaking the project. We can only assume the insurgents perpetrating such a feat were, and are, operating from within Star Fleet."

Reaction fogged through the room, taking various forms.

"A military coup?" Dr. McCoy blustered. "That doesn't make sense, Spock."

"It is only one of a series of logical possibilities, Doctor. However, it is the most reasonable, based on available data. Shortly before *Star Empire* warped out of the system, Star Fleet Command received a Code Zero priority comsync with Lieutenant Piper's biocode, specifying where *Enterprise* could rendezvous with the dreadnought. We can only assume they will announce their demands to us at that time."

"Thank you, Spock." Kirk turned to us as the computer viewscreens went blue and awaited further orders. "Federation Destroyer *Pompeii* will be joining us at the rendezvous point, bringing Vice-Admiral Rittenhouse with it."

"Unprecedented," Spock suggested.

"It *is* his baby," Kirk said. "If it was *Enterprise* . . ."

"You'd be chasing off after it with your boots unpolished and all your swords unsheathed," McCoy busted in. "I don't like the way this sounds, Jim. It smacks of rebellion."

"We won't jump to that conclusion yet, Bones."

"An' I'm not too crazy about the idea of taking potshots at a doomsday weapon with five phaser banks and triple shielding either."

Only now did Mr. Scott speak up, giving a sage tilt to his head. "He's got a point there, sir."

"Go ahead, Scotty."

He took a breath. "Anyone who could mastermind the theft of such a project is no petty adversary." Oh, I loved those funny Rs. "I cannae say I'd like *Enterprise* to be the test target of a war machine guided by people who know the inner workings of Star Fleet. I suggest a slow approach and some distance till we figger out wha' we're up against."

"I see." Kirk scanned the faces around him, and I swore, despite the circumstances, that I saw a not-smiling smile. "Mr. Spock, I see something hovering around you. Comments?"

Spock folded his arms and assimilated his opinion. "Astute, Captain. I must agree with Mr. Scott. The dreadnought is a purely military contrivance, devoid of labs, rec decks, or any facility that might distract from a given purpose. As such, there is no chance of our emerging victorious against her in conventional combat."

"Then," Kirk announced, "we'll have to be unconventional."

McCoy drawled, "Again?" All eyes turned to him, so he pushed on with opinions that might otherwise have remained unvoiced. "This all smells fishy to me, Jim," he complained. "A superstarship pilfered by people we assume are terrorists or spies, but we know they're Federation personnel. We don't know why they took it. Are they going to sell it to the Klingons? Are they going to turn on us? Are they going to hold the galaxy hostage? So the question arises; do we fight and hope for a show of strength against a vessel that outguns us four to one, or do we dangle that sugar cube you keep in your back pocket and hope they nibble?"

"Make your point, Bones," Kirk said.

"My point is the phenomenon of coincidence. They just *happen* to steal a starship on the very day we sail into spacedock, when we just *happen* to be the only heavy cruiser in the sector, when we just *happen* to be available for in-space trainee evaluations. For the first time in a solar year, Captain James Kirk is home and they know it. Or did they assume Rittenhouse would use *Enterprise* as his flagship? Is it *Enterprise?* Or is it you, Jim? Or is it all just coincidence? Spock, aren't you the man who doesn't believe in coincidences?"

Mr. Spock inhaled, sounding drily annoyed. "Doctor McCoy, your homiletics point out initial concauses, yet you fail to see that no one element can stand alone in a progressive equation. We must not only discover the sequence of events leading up to the theft of *Star Empire,* but also evaluate them and predict the events that will solve the problem passively."

"If half your brain wasn't circuitry, Spock, you'd be able to say we have to find out what happened and mend it."

"I did say that. As usual, you insist upon simplistic answers to complex situations."

Suddenly, watching this, I got very nervous. Why were they sniping at each other? Was the situation grave enough to drag vexation out of a Vulcan?

"Aren't you the one who's always spouting bald definitions?" McCoy said.

"I shall be moved to amazement, Doctor, if someday you should refrain from probing the obvious."

"Mr. Spock," Scott said with a quirkish, scolding expression, "y'must admit he hit on all the logical questions."

McCoy lounged back. "Maybe it was just a coincidence, Scotty. Like this whole affair. A great big inevitable coincidence." He skillfully ignored the look of contained aggravation rising under Spock's eye-brow.

It didn't seem like any of this was a surprise to Kirk. His face was a herding of pseudomilitary pomp and dashes of amusement, not to mention the evident respect he had for these people's opinions. I kept expecting him to stand up and make a decision; instead, he just sat and listened, jabbing the discussion on whenever it faltered. That said something about him. I wasn't sure what yet, but it was talking to me.

He turned to the backyard grin of Scott. "What about the technology, Scotty? What do you know about the dreadnought?"

"Eh . . ." Scott shrugged his opinion. "It's a fire-cracker, sir, but since we don't know who stole the bloody beast, we also don't know how powerful she is, or how dangerous."

"Spock?"

"I agree," the Vulcan said casually. "The danger quotient is directly proportional to the skills of those who have stolen the ship."

"Is it logical," Kirk said, using the word cannily, "to assume the ship was stolen by a full-capacity crew?"

"No, sir." Spock tipped his head. "Her crew complement is five hundred. The odds against so many people developing leftist attitudes simultaneously, at one starbase, without a leak, are nine thousand—"

"About the same odds as your giving us an answer without decimal points," McCoy barbed. "I think we've been baited."

Spock went on with polished, pointed stubbornness. "It is apparent, Captain, that whoever stole the ship has some awareness of her firepower and may at this moment be learning how to use it, if indeed they do not already know."

"How much of that knowledge do we have?"

Spock swiveled his gaze. "Mr. Sulu?"

This was the man Sarda was standing behind. He was Earth Oriental, and one of the most affable people around, judging by the few times we'd spoken during a special seminar he taught at Academy. The subject was "The Helm and Spaceborne Weaponry." It taught us how maneuvering a ship correlated with trajectories of phaser beams and photon torps. Martial arts was a hobby of his, enough to be considered an avocation. It was evidently in this capacity that he was here today. Sarda had been serving under him for five months now.

"I've ordered up schematics on *Star Empire*'s offense/defense systems. It's all security-one prohibited, so it'll take some time, but we should·be receiving transmission before we reach the rendezvous."

"Will that be enough time to assimilate the information, Sulu?"

Sulu gave him a dubious look. "Let's hope they think so."

"Which brings us," Kirk said, turning in increments with each word, "to . . . our Lieutenant Piper."

My face went bone-white.

"How do you fit into all this?"

Where was the spotlight? The thumbscrews? I swallowed and handed back the exact answer.

"Sloppily."

Mr. Scott chuckled. So did Sulu. Beside him, Uhura winked. Spock's eyebrow elevated. So did McCoy's, but differently. Sarda rocked on his heels. Had I made a fool of myself or scored a point?

The Captain's shoulders moved as he measured my face. There was a joining of our eyes, our understandings and sensibilities. There must have been. I couldn't be imagining it, because he straightened and said, "We're going to do something about that. Expect it."

"Captain," Spock said, "it may be impossible to assess the situation at all until we discover the identities of the terrorists."

McCoy leaned forward. "But you said they probably know how to use the thing, Spock."

"I said it was apparent. Not that it was true."

Kirk washed a soluble grin over his longtime friends, then immediately replaced it with a steady urgency. When he spoke, his eyes were gripping me. "That's all, ladies and gentlemen. Prepare for battle-stations."

# Chapter Four

RIDICULOUS. NONSENSICAL. ENIGMATIC. Unexplainable. Absurd.

In . . .

Ex . . .

Ob . . .

"Adjectives . . . adjectives . . . ."

Make a mental note to requisition new carpet. These quarters were going to need it.

Dreadnought. A stolen dreadnought. Rittenhouse, Rittenhouse, never heard of him . . . what tribblepate would commission a ship like that anyway . . . *Star Empire* . . . stupid name for a Federation ship . . . *Majestic, Embassy, Valiant, Ramage* . . . those are names for ships. My biocode! Mine. Damn.

"Excuse me."

I hadn't heard him come in. No surprise, since I wouldn't have necessarily noticed a supernova in view of my self-preoccupation. His ice-warm voice sliced through my thoughts like a meld.

"Sarda," I began. "I've been thinking about you."

His half-turn included only the barest of acknowl-
edgements. "Unlikely."

Damn Vulcan correctitude. Not only was he *correct*,
but he was also *right*. Hating to be caught in a lie, I
followed him across the room to his quarter, a painfully featureless place whose vacantness only accentu-
ated his plans not to stay long. "Do you know what's
going on?" I pestered. "Have you heard anything
new? How could they have built a superstarship at the
base without anyone knowing about it? When are we
going to reach this rendezvous point?"

He replied tersely. "I do not. I have not. In great
secrecy. Sixteen hours, twelve minutes from now."

I huffed, then hoped he couldn't hear it, all the while
knowing that he could. If I'd been an animal, canines
would have been securely affixed to his ankle. "You're
not much help."

"Help is not my purpose." He divested himself of
his uniform, neatly stowing it away, and skimmed into
a darkly intriguing meditation cloak, a hanging gar-
ment that made use of the thready physical makeup
typical of Vulcans. Shadowy purple fabric, something
like velvet, picked up the depth in Sarda's glossy,
brassy hair, and made a shocking contrast to his
bottomless topaz eyes. Sarda was pure Vulcan, but of
a race of Vulcans fairer than the city dwellers who
usually gravitated toward Star Fleet. Though there
were few Vulcans in the Fleet (more each year, however), there were even fewer of Sarda's kith among us.
Still, he was innately Vulcan. I saw that for the hundredth time as he turned to me, both hands folded
around a tattered manual. The effect was breathtak-
ingly different from the martinet who had walked in

moments ago. "If I am called for, assuming you will be here, I shall be in the aft hangar deck."

"Why there?" Intruding, yes, I was.

"Lieutenant, I will be meditating."

In his voice there was no hint of the insult he found in having to share quarters. The idea that he had to escape to the hangar deck was . . . de-Vulcanizing.

*"Kolinahr* again?" I shot at him, desperate for a score, or possibly so tense with anticipation as to drag out a cruelty in myself I hated to resort to.

He stopped before he reached the door. His shoulder blades moved closer together and his head came back slightly as he battled to control the sting. Actually it was I who winced.

Ever so graciously, he faced me. The planes of his face were made geometric by the doorway safety light. "You have an irritating habit of equating *Kolinahr* with all that is Vulcan. You are in error. I have not reached the discipline, though I hold in honor those who have. I have not achieved it, nor do I deserve to be the pawn of your inaccurate references to it. Please delete it from your vocabulary."

"I was just observing . . . drawing conclusions. You know . . . analyzing."

"Incorrect. Analysis is based upon available facts. You were speculating. You continually exude opinions, yet in fact you have learned nothing of Vulcan or Vulcans. I resent this."

The velvet swayed. There was no ceremony. It hurt that he retreated, but the bigger hurt was Sarda's.

Like a predator, I pursued. "I thought resentment was a human trait." Scales and mulch, what *was* wrong with me?

Sarda pursed his lips until control returned, and tipped his chin slightly upward again, a gesture imperceptible to anyone not watching for it. Again he turned, surrendering his escape to making a point. "I have said this to you before. This will be the last time." Not *shall*. Not *may*. Not *should*. *Will*. "You do not understand Vulcan training. As such, your assumptions fail to reach even a level of speculation. I will eliminate myself as your target by telling you this: I am only at the level of *Sele-an-t'lee*, which is only secondary adult discipline. *Kolinahr* is years beyond my reach. There is, in fact, poor chance that I shall ever attain it. Please cease enticing me to poison that which I *have* achieved."

· He was exercising much greater control than he knew, if only by not referring openly to his age. A Vulcan of only thirty-five Earth-standards was a stripling and rarely did one so young leave Vulcan at all. But Vulcan had excised him in its proper, exacting way, and he had taken refuge at Star Fleet, which quickly learned to adore a Vulcan with Sarda's peculiar talents.

That is, once I ignorantly let them know about it.

This time he made good his escape, and I let him go. He had made clear to me the continuous pain my ignorance caused him.

Merete AndrusTaurus slipped in the door before it closed, gazing thoughtfully after Sarda striding with deliberation down the corridor in that elegant Vulcan livery. Merete's short platinum hair gleamed (her eyes a laughing comparison to the brooding ones just gone.

"Evening," she said, clicking the two computer tapes she'd brought in.

"Is it?" I deposited myself on my bunk in a position suitable for grumbling.

"You all right? I heard about all the surprises."

"I'll be all right when I'm not surprised anymore."

She nodded, holding up on of the tapes. "Present. I thought you might need one." She relaxed on her own bunk, maneuvered the tape into the computer terminal and clicked it on, they lay back. I ignored the motion, expecting music or some other aesthetic recording.

Until the walls started melting.

Moss grew where the doors joined their frames, soon consumed in ferns growing like multiplying crystals. A green stream evolved and cut between our bunks, which were becoming silt beds, and with it came the aroma of seawater, the smell of brackish organic soup and varieties of life in birth and decay from protozoa to grasshoppers. Lepidodendron scale trees grew before our eyes, developing sparse, arching spires and a hair of dripping moss; plants grew vascular support systems and sucked carbon dioxide through leaf pores; conifers and cycads bloomed at our elbows. More than anything, our room was mimicking prehistoric Earth, right around the early Mesozoic Period, say mid-Triassic, with incongruent bits of pre-Cambrian tossed in for color. I half expected to see a coal forest over the mounds of club moss or put my feet down in the path of a passing coelacanth. Blue-green algae, lichen, moss, fronds, rushes, arm-long dragonflies, mats of stromatolites, sediments trapped in sparkling algae pools secreting a limestone matrix . . . all green.

All wonderful. Out of sheer empathy I almost started to sweat.

"Oh!" I propped myself up. "Proxima!"

"Do you like it?"

"Like it? I'm home! How did you do it?"

"Image projection. It's a new technology in holography. As a matter of fact, it was the brainchild of Vice-Admiral Rittenhouse himself. That was what clinched his being given full control over the dreadnought project. It's actually a weaponry concept, but it was picked up and used by recreation designers; thus, *viola,* Proxima. Or Rigel. Or Cestus. Or anywhere else you wish to spend time. It's only visual reality, but give them time."

"I thought the dreadnought design was all so secret."

She shrugged, brushing aside the image of a fern, which cooperated by pretending to waft out of her way. "Not since yesterday. It's spread like a fireglacier now. You know how contagious military data is."

We paused to watch a horsetail fern as it grew through the ceiling unti it was a good sixty meters high.

"Merete, I needed this."

"Welcome."

"Merete, are you human?"

She grinned. "I've lost my accent finally, have I? No. I'm Palkeo Est from Altair Four. We're like you, but we can't mate with you. Well . . . not successfully, anyway. We've tried," she laughed. "By the way, what is it between you and Lieutenant Sarda?"

I sensed this was Merete's way of distracting me from the mists of conspiracy I had been thrust into. Strange, but I wasn't bothered by her bluntness, nor she by mine. I was command and she was medical; bluntness was inherent in our pursuits, typical of captains and ships' doctors for generations. We would both have to get used to taking it as well as dishing it out.

Melting back into my algae bed and swearing it felt soggy, I fixed on the veins of a sigillaria and poured thoughts at her.

"I . . . we went through most of Academy together. I suppose I radiated to him out of curiosity. He never returned it, but we did become lab mates and got as close to being friends as a Vulcan will usually allow."

"Speaks nicely of you."

I shook my head, as though I had just figured it out. "I was ignorant. Sarda paid for it. He's right to resent me, my presence here . . ."

"What is it he fears?"

"There's no more fear in him. Only insult. Resentment. Memory of those." *Why?* I saw it in her expression. Was it right for me to divulge Sarda's privacy to anyone? But then, thanks to me, it wasn't a secret anymore, hadn't been for a solar year. "How was I to know it was sacrilegious on Vulcan? I thought I was doing him a favor!" Oh, that felt good. Merete observed me in silence. Once the tirade ended, I decided it was time to explain. "The Vulcan Science Academy politely rejected him. They said it would be illogical to waste his talent, yet immoral to nurture it. In other words, they turned a well-bred back on him. Star Fleet was glad to take him—you know how they feel about Vulcans—and there was me, not understanding Vulcan cultural scruples against bloodletting or punitive solutions to problems . . ."

"What is he? A mass murderer?" She meant it as a joke.

"He thinks he is." My fist struck the mattress under the image of club moss. "Damn it . . . I just didn't know. I thought I was doing Sarda a favor when I told our training captain about his fascination for . . . weapons design."

Merete made a low sound of empathy in her throat, but didn't interrupt me. In its way, it was a signal for me to go on.

"I never saw such humiliation as rose in his face when he was awarded 'the position he desired' in front of our entire graduating class. I didn't understand Vulcan morals. I had to learn by watching his face go olive with shame. Now he's not only denied by his planet's scholars, but he's ostracized by others of his kind at Star Fleet as well. Thanks to me, he's completely alone."

A synthetic breeze blew through a hall of angiosperms.

Merete sighed. "I see why your friendship ran aground. He is Vulcan, though. Maybe it's better foundered."

"Is he?" The harshness of my words forced me into silence.

Merete sensed the wisdom of shutting up. Together we sank back to absorb Proxima.

But I was still thinking about Vulcans.

This cruel tributary of destiny, and my mistake, had thrown Sarda into isolation. Back at Academy, in the privacy of his quarters. I knew Sarda spent sleepless nights trying to teach himself the disciplines only Vulcan acolytes could teach. I had watched him sink time and time again into that seclusion in our barrack—he never knew I was looking—and I sensed he was retreating into personal torture.

It had made me angry with his race.

Since entering Star Fleet, I had developed a . . .

fascination for these spirits deviling about the Academy, casting human shadows and thinking alien thoughts, philosophies so doggedly Oriental as to vault entirely into the paranormal. Vulcans.

I had some opinions about them.

For instance, this business of *Kolinahr*. Was there any practice more harmful to a philosophy? The Vulcans were in reverence of throwing away everything that separated them from intelligent brick walls. Why would a culture do that to itself? They had once been barbarians who foresaw their future and deflected it, religioning out everything that might trigger a return to violence. The price—love, enjoyment, friendship, intimacy, sorrow, release . . . gone.

Gone . . . and not. Anyone who ever knew a Vulcan, or even watched a Vulcan face carefully, knew better. It wasn't the emotion that was forbidden; it was *expression* of emotion. The emotions were still very much there, and nobody would ever convince me otherwise. They didn't show it, they didn't let it interfere with their actions; it was turned inward, but it was there. Emotion rarely surfaced in a fully disciplined Vulcan, usually only in moments of shock, pain, or unexpected physical contact. But those that did surface were pure. They were uncolored examples of emotion, bald and spontaneous. Actually it was kind of refreshing.

"Merete!"

"What? Sorry. I dozed off."

"Where did you get this tape?"

"This one?"

"Any of them. Can we get any planet?"

"Any recorded and stored by the library computer."

"You have access?"

"Of course."

"Show me, will you?"

"Just follow me."

*Enterprise*'s library had tapes.

More tapes than anybody, *anybody* would ever be able to use. Any tidbit of accumulated knowledge, extending well into the subspecies of trivia, was here in some form, or at least accessible through tie-in to Memory Alpha Colony in this quadrant, Memory Gamma in the quadrant we were approaching.

But the image projector was unique. It stood alone, proud in the middle of an array of comfortable furniture—any library was, in its way, a breed of rec hall—and begged to be used.

I put the dreadnought and the grief it brought me on hold as Merete tapped us into the system. As with most PCs, it was designed to be operated by plankton if necessary, and opened itself to her.

"What planet do you want to see?" she asked.

"Can we do it in here? Don't we have to be in an enclosed chamber?"

"No. It'll fill the area till it hits a wall," she told me, "if it's a landscape, that is. If it's a person or other contained unit, it'll just appear in proper scale. There's nobody else here now. We don't have to worry about bothering anyone, so tell me."

"Vulcan."

She looked at me. In a moment the questioning gleam in her tilted grey eyes subsided and she called up the tape. It was processed and regurgitated, and she handed it to me. "Want to see it now?"

"Please."

*Click. Beep-buzz. Whirr.*

Of course, I couldn't really hear it. I was empathizing with the damned machine.

Beneath us, *Enterprise* sizzled. From bare volcanic crust evolved red magma, heaved-up spires, regoliths and natural bridges—all red. It didn't simply appear around us; we watched it *evolve*. In moments we were standing together on the sparse, funereal surface of Vulcan.

It was a red planet beneath a sulphur sun, dusty as raw hematite and crowded with loneliness. In the distance there was part of a city, more like a gathering of dinosaurs than civilization. Primitive, it was, yet it glowered with the patina of tradition, as though it was being maintained out of respect. That didn't seem consistent with what I had assumed about Vulcans.

"What's that over there?" Merete joined me between two spires of glittering muscovite, and gestured at a multisided structure with what appeared to be gargoyles without faces at every corner.

"Looks like an ancient threshing floor," I guessed, "but Vulcans were never agrarian. Possibly it's a theatre. Maybe a temple. I don't know."

"Vulcans don't have gods, you know."

I didn't. Suddenly I was furious with myself for not knowing. Knowledge was all around me, and I didn't *know*.

"They're not very artistic," Merete observed.

"They wouldn't be Vulcans if they were. But look at the way the buildings imitate the rocks, even complement them. They must be master metallurgists too. See the inlaid scrollings of ore?" I sank down on a jutting of hematite, polished to a dull gleam by weathering and looking more like a disembodied pupil than a rock, and for a moment closed my eyes on this bastion of intelligence around me. It was such a barren place . . . yet it had spawned the greatest philosophic structure in the known galaxy. It absorbed me . . . too much.

"All right. Thank you. I've seen enough."

"Screen off."

When I opened my eyes, Vulcan was gone and the brightness of the library was painful. I took Merete's place at the terminal and punched up a definition for *Sele-an-t'lee.*

"What's that?" she asked.

"We'll see."

The screen lit up. There was no voice.

*SELE-AN-T'LEE:* VULCAN TRAINING LEVEL, AGE
   APPROXIMATELY 38–45 YRS. V.S. COMPRISED OF

"Interrupt," I ordered. "Convert to Earth-standard years."

*SELE-AN-T'LEE:* VULCAN TRAINING LEVEL, AGE
   APPROXIMATELY 25–29 YRS. E.S. COMPRISED OF LESSONS
   IN SUBDOMINANT BRAIN ORGANIZATION, ADVANCED
   PHILOSOPHY AND LOGIC, MUSCLE COORDINATION, AND
   CONTROL OF WILL.

FIVE STEPS: BELIEF DISCIPLINE/REALITY
   AWARENESS/SENSORY ACUTENESS/VISUAL
   CALCULATION/FACT ANALYSIS.

READING INCLUDE *LOGIC AND DEFINITION* BY LYRAS, *THE
INTERIOR* BY TAL LUXUR OF ROMULUS, *EQUATIONS* BY

*SCORUS, SYSTEMS OF LOGIC BY SURAK, PURPOSE AS PRIME MOTIVATOR BY SURAK.*

*ADVANCED MIND-MELDING TECHNIQUES. COMPLETE.*

"So that's what he meant," I murmured slowly. "He's falling behind."

"You don't mean he's trying to teach himself."

"It seems he is." I'd known that longer than I cared to admit. "He's a drowning man, desperately trying to teach himself to swim before he becomes completely lost. Computer, provide a general listing of subjects studied by Vulcans from age eight through adult."

*WORKING. PRELIMINARY NOTE: LAST COMPLETE ROSTER OF VULCAN STUDY AND TRAINING PROVIDED BY EARTH EMISSARIES STARDATE 7881.2.*

"Seventeen Earth-standard years ago," Merete provided, voicing both her feelings and mine.

"Well," I decided, "it doesn't matter if it's a particularly accurate listing. Go ahead, computer."

The screen lit up without hesitation, and a list appeared.

VISUAL MATHEMATICS
NEUROLOGICAL ORGANIZATION
PHYSICS
ALGEBRA
GEOMETRY
VULCAN ANTHROPOLOGY
CALCULUS
QUANTUM PHYSICS
TELEPATHIC COMMUNICATION AND ETIQUETTE

SUPPRESSION OF CORTICAL STIMULAE IN DOMINANT
   HEMISPHERE
VULCAN CULTURAL HISTORY
RITES OF PASSAGE
PHYSICAL DEPORTMENT
LOGIC AND DEFINITION
MEMORY ACCURACY
PRINCIPLES OF ANALYSIS
LOGIC PARADIGMS
CONTROL OF SUBDOMINANT CORTICES
CONCEPTS OF GIVENS
PROCESSES OF DEFINITIONS
PAIN CONTROL
PRESSURE POINTS FOR MIND MELDING

"Are you seeing this?" I muttered.

"Staggering, isn't it?" Merete leaned forward, straining to read the small letters. "I can tell you right now some of that is out of date."

"But plenty of it isn't," I said cryptically. "Computer, specify training list for Vulcan adults over the age of thirty-five Earth-standards. Include suggested readings."

Without vocal response, the secondary list appeared before us.

LOBE SEGREGATION OF THE BRAIN
DIGNITY AND TRADITION IN VULCAN IDENTITY
CONTEMPLATIONS OF INFINITY
BEHAVIORAL NEURON STUDY
ISOLATION OF THE *KATRA*
READINGS INCLUDE: *ESSAYS OF DISCIPLINE* BY SURAK
                *THE RUNES OF T'VISH*
                *ANALYSIS OF PSEUDODOXY* BY T'VEEN

"Wow," I breathed, without realizing how teenaged it sounded. "I couldn't wade through those with a phaser. Computer . . ." My hesitation belied a certain reluctance to hear more of what seemed to be mental flogging to a mere human like me. "What are the stages leading up to and inclusive of the process of *Kolinahr?*"

WORKING. *VENLINAHR* IS THE STATE OF MOST VULCAN
ADULTS. IT INCLUDES MEDITATION BY INDIVIDUAL
DISCRETION, FURTHER STUDY OF THE VULCAN DHARMA,
AND ADVANCED READINGS BY THE MYSTAGOGUES SURAK,
SCORUS, TENNE, T'VISH, PRISU, AND SELTAR. *KOLINAHR*
IS THE FINAL DIVORCE OF THE BRAIN, BODY, AND *KATRA*
FROM ALL EMOTIONAL RESPONSES. IF NECESSARY,
*KOLINAHR* MAY BE ACCOMPLISHED BY MEMORY
ABERRATION.

COMPLETE.

"Screen off." Contemplatively, I leaned back into my best position for thinking, and tugged absently at my lower lip. "Merete . . ."

"Hmm?"

"What do you know about the makeup of a Vulcan brain?"

She sprawled onto a cushion. "Enough to tell you it's not as different from yours as their physiology is. They've trained themselves to use more of what they have than most self-awares."

"Have they learned to subdivide?"

It had to be the answer.

She frowned. "What do you mean?"

I leaned forward, using my hands to hold the

thought before me. "In college, on Earth, a student learns *how* to learn, then is served up a series of courses on different subjects, most of which is forgotten but can be relearned. It seems to me that Vulcan training relies on continuity and compilation instead of ability to relearn."

"Okay so far." Merete was so casual, so unflustered, that I envied her for a moment.

Encouraged, I went on. "You saw it yourself. Once an aspect of training begins, it doesn't stop. It doesn't make room for the next aspect. Instead it continues and is added to by increasingly complex lessons, each of which must be carried on as the burden of being Vulcan piles up."

"But eventually there wouldn't be enough hours in a day to accommodate all the demands of calculating and meditating and—"

"That's right!" I was on my feet now, wading around in the mud of discovery. "That's why they must have evolved subdivided brains. One part of one hemisphere might be calculating a problem, another part meditating, another pursuing some philosophical tidbit, while yet another does the day's work and handles social interaction. That's why Vulcans are almost impossible to distract. Don't you see? Only a shock of cataclysmic proportions would be enough to upheave all those cerebral tiers at once!"

Pin a medal on me, anywhere, just anywhere.

Merete chewed the thought, folded her arms, and observed me with a look half proud and half warning. "Not a bad theory. But if I were you, I wouldn't bring it up to Sarda."

"Why not?"

"I don't think it would be wise to ask a Vulcan to admit their intellect is as much biological as it is mental. They wouldn't want to tell us they're born smart."

My enthusiasm shrank away. Reluctantly I let it go and chalked it all up to personal growth, thinking of how I would feel if I was Sarda. "Oh, Merete . . . thanks. I almost did it to him again. Now I understand why he reacted like he did every time I threw *Kolinahr* in his face. I've been playing a cruel game with him. Thanks for stopping me."

"A game? With a Vulcan?"

"With a Vulcan soul." The great window in the flank of *Enterprise* allowed me to look out into the sloe-and-jewel star field, and back into myself. "I've been trying to pinch emotions out of him. Maybe it was a game . . . or maybe I've been trying to win him over before he destroys himself trying to be part of a culture that turned its back on him. I won't tamper with that anymore. I only wish . . . I wish I could . . ."

"I have a suggestion."

"I'll take one."

"Sometime, after this business with the dreadnought is over—"

"Soon, I hope."

"There's a Vulcan embassy at Starbase One that maintains closer relations with humans who have interest in Vulcan or Vulcan nationals. You could speak to them. At least then, you'd know."

They hadn't paged me, not since Captain Kirk first summoned me to the bridge to have my heart shocked into my nostrils. My quest for distraction in those

sixteen-point-whatever hours had taken me first to
Proxima via Merete, then to Vulcan, now somewhere
else.

It was a vast place and often forgotten, much more
like a great runway than an enclosed area inside a ship,
and it was extremely dim. In fact, only a haze of
unflickering blue walkway lights provided any illumi-
nation at all, and then barely enough to navigate by.
High above, a skylight domed and allowed view of the
expanse of stars and a purplish herd of nebulae we
were passing. They must have been very large and
very far away for us to pass them so slowly even at
warp speed. Wide, insigniaed hangar doors on the far
side were the homes of four shuttlecraft, practically
starships in themselves with the new technology that
had been redesigned into them for the past ten-odd
years. On the near side were the hangars of six two-
man fighters.

It was an empty place, a place that, in the midst of
space-efficient cubicles, was unique and somewhat
disconcerting. It doubled as ballroom, solarium, lec-
ture hall, funeral hall, art gallery, wedding area, military ceremonial hall, or diplomatic arena, mutating as
needed to the many lives of a starship. Its primary
purpose, that of military and scientific launch point,
was actually its rarest duty, and there were more
cobwebs here than anywhere else on the starship. I
wondered what ancient tradition kept these decks on
the blueprints for new ships, and how long it would be
before superior transporters and independent docking
craft finally shunted decks like this into obsolescence.
Today, though, this place wore a different swaddling:
that of inner sanctum.

In the middle of all this, a lone figure knelt.

Though the distance between us was obscuring, his face turned in my mind clearly and for a moment I thought we were in contact. No . . . he would have to touch me for that, but I closed my mind anyway, just in case. There were still sensations, perceptions to guard against. Even hunches. I averted my eyes in case he could feel my gaze. Even humans could feel eyes on them.

The tape slipped from my hand into the access terminal and without pausing I manually ordered the computer to function. Instantly red haze bled across my black jumpsuit, coloring my skin and dashing the corridor with leachover. It was enough to satisfy me.

Now I opened my mind and sent along on the mental wind an offering I could only hope might be accepted.

# Chapter Five

"RED ALERT, RED *alert. Battlestations. Captain Kirk to the bridge. Lieutenant Piper report to the bridge. Red alert. All personnel to battlestations.*"

Somehow—let's hope no one ever pins me down on it—I ended up in the same turbolift as Captain Kirk as we raced for the bridge. Actually he ended up on my lift; I could never have overridden the priority code and interrupted *his* panic.

He didn't look panicked. Damn him.

He gazed at me askance, never blinking. All around us the ship pulsed with redness and the whooping red-alert klaxon; ever confined in the hurtling lift we could both feel it. It tingled on top of my skin and underneath his. It didn't show on the Captain's face, though I knew it did on mine.

"*Star Empire?*" I quivered.

"The rendezvous point, Lieutenant," he said.

"Then why—"

"When we came out of warp we spotted four

Klingon birds of prey coming about to attack position."

"To fire on us?"

"Lieutenant, they're firing on the dreadnought."

My mouth dropped open. *"Firing* on a Federation vessel? We're that close to the Klingon Neutral Zone?"

Was he enjoying my quandary as much as those little wrinkles beside his eyes said? "The rendezvous point is inside the Sabu'ka region. Disputed space. It's claimed by both sides, but not yet incorporated into the neutral zone. Entry here doesn't yet constitute a technical act of war."

"How convenient."

"For the Klingons," he added, before I could cringe at my sarcastic mistake. What, what, *what* was it about him that made me say whatever popped into my head?

"Sir, I . . . I don't understand why the people on *Star Empire* would pick a place like this to talk to us. Why would they expose themselves and us to the Klingons?"

His insignia badge glinted in the bleeding red light. "That's where you come in. Once you clear the code, maybe other things will clear up. Let's hope."

*You have no intention of just hoping.*

There was someting about his face. Something elusive. I'd seen a drawing once, a hand-drawn ink illustration for an article in an Academy newsletter. The article had a decidedly you-can-aspire-to-this bent and the drawing, though good art, was harsher, more archetypally heroic than the face I saw before me now. It had been more like someone's perception of his deeds. Definitely his face, but different.

The face before me was rendered in soft pastels. No straight lines. No hard creases. Eyes soft as dark aurelites in a plume-pool at mating time. The face of a great hero? Not this. This face didn't want the notoriety. No harsh lines at all. The strength in it differed from the strength I'd seen in Mr. Spock's angular appearance, like two sides of the same coin—one an etching of dignity, the other a work of art. As I looked into the Captain's eyes, I saw a strange personal battle going on—he couldn't wait to face those Klingons. He equally wanted to turn away and forget them. I learned a lot in that turbolift. I—

Klingons?

Real Klingons? *Live* Klingons? Alive? Not simulations not holos not pretend oh I'd rather have lunch with a Tellarite get me off this lift—

*Hissss*

"Status?"

"Captain, the Klingons are concentrating their firepower on *Star Empire*. Only one has broken off to engage us. Shields are raised."

That heavy voice. A vision floated toward us on the lower deck, near the command chair. Spock. He and the Captain shared a deep eye contact, ignoring the action of the forward viewscreen. With deliberation Spock said, "Everything is ready for you, Captain."

Something passed, shifted, between them, but it wasn't any kind of handing over. I could tell from the reactions of more experienced officers on the bridge that *Enterprise* hadn't really changed possession at all. If anything had, it was infinitely more precious.

"Thank you, Mr. Spock. Power up for evasive

action. Bring main phaser batteries to bear on targets. Uhura, get Sulu to the bridge.''

"He's on his way, Captain."

The bridge continued to bleed the red alert.

"Spock, analysis of situation?"

"The Klingons were surprised by our appearance, allowing us to disrupt part of their attack on the dreadnought, and although we still hold the advantage they are regrouping. As for *Star Empire,* you can see for yourself—"

Only then did I allow myself to absorb the sight on the forward viewscreen. A vast starship hung at a horrible angle in the distance—true, there was no "up" in space, but that ship looked . . . off kilter. As though no one had control, it pivoted drunkenly on the tip of one warp nacelle while threads of phaser fire joined it to three Klingon fighters in a macabre dance. A bird of prey looped over the dreadnought, firing, and sheared a nacelle completely off, leaving a sparkle of ion gas and ripples of iridescent melting metal. I could smell the death.

"No . . . " I backed up until the bulkhead stopped me. I stared. My eyes watered. Death. Real death. If they could cut up a supership. . . .

The dreadnought hinged around, pushed by the recoil of losing one of its three nacelles, and my throat clutched shut. The entire saucer of the primary hull was charred black, crackling with blue-hot veins of escaping energy. Destroyed. Destroyed . . .

"Bird of prey rounding on our port, Captain—" a female voice I didn't know called, shooting me with panic. A stern young woman hunched intently over the helm controls.

Kirk reacted. "Evasive! *Fire!*"

The *Enterprise* leaped beneath us so sharply that we felt it and had to hang on. We felt the tremors go through the ship as phaser fire etched across our port shields. Across the viewscreen slashed our own phasers, scoring the Klingon's green hull with damage as the enemy peeled by us so near I ducked out of reflex.

"Come about point-zero-six. Keep our forward shields to them," the pastel portrait said. Our phasers followed the Klingon into the star field. "Fire at will, Ensign Meyers." Meyers made *Enterprise* chase our enemy, relentlessly firing until the Klingon was obviously on the run. "Got him shaken, sir," she said.

I couldn't believe it when Kirk ordered, "Cease fire. Veer off. Let's free up *Star Empire*."

Why wasn't he finishing off the Klingon we already had on the run? Why leave them to come back on us later? This was a silly time for mercy, I thought.

Free up *Star Empire?* Why? So we could rescue a handful of half-dissolved corpses?

"Arm photon torpedoes. Set approach trajectory at point-seven-three-seven. Make it a tight arc."

Beside me the turbolift door hissed open and Mr. Sulu shot out, scurrying immediately for the helm. Ensign Meyers moved to the navigations console, and the less experienced officer who had been there moved back to his own station on the upper walkway.

"Welcome back, Sulu," the Captain said.

"Sorry, sir. I got held up at damage control locking down a split in the outer hull."

"Commendable, but next time don't spare the time."

"Photon torps armed and ready."

I pressed my spine against the ship's frame as we accelerated toward *Star Empire* and the three Klingon hawks that were still cutting red graffiti into it. My throat was dry, my hands shaking and sweating. All those hundreds of training drills and simulations—in the face of the real thing I couldn't even remember my name. I had to get out of here.

I tried to sound steady. "Sir . . . permission to report to my assigned post in Environmental—"

"Denied. We'll need you here to clear that biocode. Fire!"

Under Sulu's delicately aggressive touch, we looped between two Klingon ships, lancing phaser needles first at one, then the other, scoring hits that bloomed into blue fingers of lightning against their greenish hulls.

"Sir," Spock said, "shields are vacillating on aft engineering hull, port side. I shall attempt to override the damage. Mr. Scott is preparing to link power through from auxiliary."

"Ensign Meyers, help Spock. Lieutenant, take her place at navigations."

The Klingons spiraled and continued firing on *Star Empire*'s unshielded flank, shredding the alabaster hull into glowing white, red, and black filaments.

"Piper!" The Captain's voice sliced through me. "Take navigations."

I tore my gaze from the horror on the screen to his intense eyes. My legs dissolved to bubble memory. "What—? Oh . . . sir . . . you don't understand—I can't—I've never—"

"Shake it out, Lieutenant. Take that post." His tone shook it out of me.

Pure reflex pushed me down to the naviconsole, leading with my hands and muttering, "Okay, but if I screw up I'm sending you the bill . . ."

I clutched my despair and held onto it like an anchor as the three remaining Klingons vectored away from *Star Empire*'s mangled form. They turned on us.

"Keep awake, Lieutenant," Kirk's death-soft voice rested on my shoulders. My hands trembled on the console before me. "Plot negative eight-two-two," he said. He was sitting in the command chair now, his voice, his experience flowing over my left shoulder. I tried to react correctly, tried to follow orders as I'd been drilled to do, but the sight of three Klingon ships rearing before us like Triskelion's giant cobra-hawks froze my blood. My fingers wouldn't move.

"Piper," he snapped.

"But . . . that'll put us right in their crossfire. . . ."

"Plot the course, Lieutenant, *now*."

"We'll be pulverized . . . I can't just—"

Hands grabbed my shoulders and wrenched me from the chair. The hard deck grated under my thigh. Above me, Ensign Meyers's heavy eyelashes batted at the forward screen. She plotted the suicide course and fed it through to Sulu's helm. Still sitting, my legs sprawled on either side of the navigation chair, I propped myself up on my hands and craned to see the screen. There wasn't even time to stand up.

We were flanked by Klingons, descending into their nest from "above." Red glows of gathering phasers swelled on their gun ports. No ship, not even *Enterprise*, could take full phasers at point-blank range from three directions. If I could've closed my eyes, I would've. But I was fated to watch death coming.

"Sulu, fire point-zero-zero-five and execute T-minus-four thousand meters. Ringgold's Pirouette. Now."

"Executing." The crisp voice was followed by a queer lifting sensation in my stomach. The viewscreen started to rotate. No—we were rotating. The ship whined, straining against its own artificial gravity, creating a gyro effect that pinned us to our places. I couldn't have stood up with a winch.

*Enterprise* maneuvered cleanly between the three confused Klingons, almost scraping them as we turned on our thin edge in space and spooled like a giant cartwheel. Firing point-blank, we slipped through.

Their retaliation was immediate. Thin lines of red light came from three directions. But we were already gone.

"Aft scanners," Captain Kirk ordered.

The viewscreen melted, then reformed, to show the Klingons sizzling in each other's phaser slashes!

A whoop of victory filled the bridge from the junior officers. Ringgold's Pirouette. Hmm.

"A brilliant choice of battle strategies, Captain." Mr. Spock towered over me, a stunning wedged statue, never once glancing down. "Unfortunately they are heavily shielded ships and we stand minimal chance with three against one."

"Yes," Kirk murmured, contemplating the havoc onscreen. "The question is how to tip the scales. Have you scanned the fourth ship?"

"She must have been too severely damaged to continue. She has concealed herself in that cluster of asteroids and has not reappeared."

Kirk looked at him. "You do have it on scanners . . ."

"Impossible. Those asteroids read abnormally high

concentrations of Hovinga iridium. Our sensors cannot penetrate them."

"I see." He leaned forward, as Sulu hugged the ship around in a tight radius. "Lieutenant Piper, I want you to get up off the deck," he said with humiliating slowness, "take Ensign Meyers's post at the equidistance scanner, and marry it until you see that Klingon ship come out of the asteroids. You may get up now."

I crawled to the steps and got up. "Yes . . . yessir."

I knew about Hovinga iridium. It didn't block sensor energy; it absorbed it. The whole asteroid field looked like a spotty pink blur in my dynoscanner, the spots being the asteroid boulders themselves. The belt wasn't long or spread out over much space—only eight or ten large rocks with a trail of debris a few thousand kilometers long. I could only hope to detect movement among them, and only on the outskirts of the belt. The rest was fizz-fuzz.

"Captain, they're arming photon torpedoes," Sulu's deep voice announced. Calm. They were all so calm. Tea, anyone?

"Uhura, try to establish contact with *Star Empire,*" Kirk said. "See if there are any survivors. I don't want to do this if there's nothing to save. Try to maneuver us within sensor range of the dreadnought, Sulu, but stay out of phaser range of those cruisers. Spock—"

"I shall prepare to scan for life forms."

"Thank you. On your toes, everyone. This could be tricky."

The turbolift hissed again. "Doing your I-lead-you-lead waltz again, I see?" Dr. McCoy commented drily. "Christ, look at that wreck!"

"Editorials at dinnertime, Bones, not now. Are you here to report something?"

"Only that casualties are minimal right now in spite of your knocking us around in our skivvies, and Scotty's been trying to reach you. He finally called Sickbay. His com system's down above C-deck. He can receive, but he can't hail you."

"Uhura?"

"Right away, Captain. Rerouting intraship hailing."

McCoy gazed at the shredded *Star Empire* and grimaced. "So much for the giant firecracker." In the midst of what sounded like habitual sarcasm I heard a definite pain. I turned, and saw his eyes fill with empathy for the suffocating thieves. *Star Empire,* crewed by a clutch of desperate rebels, never had a chance against a Klingon argosy. If the Klingons knew anything, it was how to gang up. The doctor's hands caressed the stability of the bridge rail as he filled his heart with distant agony, knowing his power to heal could never reach so far. "Good God, Jim, why are we heading toward it?" Then he figured it out, I don't know how, and jabbed a finger at the screen while glaring at Captain Kirk. "You don't actually expect survivors in that mess of twisted—"

Uhura's announcement cut through. "Mr. Scott on audio."

Captain Kirk punched the controls on his command chair console. "Scotty, talk to me."

*"I was about to write a letter, sir. That port blast we took stressed the durasteel skeleton in the nacelle strut. Another maneuver like that could take it over tolerance. The whole rib could sever."*

"I'll keep it in mind, Mr. Scott. Lock the damage down as soon as you can. We're not out of this yet. Better get out your bag of Scottish spells."

*"Take 'em t'lunch on me, sir."*

"Your treat, Scotty. Hold us together." He put one foot up on the step, and for an instant his apple green uniform shirt took on the deep sheen of the flickering computer lights from the engineering console. His link with Mr. Scott reflected on his face, in his eyes. "Prepare for assault on both flanks."

"Shields are at full available strength," Spock acknowledged from my right, at his impressive library computer. That computer gave *Enterprise* one of its edges over other Fleet starships, having been built upon and added to, index upon index, crossfeed upon sensor track, fine-tuned to better speeds and deeper search capabilities than any other had attained. Its capabilities had compounded as his had. They had learned from each other until both were legendary. He had been the first Vulcan computer expert in Star Fleet. He had put his Vulcan mind on line with a Federation computer, and together they soared. And here I was within touching distance of them both. I felt very small. I buried myself in the dynoscanner, hoping never to be seen again. The black fabric of my jumpsuit felt cold as it clung to my body, engulfing me in my own failure, and at my ankles indignity crawled. Why didn't the Klingons come? Why couldn't they come right now?

"Dr. McCoy, Sickbay is calling," Uhura said urgently. "There's been a coolant leak in the battery, with casualties. Dr. AndrusTaurus needs you to authorize treatment with bacteria paper."

McCoy's face turned hard, his glare hitting the Captain precisely as Kirk turned to meet it. "Finish it soon, Captain," the surgeon admonished, carefully accusative. Then he wheeled and vanished into the turbolift cavity muttering something about going over Niagara Falls in a paper cup.

I turned back to my dynoscanner. Because I had turned away in the first place it took a few seconds to reorient myself to what I saw on the small screen.

I squinted at it, half hearing the disorganized harmony of those voices—Uhura's phonic enunciations calling someone to the bridge; Spock's sonorous-toned analyses; Captain Kirk's subdued response; the husky distinction of Sulu answering when Meyers asked him something. Those voices almost had a cadence when they all resounded against the bridge noises. Even in this chaos there was stability in the way these people worked together. All but one. One stranger here, one voice out of place. I cleared my throat and hoped not to have reason to speak.

Just then Sarda came out of the turbolift. He locked eyes with me for a hateful half-second, though he must have heard me paged to the bridge and couldn't be surprised to see me here. He had his uniform on now, the tenne-gold color almost matching his hair, and once again I felt silly being dressed as I was. His sleeve braids matched Sulu's, designating technical specialists, and I suddenly realized it was he Uhura had paged to the bridge. He broke contact with me and went quickly to the weapons control station.

"Sir," Sulu called. "Bird of prey firing midrange torpedoes!"

"Hold on!"

The first torpedo hit our primary hull disk on the forward starboard edge, jarring to the floor anyone who was standing, including me, Sarda, and even Spock. The Captain managed to stay afoot by holding fast to the helm. By the time I rolled over and winced through my bruises, the Klingons were firing again. The second burst shook *Enterprise* to her bones.

"Evasive, Ensign Meyers. Sulu, try to detonate those torpedoes before they reach us."

"That's a hypothetical technique, but I'll try. Lieutenant, calculate for intercept."

My heart pounded before I realized he was talking not to me, but to Sarda. Sarda's bronze head bent over the weapons console and he said, "Computing. Interjectional firing lines between ships coming to you now, sir."

"Receiving."

The Klingons broke off from the decimated *Star Empire* and came after us with vengeance. Bright red spinning balls of energy chased us as *Enterprise* dipped away. Sulu returned fire with his "hypothetical technique" and actually managed to hit one of the torpedo salvos, lighting up the space around us. Another salvo hit us and rocked the ship while a third missed and drifted harmlessly into the black vacuum. We recovered and returned fire, hammering at one of the enemy ships until it moved out of our way.

Kirk punched the intercom. "Scotty, still with us?"

*"Captain, they've hit our impulse drive a glancing blow. It's repairable, but I've got t'have time."*

"How much time?"

*"Seventeen to twenty minutes to patch up and reactivate."*

"Do your best." He turned to Spock. "Suggestions?"

"Our aft shields are weakened. We still have starboard impulse power. I can suggest only that we go with our strengths."

Kirk almost grinned at him. "Agreed. Mr. Sulu, bring the ship about."

"To attack position?"

"Exactly."

"Coming about." It was almost a sigh. There were a lot of almosts on this bridge right now.

*Enterprise* turned agonizingly slowly to face the three cruel-looking Klingon ships. The bird on our right fired. The photon bulb spun toward us. Sulu fired. Space filled with sparkles. But the Klingons fired again, too soon to compensate.

The salvo hit us. *Enterprise* rocked and groaned. Warning lights and sirens went crazy as smoke poured out of several structural joints on the bridge. Energy freed of its circuits crackled across our consoles. The smoke stung our eyes. I blinked through it, needing to see the Captain, needing his strength.

"All power to forward shields." His voice dulcified the panic. "Fire photon torpedo."

Instantly a red sparkler broke from *Enterprise* to hit point-blank on the nearest enemy ship, severing its birdlike neck from the rest of its body; in the recoil of detonation, the Klingon ship writhed, swelled, and exploded into countless billions of metallic jewels.

We cheered, or maybe it was only the breathing around me suddenly becoming loud. The two remaining Klingons rounded away from us and began a new approach, a cooperative attack.

"They're circling, Captain," Sulu reported.

"With our current damage," Spock said at the same time, "the two of them outgun us by seventeen percent. Analysis of their attack pattern indicates they intend to hit us at our weakest point, port side astern. They'll be going after our nacelle strut, Captain. We cannot effectively maneuver to keep both ships away from it."

"We can't just leave *Star Empire* until we know they're all dead either."

Sulu stiffened. "Here they come."

Captain Kirk moved tensely out of his command chair. "Just keep them off our tail."

I clung to my dynoscanner more out of terror than duty, and a strange numbness came over me, making me ready to die at the sides of these particular people, who faced death with such unreachable dignity. But the level of mercy seemed too martyrish to me—the dreadnought was a twisted hulk. No one could have survived a cutting up like that. Kirk didn't seem the suicidal type.

Unable to look, I kept my back turned from the main viewer and concentrated on my scanner, on the blurred pinkish readings of asteroids as my sensors tried to push through the Hovinga garbage. Asteroids . . . debris . . . space junk . . . bits of Klingon flotsam . . . and—a solidity. I squinted at it. Two hundred ninety thousand metric tons . . . length, three hundred meters . . . breadth, one hundred forty . . . another rock? Or—too big for a bird of prey . . . configuration still blurred . . .

Just when the thought hit me that it could be a Klingon heavy cruiser or a mothership for the birds of prey—a horrid, nasty thought—the thing suddenly accelerated from drift speed to three-quarters sublight, advertising that it sure was no natural object.

"Captain!" I spun around, unable to do more than stare at the viewscreen.

Before I could take another breath, a blue photon

ball shot into our sight and peeled away the tip of a wing on the nearest Klingon ship!

Into our viewscreen as we watched in astonishment rose a dazzling alabaster messiah, a ship vast and bulky with three thick, angular nacelles lancing out behind like scarves flying in wind, and a sculpted engineering hull any designer would worship. Her primary hull was shaped hexagonally, giving her a gemlike quality. Lights glowed red, blue, yellow, white all along polished hull rims.

Sulu almost rose right out of his seat. *"Star Empire!"*

"Fascinating—" Spock whispered.

In the space before us were *two* dreadnoughts—one razed, one hale and robust, perfectly untouched. Two!

Between us the shocked Klingons wheeled around, trapped.

"Subjacent thrusters!" Kirk called suddenly. "Z-plus-two thousand meters. Get us out of firing line and give them a clear shot."

*Enterprise* rose, leaving the stunned Klingons to face *Star Empire. One* of the *Star Empire*s, anyway. In their panic the enemy fired two shots that missed completely. One ship veered off, turning its feather-painted underbelly to us and disappearing out a corner of the viewscreen. I couldn't pull my eyes away. I couldn't breathe either. It might've been the smoke . . . all I heard was the whirr of ventilation fans clearing the bridge air, and my own heartbeat. All I saw was a superstarship cutting loose on the Klingons.

Bright blue photon balls, many times more powerful than our red ones, spun toward the Klingons, hitting both enemy ships at the same time. Their green armored skins wrinkled and shattered. Their ships ruptured, parting hull from strut, wing from hull, in a galaxy of spilled energy and explosions. Glowing debris spiralled into the void.

We were alone. With *Star Empire*.

She hung before us in engineered beauty, rising to face us ship to ship, her call letters bold against her hull: MKC 2331.

A mass sigh of relief brushed over the bridge complement.

"Captain, look!" Sulu pointed at the screen. There, as we watched, the spoiled hulk of the other *Star Empire* began, eerily, to fade away.

"It's disintegrating!" I blurted.

Spock scanned it. "Negative. It is dissipating. Pure energy. No longer receiving readings of solid mass. Captain, we are observing a projection."

Kirk pushed out of his command chair, moved around the helm, and glared at the screen as though he could get a closer look at the fading dreadnought. "Duped!"

"Extraordinary," his Vulcan counterpart mentioned.

Then, just when we didn't need any more shocks, the screen before us began to change. We watched in amazement as the new supership split like an amoeba—two ships—four ships—six—they diverged and surrounded *Enterprise* with dreadnoughts.

"What the . . . ?" Ensign Meyers began.

Kirk didn't look away from the bizarre sight. "Analysis, Spock—which one is real?"

Even Spock seemed taken aback and had to force himself to the library computer. "I have . . . never experienced such an ability in a vessel. . . . Captain, their projections appear solid to my sensors. Undoubtedly part of the technology. Energy emissions read enough for only one ship, but I cannot isolate location. A most dynamic display of computer science." He sounded as wonderstruck as a Vulcan could get. Maybe even a little more. Mr. Spock didn't seem as paranoid about expressing some feelings when the situation allowed as most Vulcans I knew. Of course, most Vulcans *I* knew were younger and had less exposure to humans. And less finesse. And less compassion. And less pliability. And less talent.

I looked at Sarda.

He too was staring at the phantom ships as they hovered around us.

"Mr. Sarda, can you explain that?" Sulu asked, putting his apprentice on the hot seat.

I leaned forward, mentally and physically, ready to defend him. This wasn't his fault—why were they picking on him?

He straightened, composing himself with some effort before facing the strange tribunal on the bridge. "It is a projection system feeding directly into our sensor banks. It operates similarly to a cloaking device, only on a reversed principle. They can confuse our sensor readings to show any item or illusion fed into the projection device at the source. The concept was originally developed for defensive purposes in combat, however it . . . may obviously be used offensively."

"And the image of the destroyed ship?" Kirk asked him.

"The projector is capable of receiving sensor readings and analyzing them, then altering the phantom in accordance with changes which would happen if the illusion were real. It recorded the trajectories of the Klingon's phaser shots, instantaneously computed them, then adjusted the image to simulate damage and debris."

Spock breathed, "Fascinating."

"Mr. Spock?" Kirk shifted his gaze.

"An unprecedented display of component-interlink capabilities. I am . . . impressed."

Now Kirk's eyes and voice became intimate. "And insulted that you weren't let in on it?"

Spock tilted his head in disclaimer, the eyebrow speaking for him.

Kirk went on. "See if you can pinpoint the energy and find out which ship is the real one."

"I may be able to trace the energy flow back to a source."

Spock turned to his console. I watched Sarda. His amber eyes dipped away from me. He contemplated the deck of the walkway for a horrible moment before retreating to the weaponry panel. I wanted to be magically across the bridge, at least standing beside him if I couldn't do any more, but we were separated by more than deck space.

Kirk eyed the dreadnought and its clones. "Uhura," he said slowly, "put me on hailing frequency."

"Already hailing, Captain. They're responding on telemetry . . . requesting . . . biocode compliance as specified."

Several sets of eyes hit me.

My spine tingled as I looked at them.

"Lieutenant, if you would be so kind?" Captain Kirk gestured toward the communication station.

"How nice of them to 'request,' " Sulu commented.

A trickle of sweat ran down the side of my face as Uhura patched me in to the voiceprint scan, retina scan, blood content readout, and pulse identification. It took forever.

Finally: *"Biocode discreet,"* the computer's soft female voice read out. *"Piper, Lieutenant Command-grade, Star Fleet Academy entry file J-34, stardate 8180.2, serial number G-61983-LRB, verified and approved."*

I sighed in relief, even though I knew I was me.

"Request communications as agreed, *Star Empire,*" Uhura hailed. She glanced at Kirk. "They comply, sir."

"A little late. Report situation to Mr. Scott and advise he has repair time. And as for our starship thieves . . . let's see who they are."

The viewscreen wavered, changed, solidified on a youthful face, soft hair, large cheekbones, deep eyes.

"Brian!" I choked.

He spoke. *"This message is for* Enterprise *command personnel, from Commander Paul Burch. We are in full possession of the dreadnought Star Empire. Do not attempt to fire on us. Our mission is peaceful."*

"Hah!" from Dr. McCoy.

Brian cleared his throat and went on. *"We have confiscated Star Empire in the name of galactic civility. We will accept an ambassadorial party of three officers, which must include Lieutenant Piper and at least one Vulcan."*

The young face on the viewscreen, a face whose nuances I thought I knew, paused for our response.

"What is the purpose of your mission?" Kirk demanded.

Brian's face went blank. Beads of sweat broke across the bridge of his nose. He was scared; I could see that, feel it. It didn't come out in his velvet voice except for a slight crack when he began speaking again. *"That will be revealed only to your boarding party. I repeat: our goal is peace and the security of the galaxy. Please . . ."* He closed his mouth tightly. The last plea—his? Or *Star Empire*'s?

"We will not comply with terrorists," our captain said. "Surrender immediately and we will consider your problem."

Brian started shaking. *"We must speak in person, Enterprise. Please comply."*

Captain Kirk gazed into that face as though Brian Silayna had just walked up and tweaked his nose. "Mr. Spock," he invited.

Spock tilted his head. "Security. Place Lieutenant Piper under arrest. Charge: conspiracy with terrorists."

I sucked in my breath, but pride and a few other satellite emotions kept me from resisting when two helmeted brontosaurs grabbed my wrists.

On the viewscreen, horror flared across Brian's face. There was a shuffle of confusion on the bridge behind him.

"Cut transmission," Kirk ordered, like a theatre director issuing a cue. The viewscreen dissolved to the star field and the hovering threat of the dreadnought.

"Let them think about it for a while," Kirk murmured. "Take the Lieutenant to deck six. Confine her to her quarters under computer guard." Kirk's words went to the security guards, but his eyes fused into mine, delivering a subliminal message. He knew me somehow—I'd had that feeling since *Kobayashi Maru*. I felt the intensity of closeness to him, but I was cold, dead, as though I was a cancer in his body and my stupidity would kill him. He would never allow that.

"Sir—no!"

Security yanked me away on my own echo.

My mind tombed in on me. Duty became torture.

# Chapter Six

STAR FLEET UNIFORMS had a special dignity even lying unused on a bunk. The rich golden fabric, outlined in black, sparkled with the triangular insignia and the wrist slashes designating rank and assignment. Captaincy candidate, mine told anyone, everyone who knew the color code and slash designations.

I unzipped the front of my jumpsuit and shrugged it from my shoulders, letting the top hang around my waist as I pulled on the uniform turtleneck and adjusted the ribbed collar around my throat. Then I gazed down at the uniform shirt and pants and thought about putting them on also. It wouldn't do to be caught out of uniform when things started prancing again.

I *thought* about putting the uniform on. I tortured myself about it. Such a proud costume, such accomplishment behind it . . . my fingers ran along the heavy material of the sleeve, feeling every test I had taken at the Academy, every trial they'd put me to, one by one seeing the obstacles they'd thrown in my path, feeling myself squeeze through every layer of the sieve of heavy competition—countless hopefuls going for their peers' jugulars to get this uniform.

And I had gotten it. Piper from Proxima was among the trickle of captaincy trainees. Piper, who had trembled in the face of an unbeatable enemy, only to watch them beaten by people whose posts I aspired to. Piper, who'd frozen at the helm, ignored orders, and been shoved aside by an ensign. Been shown up by a junior-grade attendant who happened to be on the bridge at the right time. Promotion time. But not for me. My next assignment would be in the ship's laundry.

I sat on the bunk, shoulders sagging more with each replay of my poor performance on the bridge. The memories wouldn't go away, wouldn't mellow, wouldn't change, no matter how much I tried to explain my behavior or find excuses for it.

How had Kirk done it? How had he kept a multidimensional map of space and the movements of all those ships in the front of his mind? I couldn't even conjure up the movements *we* were making without the help of a scanner, much less tell what the Klingons were doing, what they planned to do, what they thought about doing, and what they decided not to do. I didn't even want to think about what they actually did. Spock hadn't known what the Klingons were thinking, and he even had his library computer to call upon. Yet Kirk had known their minds at every turn. That didn't make sense. Spock should have been in command of his own ship long ago. Vulcans' deductive abilities outmatched any human's in speed, efficiency, and just about everything else. Most of the captaincy candidates at Star Fleet Academy were humans, and Command couldn't get away with saying only humans applied anymore. But even Star Fleet had its prejudices, apparently, biases that rose into the Admiralty, some kind of good-old-boy ethic. Somehow they kept, quite carefully, I had always assumed, most aliens from rising too high in the Fleet. If any race had the brain stuff to be starship captains, the Vulcans must have.

My shameful performance proved humans were un-predictable, no matter how hardened they were to routine.

The madder I got at myself, the more disdainful I became at the petty prejudices I sensed at Fleet Command. Sarda behaved perfectly, steadily in the face of danger. *He* should have been the c-candidate in the first place.

With a painful sigh I slipped the top of my jumpsuit back over my shoulders and zipped it up, leaving on the pullover and leaving off the uniform. Tears welled in my eyes. I forced them back, feeling my cheeks flush. A few minutes later the uniform was back in the wardrobe and I was closing the door.

Why was I here? Did Kirk actually believe I had conspired with terrorists? With traitors?

Brian.

*Brian.*

Why wasn't he on *Magellan?*

*Coward. Ask the real question. Why is he on* Star Empire?

I had to know. I had to find out. I had to *get* out. I couldn't be in any more trouble, that was sure. Certainly couldn't top myself for mistakes.

"And I'm not standing still for this," I muttered, and looked around for a way to break through the computer guard.

Almost immediately I spied the heat sensor alarm

for fire emergency and a memory flickered of a quiet, talkative, passionate morning in my quarters at the Academy. "Yes . . ."

If I tried to walk out the door, the computer guard system would identify me instantly and knock me senseless. There was no way to disarm it from here. But . . . there had to be a way to fool it.

The carpet hampered my movements as I dropped to my side on the cabin floor and detached the circuitry access panel and traced the fire alarm alert relays. Yup, there they were, just where Brian told me they should be. Ah, that wonderful morning . . . I'd learned a lot that time . . . some of it was technical.

"There you are," I murmured as I yanked out the relays that would've told the ship's fire brigade about a tripped alarm in this cabin. Now the thing could scream its electronic brains out and no one would hear.

That done, I ran to the head and got the curling implement I used to make my hair look better than it did now. "You'll work. Okay, Brian . . . here's hoping you told me everything." Back at the fire sensor, I let the implement heat up and held it against the sensor filaments until they reached melting point, turned brown, red, and sizzled. At the locked door the alarm light started flashing, but I had disarmed the klaxon. *Brian . . . you'd better be—*

The cabin door hissed open. Even a computer guard wasn't allowed to trap a prisoner in a burning room.

"Weeeeow!"

The implement went sailing back into the head and clanged against the urinal, then to the floor. I was long gone before it fell.

\*  \*  \*

The transporter room on deck six hadn't been used in weeks. Everything was shut down completely and it took me a few minutes to reactivate the platform. Time mattered. I was safe unless the Captain or somebody tried to talk to me in my quarters; the fire alarm filament would cool and, assuming the crisis was over, the computer guard would seal the door back up. An irresistible grin touched my lips when I thought of the confusion once my escape was discovered. That little ploy was sandbox strategy. Anyone who knew how the fire system worked could've done it; anybody who had an engineer to explain the little flaws, that is. Captains had engineers. Kirk had Scott. I had Brian Silayna, once.

Something was going on here. My skin almost fell off when the door parted with a sibilance and someone came in.

"How did you find me?" I gasped.

"Through logic," Sarda said, depositing a heavy uniform parka on the transporter console. It was an extra. He had one on. "You were absent from our quarters. Logic suggested you had not escaped without plans to reach *Star Empire*. This is the closest transporter r—"

"Is that parka for me?"

"Obviously. As is this phaser."

"Why?"

"For warmth and for defense."

"Not why those. Why *you?*"

"I presume you mean—"

"Why are you here?"

He inhaled slowly, hating to explain. "It is illogical for them to assume you to be an accomplice to terrorists."

"You . . . don't believe I am?"

"It is not part of your character."

"I'm glad somebody thinks so."

"May I ask your plans?"

"Just one. I'm going to get to Brian Silayna on *Star Empire* and lay on that ticklish right foot until I get some straight answers. There's something more to this than just a terrorist plot. Brian's no militarist, I know that for sure. I've got to take the initiative, Sarda. Kirk didn't put me under computer guard for no reason."

He looked puzzled suddenly. "I fail to understand what you mean by that."

"Oh, come on. Any numb-nut can outthink a computer sentry. He must have known I would, Sarda, he must have. I don't know why, but he expected me to break out."

"Your line of thought has no logical basis, Lieutenant."

"That's right. That's why it works. Listen . . . thanks for the parka and the weapon. Will you operate the transporter for me?"

"It would be to no avail. When you were taken from the bridge under guard, *Star Empire* dissolved its clones and moved off to the edge of sensor range, well out of the transporter's reach."

"What? Damn . . . Kirk didn't fire on them?"

"He refused to fire on a fellow vessel until motivations are crystallized."

Making a dangerous alternative start to form in my mind, I grabbed the parka and headed for the corridor. "Let's hope he holds that thought."

Minutes passed in a flurry of turbolifts and tube accesses as we tunneled our way through the bowels of *Enterprise*. Soon, under Sarda's touch, the hangar deck flooded with yellow-white lights and we were opening the panels on the starboard hangars. And there sat the fighters. These weren't one-man Tycho fighters, but the newer Arco Class attack sleds, designed exclusively for starships when *Enterprise* was refitted during the fourth year of her exploratory mission. They were two-seaters, low-nosed and fast. Half of the eight-meter length was engine, to power a 360-degree thruster, two forward phasers, and two side-mount photon slings.

While starships and service vessels got heroic names like *Enterprise, Defiant, Constellation* and *Intrepid,* these runabout fighters were christened less flattering tags: *Zipper Fly, Stocking Cap, Wooden Shoe, Honey Bun, Rock Slide,* and *Runamuck.* Strangely enough, the chubby work-bees hangared opposite us usually got even less likely names like *Dante, Prodigy,* and *Gray Matter.*

"Those people in the dubbing department at Star Fleet must get bored," I commented, climbing the wing of *Wooden Shoe.* The hatch finally opened with some difficulty. The fighters weren't very well maintained, it seemed, since they hardly ever got used in actual combat. Bureaucrats. Somewhere, somebody was still paying somebody else to put nuts on bolts because somebody else was sentimental about the "skill."

"Can you get the hangar bay doors to open?"

"I shall attempt it." Sarda found the control panel and patched it through to the bay doors. "Yes, it can be done from here."

"Go ahead. I'll power up the sled."

*Wooden Shoe*'s two seats were fitted for optimum function and freedom of movement, but not much for comfort. I settled into the pilot's seat at the left and buckled myself in. "If only I can remember how to do this. . . ." There weren't any choices; I *had* to remember. Moments later the ship began to hum around me as power surged through its shell. I taxied out to the flight deck and waited for deck to depressurize and the vast, scalloped bay doors to open. My hands were ice cold. I was throwing my commission out the garbage chute and maybe even my life.

The sled jostled slightly, shaking me out of my thoughts. As I looked around for the problem, I felt a telltale shift of air and the suction sound of repressurizing.

Without turning, I said, "I can handle it from here on."

The seat beside me rotated and when it turned back, Sarda was in it. He said nothing. He must have keyed the deck depressurizing unit to give him a few seconds to climb on board with me and seal in.

"Sarda, they asked for me."

"You," he said, "and a Vulcan." His expression was unreadable. He slid a communicator across the panel to me.

I stared at him. "Absolutely not. Get out."

"I am not obliged to follow your orders, Lieutenant. When we clear *Enterprise* I shall consider you my commanding officer, since inevitably one of us must be in charge. Logically that individual is you."

The immediate urgency parted for a warm pause. I surveyed his plastic expression and felt a molten core behind its Vulcan stoicism. His amber eyes met mine not in camaraderie but in defiance.

"Why, Sarda? Why would you risk everything for me?"

His hands moved on the controls. Before us the immense docking bay doors made a loud hydraulic *chunk* and started to open. A thin line of black outer space appeared and got wider. I waited for his answer.

"Nothing I do is for you," he said coldly. "I have . . . other motivations."

My voice was solemn as a whisper. "You don't know what you're getting into. Stay on *Enterprise*."

*Wooden Shoe*'s engines whined under his touch. "Out of the question."

I took the controls. The engines roared in our ears, begging to be released, to fly. I engaged thrusters and raised the ship off the deck floor to a hover position, ready to—

The bay doors stopped opening. Orange lights flashed along the panels.

"The override!" I shrieked. "They're onto us!"

"The doors are closing."

*Damn, damn, damn—* "Not on me they're not. Give me full power. And sit back."

*Wooden Shoe* nearly tore itself and us apart trying to go from dead hover to full throttle. We shot toward the closing doors.

"Piper—" Sarda gripped his seat arms.

The fighter roared toward the bay doors, toward what was now only a slit of space not even as wide as we were.

"I see it." With a wrenching move that defied our balance gyros as well as *Enterprise*'s artificial gravity, I turned the fighter on edge. Engines straining, *Wooden Shoe* skimmed between the lips of the bay's maw as they snapped shut behind us. Space opened wide and we sailed into its black panorama.

I sank back into the seat and started breathing again.

"Keep us at half throttle. By the time they realize we made it we'll be out of tractor range and they won't be able to pull us back."

"They will, however, be able to fire on us."

Kirk's face filled my mind.

Within seconds we were out to optimum phaser range. And by then I had an answer for Sarda.

"He won't fire on us."

Sarda questioned me with a glare.

"I know he won't," I said.

"How do you know?"

"A guess." Sarcasm rose in my tone. "Is that all right with you?"

"Intuition is recognized as a command prerogative—"

"Don't say I'm in command."

"I beg your pardon?"

"Just don't say I'm in command! Just don't. I don't even want to hear it."

Disturbed, he turned back to the navicomp and plotted a course for the new position of *Star Empire*. Our fighter could outrun a starship at sublight, so *Enterprise* couldn't chase us if she wanted to. If *he* wanted to.

*He won't.*

"What happened on the bridge after I left?"

"*Star Empire* moved off—"

"I know that. I want to know the rest of it."

"*Star Empire*," he repeated with extra firmness, "retreated and Captain Kirk contemplated pursuit but decided against it. Uhura advised him we were receiving subspace hailing from Vice-Admiral Rittenhouse aboard his flagship, *Pompeii*, which is on its way to this sector. Rittenhouse ordered Kirk to abate any interference with the dreadnought, but only to hold it in this sector until reinforcements arrive. I gathered the Vice-Admiral has called in starships from all over the quadrant. Kirk's hands are tied."

I stared at him until he nearly twitched. "Other *starships?*"

"Affirmative. *Potempkin, Lincoln,* and *Hornet* specifically."

"It's that critical?"

"Evidently."

"But why? This is crazy. What is it about this that warrants the attention of that many heavy cruisers? Pulling other starships off assignment . . . ?"

"We are now out of phaser range from *Enterprise.* My congratulations on your 'guess.' "

His approval sent needles down my spine for a crowd of reasons. A fully trained Vulcan wouldn't have offered congratulations or any kind of laud at all. If I hadn't known Sarda's problem, I would've felt good at his comment, but I knew he could say such a thing only because of his lack of training and my ignorance, largely because of the harm I had done him, the distance I had put between him and other Fleet Vulcans. I felt cheap accepting the benefits of his pain.

"Thanks," I mumbled.

*Wooden Shoe* streaked through open space, past the sensor-fouling asteroid belt, toward the thing in the distance that looked more like a toy than an outsized star vessel. More toy than threat.

"May I ask how you escaped from the computer sentry?" Sarda wondered as *Enterprise* shrank on our aft scanner.

I shrugged. "I gave it a hot foot." A strange ambiguity crossed his face, making me get through my reluctance to explain. "Brian Silayna . . . a long time ago we had occasion to be . . . noticing details in my cabin at Fleet Headquarters. He told me how the fire system might be able to override a computer guard because the sentry system wasn't allowed to trap a life form in a burning room. It's a glitch in the system design. I just disconnected the alarm so the bridge wouldn't be alerted."

"Engineer Silayna has a talent for system crossover uses."

"He . . . certainly does." The *Star Empire* filled my vision, my whole mind. Within it, Brian. Why hadn't he told me? Why hadn't he let me know he was involved with insurgents? My heart thumped a thready rhythm of desperation, loneliness, infirmity.

Sitting beside Sarda intensified my loneliness. Particularly obvious was his refraint from applauding my ingenuity at putting Brian's hypothesis to use. I didn't know what I liked less—his approval or his silence.

"Sarda."

"Yes?"

"Why didn't the Klingons' phaser blasts go right through the projection of *Star Empire?*"

"Because the projection was not in space at all. It appeared only within the ship's sensors, adjusting the appearance of the phaser beams."

"So anyone out in space would see phaser lances shooting out without effect."

"Correct. *Enterprise*'s sensors 'saw' what the image projector told them to see."

I shuddered. "That's . . . a formidable weapon. No wonder the dreadnought was top secret."

Through tight jaws he said, "It was not intended to be a weapon. It was created for defense." He said it with a strange, unlikely intensity, and coupled the gruffness with an un-Vulcan snap of the navigation perimeter switch. "Like the synergist," he added with frightening bitterness.

I swiveled slightly his way and leaned toward him, hoping to bridge the gap. "What's 'the synergist'?"

His embarrassment was plain and it quickly pushed him back into his shell. But not soon enough to get him out of answering my question, especially since I refused to turn away, and leaned nearer. He became more and more uncomfortable. Finally he recited, "A synergist is an element which changes into a different element under the proper circumstances."

"But you didn't say 'a' synergist. You said 'the' synergist. Tell me, Sarda . . . or would you rather I find out for myself?"

His glance told me he knew I was just bulldog enough to do that. Seconds ticked. He wrestled with himself, trying to decide if he wanted me to hear it now, in his version, or later in the version of the Starbase's official library banks. I could hack into that system. He knew I could.

"I . . ." He had to clear his voice. "I received a Special Commendation for research contributions recently—"

"Sarda! That's incredible! Why wasn't it announced at Academy? I didn't hear a thing abo—"

"Because I insisted it be kept private."

"But an honor like that—"

"Is no honor to me."

"But why not? That kind of recognition could carry enough weight to get you back into the Vulcan Science Academy!" Before gushing any further, I picked up the weird jade flush in his cheeks and realized I'd said the wrong thing. Again. Gosh, big surprise. Speaking softly, I asked, "What was the project? This synergist?"

He actually sighed. "I developed a synergist which turns nitrogen in atmospheric compounds instantly poisonous."

I let out a low whistle of appreciation. "That's quite a . . ." *Weapon. Oh, damn. Another problem.* "I see."

His resolute silence was agonizing.

"Did you discover it by accident?" I asked.

"I was searching for a synergist," he admitted; "however, I hoped to discover an element which would render toxic substances inert, not turn beneficial compounds lethal."

*In other words, my lost Vulcan friend, you got a high award for an achievement that can only be regarded as dishonorable and shameful by your home culture.* I thought about the strange twists of fate bothering his awkward position between races. He walked a strange tightrope indeed, partially because of . . . guess who. "A defensive substance, not a terrible weapon," I murmured. "Sarda, don't blame yourself for humans' funny priorities. It's not your—" My voice caught in my throat. *"Defense?*—like the image projector? You! You developed the image projector! Didn't you? Didn't you? That's why Commander Sulu made you explain it to the Captain!" His cheeks flushed deeper jade and his eyes turned hard as gemstones.

I slumped back in my seat, drained. "Yours . . . so why is Rittenhouse getting the credit for it?"

Sarda's lips narrowed into hard, flat lines. He remained silent as a statue.

I knew. "Because he *took* credit for it. Right? He took it away from you, didn't he?"

When he spoke again his voice was tight with the battle for composure. "I was compensated for it."

"Meaning you were paid. Sarda, that smells! What's a fistful of credits compared to the recognition you'd get for such a fantastic device?"

"I want no recognition for developing a weapon of that magnitude."

"You didn't intend it to be used as an aggressive tool. And today's events proved you right. The projection was a perfect decoy. It let *Star Empire* lure the Klingon sentry ships out and get the drop on them."

"It is a dangerous device, too easily perverted. I should never have attempted its invention."

"Wrong. You're totally wrong! A starship could be misused too. Medicine can be misused. Any good thing can be. Don't torture yourself. Even Vulcans should realize the need for weaponry, Sarda. It's not your fault you were victimized by a power play of rank. You *should* get recognition for it."

A thick amber glare bored through me. "Was that your logic when you announced my propensities to our superiors at the Academy?"

I winced, remembering that terrible misjudgement, and gazed back at him in sorry shame and abrupt silence.

"Please do not repeat your generosity," he said harshly, and turned away.

Elegiac distance soon reestablished itself on Sarda's face, in his movements, and in his eyes. As for his voice—he refrained from talking to me or acknowledging my presence in any avoidable way. I had managed, unintentionally again, to completely humiliate him.

There was nothing I could do to heal the damage, but I was getting the idea these uneasy moments weren't entirely my fault. Sarda *shouldn't* feel as he did. There *was* great value, positive value, in his talent, and he could do tremendous good with it. Of course, he was trying to make it beneficial, but his inventions kept fouling on the natural human propensity for using military superiority to back up human principles.

*Our* principles. Of all the races I could've been born into, I had to be human.

"Do Arco Class sleds have destruct sequences?" I asked him.

"All Federation vessels are required to have—"

"Then I want to key into it. Code it into our communicators with a fifteen-second detonation delay."

For the first time in several minutes his eyes locked on mine. "I see no logical reason to expect a need for such an encoding," he said in a tone of voice that might have been his version of shock. Clearly he never took me for the kamikaze type. "We shall be boarding a vessel which must be returned to Star Fleet intact; therefore I—"

"*If* we can return it intact."

"I resist your logic."

"Then blast logic. Call it an order, Lieutenant. Call it whatever makes you set that code." Tension laced my words with undue force, but I didn't feel bad about it. I didn't care if he liked my orders or not as long as he followed them. He said I was in command. Then command I would. Since the earliest Phoenician ocean crossing, vessel captains had forgone any concern about being liked by those they commanded. Cold. I had to learn to be cold. Suddenly I envied Sarda's luck at being Vulcan, even though he felt less than privileged.

Unable to hold the iron hardness for long, I reacted to his eloquent silence by way of an explanation. "It's an old human tactic of anticipation. We call it 'covering your ass.' "

"It sounds unreliably colloquial."

"Maybe. But I'm not going any farther into this mess without stacking my deck. I just want to make sure we can get out as well as get in."

"But they insist their mission is peaceful."

"I'm not in a mood to believe everything I hear. Even if Brian Silayna is the one talking."

"He did seem unusually stressed." Sarda completed several computations, crossed indices in the sled's computer, and locked it in. "Destruct code isolated and tied in," he said, "as ordered."

We shared a bare gaze, but I refused to apologize. In another minute he had keyed the destruct code into our communicators, giving me something to bargain with once we reached *Star Empire*. The situation wasn't trustworthy enough to go into empty-handed.

"All we have to do now is sit back and get to that ship. Increase speed to three-quarters sublight."

"Increasing. Warp point-seven-five in thirty seconds."

The sled moved gracefully faster, engines humming behind us as we increased speed, an enjoyable, orgasmic sensation even in the unresisting vacuum of open space.

Suddenly we were both hit with a stunning instant of

pain. Pressure filled my head and I jolted forward against my restraining harness. Only the straps kept me from slamming into the control panel. Sarda was speaking but I couldn't hear until the buzz in my head cleared, leaving only the whine of struggling engines where moments ago there had been a satisfied thrum. I jolted back into my seat.

"What is it? I didn't hear—"

"A tractor beam." Sarda struggled with the controls.

"From aft? *Enterprise?*"

"Negative . . . from port. A ship coming out of warp." He intensified his scan capacity and drew in the magnification. "A Saladin Class MT-one Federation Destroyer . . . NCC-four-two-four . . ."

"*Pompeii*. Have they got us?"

"They have us," he stiffly said, turning his gaze into the space outside, "utterly."

I leaned forward and peered out. A blocky hull hung just over our port side. Though immense, the destroyer wasn't as massive as a starship, nor as streamlined; *Pompeii* was a chunky gathering of weapons, burst-speed, and cramped quarters. Its size drove home the true giganticism of *Enterprise*. I felt like I was piloting the tiniest moving vehicle in the quadrant.

And *Pompeii* had us.

"Do you wish me to hail them?" Sarda asked.

We were being sucked into *Pompeii*'s docking bay, crawling along the destroyer's endless grey-white hull and the Federation registry codes as tall as I was.

"No." I finally answered. "I don't want to talk to them before I can look them in the eyes and see what I'm dealing with."

He didn't understand and I made no attempt to give

him a crash course in human instinct. Soon the tractor from *Pompeii* began to strain our engines so badly we had to shut down and submit, rather contritely, to their control.

Indignation filled my mind. They had no business yanking another vessel out of space without a single formality. Power without authority drew us into its bowels, raping the integrity of my ship. Just a little, insignificant attack sled, okay. But *Wooden Shoe* was mine. More than that, even. My ship was *me*. Maybe I had stolen her, but at this moment *Wooden Shoe* comprised my whole universe, since I had given up any chance of being welcome back on *Enterprise* and had no guesses yet about *Star Empire*.

"I don't intend to stay here," I told Sarda as we settled onto the deck and waited for the bay to pressurize around us. "Don't take off your parka. And hang on to your communicator at all costs. Give them your phaser if you have to distract them. No—I have a better idea. Give me your communicator."

"For what purpose?" But he did hand it to me.

"A decoy."

"We have no reason to suspect the Vice-Admiral might confiscate our implements." There was a definite unspoken "do we?" attached to his statement.

"If he's been talking to Captain Kirk, he's going to consider us escaped conspirators with the terrorists, if that's what they are." I watched three security people, two men and a woman, walking toward us, phasers drawn. "Oh, yeah . . . they think we're trouble. We're going to have to break out of this ship, Sarda." I turned to him. "I could do it alone . . ."

"Not necessary. I have committed myself. *Star*

*Empire*'s extended use as a military device is partially my responsiblity."

"And if I phasered you to death, would we blame the designers of the hand phaser?"

His response was sucked away as the sled hatches whined open and we were invited to debark.

"Your weapons, please," a long-bodied security ensign ordered. We gave him our phasers, which he immediately shifted to a blond woman, who deactivated them. "Vice-Admiral Rittenhouse wishes you to join him in the briefing room. Come with us, please." The invitation was pleasant enough, but they still surrounded Sarda and me while escorting us through the destroyer's narrow corridors. My whole metabolism tingled in unexplainable warning, not to mention exasperation, at this sidetracking. I had to get to Brian and wring out some straight answers. I was the only person they trusted to tell the truth—why else would they have specifically asked for me? Brian had to be at the bottom of that. Hardly anybody else even knew of my sudden transfer to *Enterprise*.

As we came out of the docking bay into the corridor I found myself face to face with a large non-Fleet, non-Federation emblem on the wall across from me. It looked like a stylized Greek letter, but I wasn't sure.

"What's that?"

The security lieutenant said, "It's Vice-Admiral Rittenhouse's personal command emblem."

"I've never heard of anything like that."

"How many vice-admirals have you served with?"

"Hmm . . . must be nice." I sighed at the privilege of high command and followed him on down the corridor.

The briefing room doors slid open before us, and the

security man stepped to one side, funneling Sarda and me through first.

Before us, at the head of the conference table, sat a massive snowy-haired man with a grandfatherly face and small, flickering green eyes. Behind him stood a dignified black man in civilian clothes.

"You must be Piper," the older man said.

"Yes, Vice-Admiral," I answered.

"Ah, you know me. Good. Sit down, please. This is Dr. Boma, my astrophysicist and civilian liaison." Other than that he made no explanations about Boma's presence, nor did he even glance at Sarda. I didn't introduce my Vulcan companion because I assumed they knew each other—bitterly well. But the more I watched Rittenhouse's face as he talked to us, the less he seemed to remember Sarda at all. Had credit for the image projector shifted without their ever even meeting? "I'm sorry we had to snatch you up so unceremoniously," Rittenhouse said. "It's critical that no unauthorized contact be made with the insurgents until I find out what their game is. Captain Kirk received strict orders against any contact—"

"Captain Kirk didn't authorize our actions, sir," I said. "I acted on my own judgement. In fact, Lieutenant Sarda isn't responsible for his presence. I ordered him to come with me and told him Captain Kirk had assigned me to go to *Star Empire*. I'm responsible entirely."

Sarda opened his mouth to tell the truth and claim his right to self-incrimination, but I found his arm under the table and squeezed a firm shut-up. Sharing blame in a situation like this wouldn't lessen the severity.

"Sarda?" Rittenhouse looked at him. "Don't I

know that name? Oh, yes, the young scientist who helped with the projector device. At any rate," he looked back at me, "Kirk tells me you are the person whose biocode cleared communications with the terrorists who stole my dreadnought."

"Yes, sir, I am."

"Do you have any idea why? The obvious assumption is that you're in league with them in some way."

I started to speak only to be cut off by Sarda. "Such a conclusion is not obvious at all to anyone who knows Lieutenant Piper personally."

Rittenhouse grinned softly, as though remembering some pleasant encounter years past. "Your loyalty to your friend is commendable, Mr. Sarda. And I'm inclined to believe you. This is an unusual situation, without precedent to call upon. We're all playing it by ear, which allows me to give you the benefit of the doubt. The *Star Empire* is in the hands of dangerous people. Volatile insurrectionists. Paul Burch was my personal adjutant on the dreadnought project and I didn't want to admit it when he started to . . . change."

I tried not to lean forward like a fish catching at bait. "Change, sir?"

The Vice-Admiral's eyes shifted slightly down, a helpless sadness filling them. "Paul had been with me since his Academy days. Started as my official translator on assignment to Gamma Hydra. He was completely loyal, the most accommodating assistant I ever had. Supported me at every turn, came up the ranks at my side . . . I taught him everything I knew. Then we started the dreadnought special project. In retrospect, I suppose he expected me to promote him again and make him overseer of the project, but I took that option upon myself. Evidently Paul never got over it.

He became increasingly neurotic about his duties and paranoid about me. His bitterness has escalated to this unforeseen tragedy. He's . . . unstable. I have to suspect he's become sociopathic."

The chair back pressed into my shoulder blades. "Then how do you . . . how could he have convinced the others to help him steal the dreadnought?"

"Oh, his mental unbalancing wasn't overt to anyone who didn't know him well. He didn't let it show, almost as though he perceived himself changing. I suppose it was a mistake, some effort to return all the years of loyalty, but I didn't log any of the bursts of temper, the neurotic periods of silence, the little attempts at sabotage . . . protecting him was almost instinctive. I regret my delays now, of course," he admitted quietly. "If I'd done my duty instead of acting parental toward Paul . . . maybe we could've helped him. Saved his commission. I'm afraid there's no hope for that anymore. All we can hope is to stop them before they turn a supreme peacekeeping force into tragedy."

"Sir, why are you telling us this?"

He sat back, realizing he didn't need to explain his motivations to junior officers. Nerves, I guessed. It was difficult to straddle between the details that could turn a mistake into a galactic incident. Then he bothered to explain his explanation. "I'm hoping to save you, Lieutenant."

"Sir?"

"If you're a victim of circumstance, then you need to know the facts if you're to help us resolve this unfortunate circumstance. If you're indeed one of the terrorists, then you've been inveigled by Paul's charms and you don't realize the sad mental problems that motivated him to steal *Star Empire*. He's a most persuasive man, Lieutenant Piper. He's already botched his own career. I can't allow him to take a crew of impressionable young men and women down with him. We *must* regain control of *Star Empire* before he uses it in some diabolical, destructive way. If he tries," he said with pained force, "we'll have no choice but to destroy it."

Plainly he saw the shock fall across my face at such an idea. Cut *Star Empire* out of the sky? Words failed me entirely as I gawked at the prospect, and Sarda's stunned silence filled a cold space beside me. Rittenhouse stood up, leaning forward on the table and saying, "I'm counting on you to help us avoid that situation."

Responsibility and empathy for Rittenhouse clutched my heart, reminding me again how very human I was. He seemed so helpless, so hurt by Paul Burch's strange turning, yet he was trying his best to salvage his friend, or at least those Burch had convinced to follow him.

*Brian, why you? What did he say, what words exist in the universe that could charm you, of all people, into throwing away your career?*

I shivered, knowing Brian. Burch must be a compelling person to turn Brian Silayna off his prescribed path. Was Brian trying to recruit me? He must have known I'd never follow a ringleader. And why had they asked for a Vulcan? A long gaze at Sarda didn't provide any answers. Only another question: why wasn't *Star Empire* moving off? If they wanted the dreadnought, its power, its value as a bargaining chip, then why were they just hanging out there at the edge of our sensor sphere? They had what they wanted, didn't they?

The questions started to make me dizzy. I closed my eyes for a moment, torn between wanting to help Rittenhouse bear this awesome burden and a mad wish to file for transfer to the nearest ore freighter.

"Lieutenant."

"What? Oh. Yes, sir?"

"What do you know that made the terrorists ask specifically for you?"

Swallowing a lump of embarrassment, I shrugged, "I haven't found out yet. I planned to have them tell me when I docked with them. Although . . . I don't think it's very important."

"Oh?"

"Well, the person who sent the message is, or *was* . . . very close to me before my transfer to *Enterprise*. He may just want to recruit me."

White eyebrow puffs lifted in sage understanding of exactly my meaning of "very close." "We'll see," he murmured.

*"Bridge to Vice-Admiral Rittenhouse,"* the intercom said.

"Rittenhouse here."

*"Captain Kirk hailing from* Enterprise, *sir."*

"Pipe it through, Ensign Booth."

*"Captain Kirk, on discreet."*

*"Kirk here."*

"Captain, I have your two young emissaries here with me now. Would you like to have them beamed back? No, on second thought I may need them here to ensure communication with the terrorists."

*"May I ask what you're planning to do, Vice-Admiral?"* Kirk's voice felt like an anchor to me.

"I'm going to try talking some sense into Paul Burch. I may be able to convince him of the futility he's taken on."

*"And if you can't?"*

"Then we'll do whatever we have to do," Rittenhouse said. "War is an investment in peace, Captain Kirk, a necessary sacrifice for the good of all."

*"Are you implying we may have to destroy the dreadnought?"*

"We can't leave it in the hands of a vindictive maniac. Paul Burch is mentally unstable and he's stolen a device capable of destroying life on a systemwide scale. Better to cut them short here and now. I don't like the idea of taking life any better than you do, Kirk, but sometimes we have to sacrifice our minor principles for a greater ideal."

In my mind I could see Kirk pacing across the bridge, his brow knitting slightly, maybe frowning a little at the same uncertain coldness that also shivered down my arms. Sacrifice *whose* principles for *whose* ideals?

I squinted thoughtfully, imagining Kirk locking eyes with Spock in silent conversation. I imagined Spock's head tilting, the eyebrow lifting. When Kirk spoke again, his tone was full of that communication. *"I hesitate to fire on another Federation vessel until we know what's going on."*

Rittenhouse's mouth flattened into a line. "We do know what's going on. All we have to do is our duty. *Star Empire*'s crew must be stopped. Here and now. Before they go on a bloody rampage. This is a direct order: pinpoint your phasers on the primary life support systems of their two major hulls and be ready to fire on my signal. Kirk, of course I hope we don't have to do this. But if we're forced, we must at least try to salvage the Federation's investment in the ship itself."

In my mind Kirk looked at Spock again, with that same perplexed underlying suspicion. *Logical,* Spock said, I'd have bet, but the way he said it was dubious, doubting something in Rittenhouse's decision, some sniggering problem in the motivation. Kirk and his Vulcan counterpart were sensing—or was it just me? Just my imagination? Save the ship, kill the crew. Logical. But would logic be enough in a situation like this? Rittenhouse seemed like an innately concerned, kind, experienced man, but I wondered if he had been away from actual space duty too long.

*"I assume,"* Kirk began again, *"that we'll exhaust all other alternatives before we resort to that, Vice-Admiral."*

It wasn't exactly a question; in fact, it wasn't a question at all. Kirk was diplomatically refusing to fire on *Star Empire* without overwhelming reasons. Rittenhouse picked up on it.

"If you find yourself reluctant, Captain," he said, "you may return to headquarters and consider yourself relieved of this situation. There really was no reason for Command to order your pursuit of the stolen ship at all. I have several starships on their way here which are under my direct command per the Special Powers Decision, Star Fleet Regulations, Section forty-one-B. Thank you for your help in restraining the thieves."

Sarda tensed beside me. I nodded. Never had either of us heard of anything like this. Dismiss a starship in a hairline situation? I found myself silently begging Captain Kirk not to go, to stay here even if it meant defying orders directly. He *had* to stay. If he left, I'd be—

*"We're not leaving, Vice-Admiral."*

I almost passed out with relief.

"Are you defying me, Kirk?" Rittenhouse's gentle green eyes hardened.

*"No, sir. But Enterprise is in this whether we like it or not. For some reason the people aboard the dread-nought asked for us specifically. If we leave, they may be provoked into just the actions you're trying to avoid."*

The little Kirk in my head turned to the little Spock and the little McCoy behind him. *Touché*, the little doctor congratulated. *One helluva chess player, Jim.*

I started breathing again.

Rittenhouse realized he was in a corner, and inhaled slowly while he made a decision. He looked briefly at Dr. Boma, then punched the intercom button again. "Very well. But remember this is my project. I'm in charge . . . Agreed?"

Could he be referring to Kirk's renowned propensity for taking over in times of difficulty?

*"You're in charge, Vice-Admiral. Kirk out."*

Rittenhouse flopped back and sighed, but not in relief. "He doesn't understand."

"Sir?" I prodded.

He shook his head slowly. "Kirk doesn't compre-hend the value of the dreadnought itself. The Federa-tion needs that very unique power, especially the way things have been going in the galaxy. The Klingon negotiations are snagging, the Orions pushing their neutrality to a point of doing more harm than good . . . the galaxy is an inefficient puzzle of fragments. *Star Empire* could change all that."

That cold feeling came back to me, redoubled. "I don't understand."

"Don't you? Think of the accomplishments we could make if we all had the same goals, if we all pulled together . . . the unlimited glories if only the Klingons, the Romulans, the Orions could join with us in a singular movement toward the good of all."

"But, sir, they could. They don't because they want their sovereignty. And according to the Articles of Federation, they have that right."

"Do they?" He got up and circled the table. "The right to fragment the galaxy? The right to hold back progress? To be a constant threat? Why, with a fleet of dreadnoughts, we could unite the races of the galaxy, create one marvelous conglomerate. Imagine the progress, Lieutenant! Not a child without food, without medical care. In medicine alone, merging of sciences would allow a surge of advances to match the rediscovery of the Fabrini lexicons. Technology could move forward without espionage. There would be no more need for petty secrets, Lieutenant."

"It sounds . . . very nice, sir."

"It's a goal we should all be striving for. Of course, such things are the tasks of diplomats, not mere soldiers like you and me. We are pawns to greater schemes, and our duty now is to get that magnificent piece of engineering back into capable hands. I'm going back to the bridge. I want you two to stay here in the briefing room until I call for you. Understood?"

"Yes, sir, we understand."

Dr. Boma followed him out, and soon Sarda and I were alone.

Distractedly I got up and wandered to another print

of the Vice-Admiral's personal emblem, emblazoned on the door. It was gold, outlined in red, very majestic. "I hope nobody ever puts me in a position like the one he's in right now," I murmured. "I used to think it would be wonderful to rank that high in the Fleet, command so many people . . . I guess the higher you climb in the system, the more it ties your hands. Even Captain Kirk can't take action."

"Captain Kirk covered for us."

I turned. "What do you mean?"

"He obviously avoided telling the Vice-Admiral that you were under arrest."

"You're right. Why would he do that? What is it he sees in all this that I'm missing?"

"Nothing I am aware of."

"But there *is* something. Something about Rittenhouse that seems familiar to me. What was it he said about the Klingons, the Romulans, and Orions?"

"He spoke of the unlimited accomplishments if there could be unity in the galaxy."

The personal emblem seemed to swell toward me as I stared at it. Suddenly I understood something too terrible to believe. "No! He didn't. He said unlimited *glories*. Singular movement . . . a galactic homogeny or something. And he talked about a whole fleet of dreadnoughts!"

"It seems unusual to you?"

"It seems familiar. Like a pattern I studied for my captaincy dissertation. A very dangerous pattern."

"What is your hypothesis?"

"There's something about him. All the signals are here. The personal emblem—I've never heard of a flag officer establishing a personal emblem. And the name he chose for the dreadnought . . . he wants an excuse to get rid of the crew and get the ship back so he can use it to take power in the galaxy!"

Sarda looked at me as though I'd just suggested he stand on his head and sing love songs to Andorians. "That is an extraordinary leap of logic. No one ship, regardless of power, can possibly effect an aggression upon the entire civilized galaxy, Piper."

I groaned. "Pretty farfetched, I guess. Still . . ." Once again the Vice-Admiral's emblem absorbed me thoroughly, making me tremble with whole-souled warning, but in no way I could pin down.

A presence filled the space at my shoulder before I realized he had moved at all. "Your human insights are at work upon you?"

"That or my human imagination. I don't know which is more faulty. It sounds crazy, I know."

"They are telling you something about Rittenhouse which is eluding me?" It must have been difficult enough for him to admit human insights existed, much less admit his lack of them prevented a knowledge, but he said it inquisitively, not tersely, and urged me to answer. "Say what bothers you."

"I think he's trying to get in the back door."

"I do not understand that phrase."

Facing him fully for a long gaze made the connection I needed. "Let's see if the computer understands it."

"What do you hope to learn from the computer?" He followed me to the conference table console and remained standing behind me when I sat at the access controls and turned them on.

"We know Rittenhouse has the dreadnought project. Let's find out what else he's got. Computer."

*"Working."*

"Library tie-in. Read out current duties of Vice-Admiral Vaughan Rittenhouse."

WORKING. CREATOR AND DIRECTOR OF SPECIAL

PROJECTS—CLASSIFIED . . . DEPUTY CHAIRMAN, STAR

FLEET MILITARY STAFF COMMITTEE . . . ADVISOR, FLEET

OPERATIONS . . . MEMBER, LOGISTICAL SUPPORT

COMMITTEE . . . ADJUNCT ADVISOR, ADVISORY BOARD FOR

GALACTIC EXPLORATION.


COMPLETE.

_____

"Well, isn't he the busy little bumblebee."

"I am unfamiliar with that classification; however, if you mean to say the Vice-Admiral is exceptionally active in military government, I agree with your estimation."

"Thanks."

"You're quite welcome."

"Let's see where those committees fit into Star Fleet Command. Computer, supply visual schematic breakdown of Star Fleet Command."

A few seconds ticked away as the data was called to the top. Then we got a screenful:

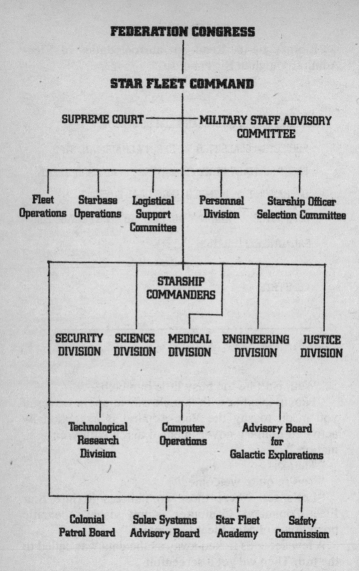

**FEDERATION CONGRESS**

**STAR FLEET COMMAND**

SUPREME COURT —— MILITARY STAFF ADVISORY COMMITTEE

Fleet Operations    Starbase Operations    Logistical Support Committee    Personnel Division    Starship Officer Selection Committee

**STARSHIP COMMANDERS**

SECURITY DIVISION    SCIENCE DIVISION    MEDICAL DIVISION    ENGINEERING DIVISION    JUSTICE DIVISION

Technological Research Division    Computer Operations    Advisory Board for Galactic Explorations

Colonial Patrol Board    Solar Systems Advisory Board    Star Fleet Academy    Safety Commission

Sarda gazed contemplatively at the schematic and said, "Interesting. Those committees are among the most powerful in the military government."

"A man that ambitious might be tempted to stack his deck."

"I beg your pardon?"

"He can't be everywhere at once, can he? Is it logical to guess he might try to put his own followers in power where he couldn't have influence himself?"

Sarda's brow furrowed. "If your instincts about him are correct or nearly so."

"How could we find out?"

"Perhaps there are correlatives between upper-echelon officers currently answerable to Rittenhouse or formerly under his command."

"I'll see."

"A time limit should make the information easier to handle."

"Let's try the past three Earth-standard years. Computer, correlate as specified and put the roster on screen. Only officers with current ranks of commander or higher." The computer's answer was:

CAPTAIN STEPHEN LEEDSON

ADMIRAL RAN ARMSTRONG

COMMANDER LU SING QUAID

COMMANDER CHIRITA DUR TAHR

CAPTAIN SUKARU TUTAKAI

COMMANDER ELIZABETH CONNOLLY

CHIEF ADJUTANT STAV

CAPTAIN ROY NASH

COMMANDER IRENE FOGEL-MALONE

COMMANDER SUSAN YIN
COMMANDER ADEB BEN ABDULLAH
CAPTAIN NIDITORICUMTU RO
COMMANDER PAUL BURCH
FEDERATION UNDERSECRETARY FOR THE INTERIOR NIGEL
   SWENSON

"Wait a minute . . . wait a minute. Look. Leedson
. . . Tutakai . . . Nash . . . Yin."

"Fascinating—three starship captains and a starship
first officer. Also, I believe Admiral Armstrong once
commanded the *Constellation*."

"Three out of twelve current starship captains. And
didn't you tell me—"

"Indeed. *Hornet, Potempkin,* and *Lincoln* are the
ships Rittenhouse said are on their way to this location."

"Rather an amazing coincidence, wouldn't you
say?"

"Quite."

"Quite and a half." I asked the computer to specify
present duties of everyone on the list not commanding
a starship, and found some very interesting, and frightening correlatives. "Sarda, do you see this? Lu Sing
Quaid is chairman of the Starship Officer Selection
Committee *and* a member of the Logistical Support
Committee at Star Fleet Command! Admiral Armstrong is the Star Fleet Representative to the UFP
Congress. Chirita Dur Tahr is in consideration for the
ambassadorial post from her home system."

"It seems Vice-Admiral Rittenhouse has maneuvered his influence with assiduity."

"He's got his fingers into everything. Could a vice-admiral influence the selection of representatives in those groups?"

"Easily."

"Computer, where does the Star Fleet Representative fit into UFP Congress?"

*Pompeii*'s computer wasn't nearly the equal of the one on *Enterprise* and took longer to trace down that information, giving me time to break out in a nervous sweat. Even Sarda shifted positions a few times, although I didn't think he quite understood the alarms that were ringing in my head about Rittenhouse and this weird, familiar pattern I thought I was seeing and hearing all around us. Finally the computer found our diagram.

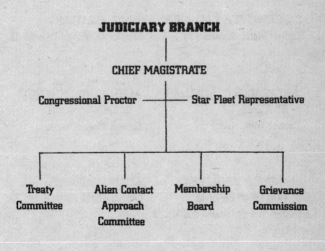

**JUDICIARY BRANCH**

CHIEF MAGISTRATE

Congressional Proctor — Star Fleet Representative

| Treaty Committee | Alien Contact Approach Committee | Membership Board | Grievance Commission |

# UNITED FEDERATION OF PLANETS

## GENERAL ASSEMBLY

UNITED NATIONS SOL SYS-
TEM
Contact World: Earth

UNITED PLANETS OF 61
CYGNI
Contact World: Tellar

EPSILON INDII STAR EMPIRE
Contact Cluster: Kohlhase

FIRST FEDERATION
Contact World: Tholus

CAMBORN SECTOR ALLIANCE
Contact World: Antares IV

PELIUS COALITION
Contact World: Tau Lacertae IX

AGGREGATION OF RIGELLIAN
SYSTEMS
Contact World: Rigel 4

ALPHA CENTAURI CONCOR-
DIUM
Contact World: Procyon

PLANETARY CONFEDERA-
TION OF 40 ERIDANI
Contact Worlds: Vulcan and Tau
Ceti

ALTAIR QUADRANT
Contact World: Altair 6

"Hmm . . ." I found myself hmming. "Looks to me like the kindly Vice-Admiral has his finger on the carotid artery of the civilian government as well as Star Fleet Command. Or maybe I should say he's got his knife on it. The Star Fleet Representative sits pretty high on that totem pole."

"A difficult perch to maintain," Sarda mentioned, "without great caution."

He made me grin, and I stopped sweating. "We've got to warn Captain Kirk. We've got to make sure Rittenhouse doesn't convince him to leave the sector."

I stood up, fumbling in the various pockets on the uniform parka's heavy exterior lining for one of the communicators, but before I found it I was slowed by a strange feeling, some odd awareness of extra thought, more than my own brain could exude, and I raised my eyes to Sarda. For a long time we exchanged that gaze, a tense, knowing kind of unity. Dangerous, yes; we were committed . . . almost. Did he want to stop before the commitment took us both forward into disaster?

As I suspected, he seemed to know my thoughts. Protocol wouldn't allow him to meld with me, to breach the deeply personal zones and boundaries between our minds, but the extrasensory communication was there, I swear it was.

"Am I wrong?" I asked, not knowing for sure just what question I was asking him.

A long breath flowed through him before he would answer. "We . . . are making gross assumptions," he warned, "without sufficient evidence. The Vice-Admiral may very well be no more than a supremely dedicated and active officer. I can find little logical support for your guesses, nor do I understand completely your bases for making them since I have tried to limit my contact with humans in spite of . . . circumstances. And yet . . ."

I latched onto those humanlike pauses of unsureness and wondered whether he would go the way of logic, which said I was out of my mind, or follow me into the fog of intuition.

"Yet," I urged.

"I see no harm in suggesting to Captain Kirk that *Enterprise* take care to remain in this sector."

He backed off, mentally and physically, as I had felt him do so many unfortunate times. The loss was acute, a hard ball in the hollow of my gullet. He might have felt the pain; I know I did. Bucking down the urge to follow him and pull him back into my sphere of sensation was the hardest job of resisting I had ever done. Almost . . . we had almost touched, almost understood each other. *Almost*.

I was beginning to really hate that word.

The communicator flipped open. Distractedly I tuned it to the right frequency, pretending not to feel Sarda's dense wall. "Piper to *Enterprise*."

But instead of Kirk's dulcifying response or Uhura's acknowledgement, the only sound was that of the briefing room door breathing open.

"Close it." The strong order made me realize Boma hadn't spoken at all before now. He held a phaser on us. Beside him stood Rittenhouse.

"Close the communicator, Lieutenant."

I remained still. "Sir, I've never had a phaser held on me before and—"

Boma grabbed the communicator and snapped it shut, knowing what I was trying to do, and with a disgusted expression stuffed it into a pocket. Rittenhouse searched Sarda for his communicator but found none.

"I thought I saw a perceptive glimmer in your eyes, young lady. I've only seen it a few times before, and I've had to take steps to protect the future of this galaxy."

"Then I'm right," I murmured, chilled to the toes at the prospect. I hadn't wanted to be right.

"The galaxy is ready to grow up, Lieutenant. You, move over there beside her." He motioned Sarda into the line of Boma's phaser. Boma posed a stern, inflexible presence, trenchant even though he wasn't saying much, a silent determination that piqued my curiosity. Men like Rittenhouse could entice followers with dreams and promises, but the steadiness in Boma's black eyes told of other motivations too. He was acting the myrmidon role, phaser held rock-steady, but he was no unquestioning puppet. While Rittenhouse talked, I found myself staring at Boma, looking for . . . truths?

"You're an unusually discerning person, Lieutenant Piper," the Vice-Admiral said. "My compliments on your rare insights. I can only hope they're not too contagious. I'd hate them to catch on before my goals are realized."

"Meaning before you can carry out a coup at Star Fleet? That's what the dreadnought is for, isn't it?"

"Not exactly. What I'm planning is necessary. The Federation is ineffective and will be until it comprises the whole known galaxy. My way is a better way for everyone. Get your hands up. I know better than to trust an independent thinker."

"This way, both of you." Dr. Boma stepped away from the door and herded us both through it into an empty corridor.

"The Klingons first, right?" I prodded when Rittenhouse came out. The answer hung on his face. "Don't do it, Vice-Admiral," I went on. "They have the right to self-determination too. What you're planning hasn't ever worked." In an odd way I was pleading, not warning. The false threat in my tone helped cover for my own stupidity. They'd left Sarda and me alone on purpose, to see if we would do just what we did. I would've listened in too. I wanted to kick myself for underestimating them.

"I can make it work, Lieutenant." Rittenhouse narrowed his green eyes, full of youth despite their aged casing, and wistfully added, "I can keep it pure. Put them below, Boma. Then join me on the bridge."

We watched him go.

"Move." Boma's phaser nudged my shoulder. Sarda was in front of me.

"Why are you doing this?" I asked him, moving slowly, letting Sarda pull ahead. "You're not the type to be enchanted by utopianism."

"How do you know?" He seemed amused.

"I can just tell. And you're a civilian. What could Rittenhouse offer you?"

"More success than I've had in the past."

"A high rank in some new fleet? That's how the song is usually sung."

"You're a unique young person, Lieutenant, the

Vice-Admiral's right about that. But you talk too much."

"Yeah," I agreed, "and I try too hard. *See?*" My arm swung in an arc and I put my whole weight into an awkward body slam. Boma grimaced as we crushed up against the hull. I tried to knock his hand on the bulkhead strut to make him drop the phaser but somehow he kept hold of it and surprised me with a deliberate twist to the left that broke my leverage. I tumbled backward, off balance, and skidded hard to the floor. He brought the phaser down to aim square at my throat. In desperation I shoved my legs between his and jerked him to his knees. His arms flew up as he struggled for control, but by then Sarda appeared and reached for the key nerves on the side of Boma's neck. Boma squirmed to one side, but too late. He grimaced and shouted a bitter "No!" before crumpling under Sarda's hand.

The same Vulcan hand hauled me to my feet.

"Thanks," I muttered, straightening my twisted parka.

"Your deductions seem to have affected them," Sarda observed.

"We hit home, all right. I'd rather have been wrong, Sarda. This is terrible for Star Fleet, you know? Either way we're in for a major shakedown. Come on. We've gotta get out of here." I stepped over Boma's inert form and jogged down the hallway, trying to decide where I was going, and ran flush into pain.

Blue-green lights. Energy . . . frozen spine—pain—I yelled Sarda's name before my throat closed up— hands in front of me . . . my own hands, white and bloodless—nerves burning, fraying—my head snapped backward as my spine constricted. I felt myself falling forward, slipping to one side. A heartbeat thudded in my head—*ba-boom—ba-boom*—knees buckled . . . no feeling in my feet . . . consciousness dribbling away . . . *ba-boomp—baaa-booomp—baaa*—

My mind guttered, and winked out.

# Chapter Seven

THE DREAM WAS uncomfortable. A dark place, cold and confusing, full of two-sided masks with strange faces inside, crushing my thoughts with their presence, too close, too tight, and the pain came back.

Roaring in my ears—too loud to think. I drifted upward toward a dimness. Not light, exactly, but a place other than this. A place to go, a place for me to feel again. I grasped onto the pain with my fragmented mind and pulled myself up toward that dim place. It was a hard, long fight. My life clung to the thread of pain and the terrible deafening bawl.

The sound changed even as I wished it to go away, but it didn't stop, changing instead to a sucking noise, like planet-sized bellows sucking and gushing—*sssssssssss-chuuuuuuh-sssssssss-chhuuuuuh*

"No—*Oh!*"

I clapped my eyes shut, one hand streaking to my cracking lower back. Stupid . . . sat up too quickly. "Oh . . . ooohhh . . ."

"Move as little as possible."

What was Sarda doing in the loud place?

The only thing worse than sitting up too fast would have been lying down again, so I leaned forward and pressed my pounding head between my fists. "Oh . . . brother. I always wondered what phaser stun felt like . . ."

Sarda gently maneuvered me into a position that let me lean back, supported by a blank grey wall. There were other walls here just like this one, I noticed as I blinked sight back into my eyes.

"Rittenhouse?" I guessed.

"He evidently assumed we would attempt to break away from Boma. Are you hurt badly?"

"My back feels like splintered wood. He must have hit me square in the spine." I blinked more and squinted into his amber eyes, sure I saw anxiety deep behind the Vulcan shields, and I wondered about the reason for it. "Was I out longer than normal for a phaser hit?"

"Only seventeen minutes."

"Then why . . . never mind. Nice little brig they've got here. I won't be able to computer-fool my way out of this." The cubicle surrounded us in a lead corrunite shell, except for the wall to my left, the opening, through which we saw an empty corridor. We would've been tempted to walk right through were it not for the bright blue glowing rim all around the portal, showing the disruption field in full operation. A very nice, complete little brig. I ignored the force field's threatening hum and pulled at my ankles. "My legs aren't with me yet."

Sarda relaxed slightly, exuding what must have been the Vulcan equivalent of a sigh of relief. "The human neural network begins to reactivate from phaser stun virtually as soon as the blast ceases. Sensation should return to your extremities in a few minutes, at which point we will attempt escape."

I shot him a look. "You think we can actually bust out of here?"

He tipped his head, meeting my gaze fearlessly. "No," he said flatly, "but you do. Doubting I can stop you from so futile an attempt, I shall help you."

Though I tried not to smile my thanks for his faith in me, my mouth curled into a grin as I said, "Always knew there was more to you than logic."

He straightened, barely perceptibly, retreating, but not as much as before. Luckily he didn't bother to argue that logic was his sole motivation, since we both knew better. "May I vent a curiosity?"

"Sure. Go ahead."

"To what were you referring when you told Rittenhouse that 'it' would not work? You mentioned a coup at Star Fleet . . ."

"That would be only part of it. A big part, but—well, Earth history has good examples."

"I am disturbingly ignorant of Earth history."

"You don't know the events that led up to the Third World War?"

"As I indicated, I do not."

"Well . . . freedom isn't something people just give up one day. It trickles away, bit by bit, without anyone really noticing soon enough." Seeing his quandary, I offered, "Let me give you an example. In the prosperity of the late twentieth century people kept handing over deciding powers to their governments, sometimes even demanding government intervention. Can you imagine actually *asking* bureaucracies to take over?" Disbelief crossed Sarda's face. As a Vulcan, he couldn't even conceive of such a thing, so I kept on explaining since interest lay behind his disbelief. "It started with the most basic of rights—property. The right of the individual to the fruits of his own labor went under in the face of the needs of his society."

"Were there not objections?"

"Sure, strong ones, but too late. Those who benefited from sacrificing the individual to society were too powerful. Some groups became so powerful that nobody could compete anymore. So more government help. The pile got bigger and bigger, but it was just a fat horse. The more it got fed, the less work it could do. You heard Rittenhouse talk about a common-good sort of ideal? This is the same thing. After a while the only way to survive in the "new" system was through joining a powerful group—a labor union, like I said, a religious organization, a political unit or business conglomerate that had gotten itself special insulation from competitors. Eventually individuals fired by self-interest just began to disappear, replaced by those groups, each fighting for a different way to promote the common good, which of course translated into whatever was best for themselves. The economic system fell like a house of cards. If society had problems, they blamed it on parts of society who were disruptive, the same people who just happened to have different viewpoints from theirs. So they pushed for control of those others."

"Like the Klingons," Sarda murmured.

"And everybody else who doesn't go along with his plan," I agreed, glad he could grasp so senseless an idea. "The harder the struggle, the tighter the control."

"The deeper the loss of freedoms," he finished for

me. He dropped his gaze. "The Vulcans would be among the first to struggle. And we would never cease struggling against such foolish unity."

I answered only with a silent nod.

"Strange," he said, "that no one questioned the basic philosophy."

"What do you mean?"

His brow knitted. "There is no such thing as 'common good.' The only good is in what the individual finds best for himself. If he does no harm in his practice, why would others seek to control him?"

"On Earth, it was because the others wanted what the individual had earned. Somehow they made themselves believe he didn't deserve what he worked for, if it went too far over what someone else had, even if that second person hadn't put much effort out on his own behalf. It became easier to get the government to steal for you than to work your way up."

"Inconceivable."

"It is to me too." The bench creaked as I leaned back in thought. "To everybody on Earth. That's why we guard our personal freedoms so dearly. We came too close to handing them over, and losing them forever."

"Did this . . . change of structure occur swiftly? All over the planet at once?"

"Well, Earth's a big planet, but it did hustle right along once it started. It started on the Asian continent and spread to Europe, the Africas, over to South America, and eventually the North Americas. Wherever it went it squeezed the life out of the economy by enslaving successful people to placate those who didn't produce."

"A viral effect?"

"More like a plague. Or a drug, might be the better way to say it. The addict keeps asking for more. The worse things got, the more the government interfered. After a while, nobody bothered to be an entrepreneur anymore. Oh, they got their utopian one-class society, all right, but the one class was poverty. The black market went wild. Politics became more powerful than personal initiative. People lost the idea of individual action and started looking for great leaders."

"The eugenics experiments of the 1990s?"

I nodded heavily. "I'm glad I don't have to explain to you about *those*."

"A most . . . shameful time."

"Oh, the worst was yet to come."

"Dictatorships?"

"Like bees' nests. Democracies turned into little dictatorships. Some of them weren't so little, really . . . The worse the economies got, the more those dictators concentrated on taking care of themselves, never mind the people. They started looking for scapegoats, blaming each other, blaming various racial groups or ideological units—"

"Disgusting . . ." He actually shuddered.

"Have you heard of Li Quan?"

"Not in any detail. Only in references to excess."

"He popped out of the western United States and used the border skirmishes between the dictatorships to carry out a global coup. He wanted to be a benevolent dictator, he said. Unify all people under one flag, he said. The good of all, he said. Total sharing, food for all, planetary consolidation . . ."

"What occurred?"

"Sarda, that system doesn't work! It sounds generous and perfect, but no matter how often it's been tried, it never *operates*. Li Quan kept talking benevolence, but the only way government control works is to turn everything into a law or a regulation, which means you have to bring in a military order to keep people in line, which means anybody who disagrees is automatically a criminal. His benevolent dictatorship started as a police state and escalated into a global bloodbath. And all the while he talked about his perfect order, how great it would be for all the people. Of course, in the meantime the people were starving because the economy was shot." I leaned forward intently as Sarda's brow knitted in lack of perception. "Don't you see? Rittenhouse is gradually taking control, gradually putting his own people into key positions. Admiral Armstrong as Star Fleet Representative to the Federation Congress, one step below the Chief Magistrate, three of his people commanding starships, himself chairing the Military Staff Advisory Committee at Fleet Command . . . and *Star Empire* to light the fuse. The dreadnought isn't the beginning of a science—it's the end of a long fuse!"

"A galactic military incident with the Klingons . . . ," Sarda murmured as he added it all up. "Li Quan's global skirmishes. The perfect excuse to launch a military upheaval at Star Fleet—"

"Establish martial law," I added, "and disband the civilian government."

"Remarkable. . . ."

"Sarda, he means to dissolve the Federation itself."

We stared at the wall, imagining the distant form of *Star Empire,* and I found that although I understood the processes I was so verbosely explaining to him, I was just as shocked as Sarda was by the idea of their actually happening to us. Rittenhouse drifted back into my mind, a gentle, grandfatherly kind of man who could make anyone trust him. I shook my head slowly. "He really thinks we'll be better off if the galaxy is directed by some central character. Himself."

Sarda turned when I said this. "He does not perceive the error?"

My right shoulder lifted in a tired half-shrug. "His belief that we should all invest ourselves in the common good will force him to violently subjugate the Klingons and Romulans; he knows that. What he doesn't realize is that vast parts of the Federation planetary systems won't hold to his view of the ideal society, and they'll fight too. We'll fight. He doesn't imagine himself at war with the Vulcans or other humans. He'll be forced to war beyond imagining, and finally to enslave everyone. He doesn't see it, but it will happen. It always has."

The impact sat on us like a grey numbness. I had to force my spine to relax again as we sat side by side and absorbed the terrible realization of my outlandish guesses actually turning out to be true. They must be true—Rittenhouse hadn't argued with me, and he certainly knew what I was implying.

Beside me Sarda battled to accept the full-scale foolishness my intense, emotional, too human race made itself vulnerable to, his face hardening, his eyes growing shallow and cold with empathy he would have denied. I saw anger grow as I watched him, his lips pressing tight, his stare filled with the hard floor beneath us, though he wouldn't have given in to it. There no longer existed any target for his anger from those awful times. Li Quan and his followers were generations dead. World War Three had shown mankind once and for all to let their society grow as a tree grows, free of pruning, free of artificial aids. Since then, since nearly making the biggest cultural blunder in the history of any known race, humans guarded their personal freedoms fiercely and had pushed out into space to guarantee those freedoms to others. Noble in the end, they had made gross mistakes which embarrassed me now in front of my Vulcan companion.

He shook his head the tiniest bit. "Such waste," he breathed.

I nodded. "That's what happens when society makes decisions instead of individuals."

"Society, of course, meaning whoever is in control at the time."

"Yes . . . the loudest lobbyists, political armtwisters, ideological cults, pro-protectionist powers . . . the father-protector syndrome. It's a human failing."

"I have never understood religions."

"Me neither."

"You seem to know a substantial amount about that period."

"Yeah . . . captaincy candidates have to concentrate on one section of history from a major Federation power and do a dissertation on it. Mine was 'Political Collectivism As Causal to Earth's Third World War.' So this is my subject. Sorry if I'm ranting. I don't mean to."

"I did request an explanation. Your apology is misplaced."

"In that case, I'm not sorry." *Just embarrassed.*

Sensing some intent of mine that I wasn't even aware of yet, he clasped my arm and hauled me to my feet, then held me as I wobbled through a dizzy wave and moaned at the numb ache in my back. I avoided eye contact; he didn't need any extra humiliation from his concern for me, so I did him the favor of pretending not to see it. A thanks would only have reminded him of his less-than-complete status as an adult Vulcan. "He must've had that phaser set on full stun," I groaned. "Any more energy and I'd be deader than I feel."

"Or less alive than you look."

My squeezed-shut eyes flashed open and this time I couldn't keep down an ear-licking smile. I grabbed his wrist. "A joke? You—joking?"

He managed to remain deadpan. "Negative. Vulcans never joke."

"I'll remember that, old bean."

"I am not a bean."

"Not yet." I shoved myself off the wall, fighting my legs all the way to the brig portal, and stopped just short of the force field. Except for the blue-lighted rim, the field was invisible, but I could feel its energy jumping around my body as I stood near it and its message was clear: forget about getting through.

"Suggestions?"

"I have none. Star Fleet does not often use its brig facilities but the technology behind them is state-of-the-art at all times. I regret my ineffectual presence."

"Your presence isn't ineffectual, Sarda. Not to me anyway."

In fact the only thing between me and severe depression was Sarda's Vulcan steadiness. What was I doing here? A day ago I was just a cadet, safe and buffeted by the years of gradual experience ahead of me before I had to face any real crisis. How in a matter of hours had I ended up at the hub of a military convulsion? All my life there had been a Star Fleet, a Federation, casting their protective cloak over our growing settlements on Proxima, providing a stable root for all their quivering branches, like me. What would I have to go home to after this? Proxima lay on the edge of Federation space, quite secure, until now. If Rittenhouse and his cronies took control, it might be years before the government fabric settled down. The galaxy would be a grab bag. Forces from all over would clutch at ground. My ground. My dripping moss-forests, my lepidodendrons, my fern ponds. My parents. Gone?

The small bulk of Sarda's communicator pressed against my thigh, still hiding in the side pouch of my parka. Such a small instrument. Yet with it I could key into the self-destruct mode on *Wooden Shoe* and with a touch destroy *Pompeii,* stop Rittenhouse in his tracks. That was worth dying for.

I pulled out the communicator and stared at it, my eyes blurring the mesh cover into a fuzzy gold square. It was warm in my clammy palm, as though carrying life of its own. I would do it. I would blow *Pompeii* to Orion. My only doubt was how strongly Rittenhouse led his people. If he died, would the coup die with him or would his cronies carry on? If I could only tell Captain Kirk . . . he'd make sure things were deflected at Star Fleet, get it all cleaned up, make it safe again.

I would never know if Sarda knew what I was thinking, the weights and balances shifting in my mind. He should've hated me for such thoughts, since his life lay here in my hands too. But his reaction held no resentment, and certainly no lack of courage.

His fingers closed over the instrument before I could open it, making no effort to avoid contact with my hand. Regretfully he said, "Useless. The brig is insulated against outgoing beams of any kind. Phasers also, if I recall the technology correctly." He eyed me intently, quite knowingly and with unexpected agreement, even sympathy. "There is a high-energy interior forcefield."

"Even a phaser wouldn't cut us out of here?" I sighed, recovering from near-suicide. "Damn. You'd think Star Fleet could arrange to be inefficient in one little area, wouldn't you?"

"Such an aim would be—"

"I know, I know." The wall drew me over to itself when my legs started to give out.

Sarda guided me down to sit on the floor again. "You should rest. Conserve your strength."

"I might as well. There doesn't seem to be much else to do in here. We do have to get out. I don't think Kirk has picked up on Rittenhouse yet, if he ever will, and we've got to tell him."

"Are you planning to escape back to *Enterprise?*"

"No, I still want to get to *Star Empire* and get to the root of all this. We have to find out how much is true of what Rittenhouse said about Paul Burch. Burch could be just as bad. A competitor."

"Unlikely. His call to *Enterprise* for support indicates quite different motivations, Piper. I would not be concerned for Engineer Silayna."

*Vulcan throughout, are you? That's not Vulcan generosity peeking through your shell. But thanks—I need it.*

"There's one other thing I can't figure out."

"Which is?"

"Boma. Have you ever heard of him? Neither have I. And what's a civilian liaison? Have you ever heard of that classification? I haven't. But I guess it isn't odd for a member of the Admiralty to handpick his adjutants, is it? I didn't think so. Rank has its privileges, right? Sure it does. And did he handpick those three starship captains? Were their captaincies rewards for fealty to him? Because if they were Star Fleet is in deep—"

"*Piper.*"

"What? I'm trying to think."

"And I am trying to save you from it. Please remain calm." He inhaled deeply and recovered from my thought processes, saying, "Humans can certainly be dithyrambic at times."

"I was just trying to be logical."

"Please avoid such attempts in the future."

"I'll try to stick to intuition."

"It does seem more within your grasp."

"I'll remember."

He started to say something else, but at that instant the hum of power running through the ship drooped away, taking all the lights and the force field's blue frame with it. We were in total, disconcerting darkness, very suddenly.

"What . . . a power failure? Is someone firing on us?"

Sarda answered only with a shuffle of hurried movement in the blackness. A swish of air rolled at me before I realized what he was trying to do. "Sarda! Don't—" I grabbed for him through the blinding darkness, but only caught the cuff of his pant leg as he shot by me. A second later I would've been doing the same thing, but the idea of his taking the first risk turned my stomach. I inhaled to yell again just as the power flickered on—the blue field came on first, and all I saw was a bizarre glowing silhouette of Sarda as the beam caught him on his way out—off and on again, full strength. The hum came back. The force field sizzled around Sarda's body for agonizing seconds, then spat him out into the corridor since enough of his mass was on that side of the repellent screen, and slammed him like a rag doll into the opposite wall. He crumpled.

"Sarda!" Only the sight of what the field had done to him kept me from running right into it. "Sarda!"

Slowly, too slowly, he began to move, plainly struggling with every muscle that would still work. I ached from the hard concentration on his face as he forced his legs beneath him and crawled up the wall to a standing position. He leaned heavily against the bulkhead, breathing hard, concentrating even harder. Seconds crept by. I called his name again. He pushed away from the far wall and came within an inch of falling back into the blue field before swaying to the control panel outside our cell. The effort to remember the pattern for shutting down the force field showed in his face, but in an instant the field died back and I caught Sarda as he slumped down.

"That was really stupid," I said. "Wish I'd thought of it. Are you all right?"

"Will be . . . fine . . . was necessary . . ."

"Hold onto me. Come on. I've got to get you out of here before they figure out what happened."

"Have no idea . . ." He paused and strained to speak clearly. ". . . what caused the power failure."

"Neither do I, but it's a fair guess somebody around here is out to do us a favor. Lean on me. Just pretend you're moss on a rock."

"There is no . . ."

"No moss on Vulcan. Use your imagination."

I grasped his upper arm and slipped my other hand around him, glad he wasn't fighting my help. The fact

140

that he leaned quite heavily against me was helpful but worrisome. He must really be hurting.

We threaded our way through the bowels of *Pompeii,* the cramped corridors making it difficult for us to hide from passing crewpeople and taking precious time when we did duck into some niche or antechamber to wait out a dangerous encounter. Sarda tried to mobilize himself and I gradually helped him less and less, for his sake, offering only a hand for steadiness and resisting the temptation to steer him along. The difficult part was keeping my solicitous gazes to a minimum. We had to get back to the docking bay, to the Arco sled, and get off this ship.

A simple enough goal. Until it got complicated. We started around a corner, only to have me slam Sarda backward again. A crowd of people were filing into the briefing room where Rittenhouse had originally put us. I held Sarda against the wall—more out of nerves than need—and peeked around the bulkhead strut.

Captains. Three I didn't know. With their aides. Rittenhouse . . . *Kirk!* After him came Spock . . . Mr. Scott . . . Dr. McCoy . . . here on *Pompeii?* Why? Those three captains must be Leedson, Nash, and Tutakai. So Rittenhouse's clique of soiled starships had arrived. My heart dropped to my boots.

"I've got to find out what's said in that meeting! Sarda . . . how are you making it?"

"Recovering. However, I would not recommend full encounter with a restraining field for daily consumption."

"Let's find engineering. We've got to tap in on that session somehow. I wish to hell Scanner was here."

\*     \*     \*

The engineering deck was only seconds away. *Pompeii* was neither as spacious nor as comfortable as *Enterprise*, which made consolidation of area necessary. Sarda steadied himself perforce and we walked handily into the Intraship Monitoring Section, past a handful of engineers and tecnicians.

"Hi," I greeted when they looked at us. "We're supposed to check on that power failure. Anybody got any ideas? I'd hate to go back above and tell them I didn't even know where to start looking. You know how security chiefs are."

They muttered at each other for a few horrible seconds, then one of them waved a Cogan wrench toward an access stairway and the electronic panel it led to. "Try up there," he suggested with an invisible shrug.

"Thanks. I owe you a brandy."

"Make it Denevan and you've got a deal."

I worried about Sarda as he followed me up the access ladder, but didn't help him for fear of tipping the crewmen off that something was up. When we reached the control panel he leaned on it and closed his eyes briefly, soon straightening to his usual posture. He said nothing about the look I was giving him.

I narrowed my eyes on the panel of colored buttons and switches. "There's a visual access screen over there. Do you know any way to home in on that meeting?"

"I know many reasons why we should *not* be able to do it, but little about overriding them," he said. "However, I do have an alternative. Open the communicator."

I did what he said, and moved aside while he tampered with the codes and signals in a manner I didn't recognize. All I knew for sure was that those weren't intraship signals. "What are you doing?"

"We should get a response in a few seconds."

"What response? Who were you contacting?"

He had faith in his own arrangements and let them be his answer. Our mutual eye contact was broken as two pillars of shimmering bands of light whistled out of nothing onto our platform. Surprise kept me even from glancing down to the main deck to see if anybody else noticed, but evidently the other engineers had dispersed and weren't around to see the forms materialize.

"Scanner! Merete!"

"Howdy."

"I can't believe it!"

Merete smiled. "After things settled down on *Enterprise*, we just waited in the transporter room for your signal like Sarda asked us to."

"Sarda . . ."

A Vulcan non-shrug met me when I turned to him. "I presupposed we might require help. While it would've been illogical to tell a senior officer of our plans to leave *Enterprise*, it would also have been illogical to tell no one at all. You might say I was employing an old human tactic."

I shook my head in awe and plowed through my confusion. "Scanner, there's a meeting going on one deck over us on the aft starboard side. Do you know enough about sensors to tune in on them without their knowing it?"

"Sure can give it the old Academy slap shot." He stepped past me and Sarda, pausing to land Sarda a loud, unexpected Tennessee clap on the back and a barroom squeeze around the shoulders. "Say, Points, how y'all doin'?"

Merete and I stared, holding our breath, watching Scanner's emotions surge through Sarda's unguarded mental connections. Sarda endured the contact as dispassionately as possible, unable to help an annoyed glance ceilingward and a slight grimace. I couldn't believe Scanner didn't know it was rude to touch a Vulcan socially. The look on his face said he figured a little country tactility couldn't hurt the universe any, for Vulcans or anyone else.

Sarda didn't exactly agree. But he didn't react either. Scanner patted the stiff Vulcan shoulder and said, "Bin havin' yourself some kinda adventure, eh? Well, let's see what's goin' on." He sat down at the controls and put to work all his hopes of someday being assigned to a ship's sensory. Evidently it was no hollow ambition. He knew what he was doing.

I moved to Sarda, keeping down a grin at his thoroughly peeved expression. "You okay?"

He gathered himself and sighed, "He is . . . rabidly emotional."

"I think I got somethin', Piper," Scanner called. "This your meeting?"

On the viewscreen appeared a swarm of Fleet uniforms of a few varying styles. The four of us crowded around and watched.

"There . . ." I pointed. "See where Captain Kirk and the others are talking to Rittenhouse and Tutakai? Can you narrow in on their conversation?"

"Give it a try . . ."

The screen flickered, focused in on somebody's

shoulder, then an ear, then backed off to encompass the group of *Enterprise* officers at the near end of the room. Behind them a yeoman was pouring coffee.

"Looks more like a high-echelon tea party than a tactical conference," Merete noticed.

"At least they have not yet convened," was Sarda's observation.

I leaned nearer. "Tune in the sound, Scanner."

He tuned in the audio just in time to catch Rittenhouse addressing Kirk.

"Captain, pardon my asking, but what is your ship's surgeon doing here?"

Mr. Spock unexpectedly butted in with, "I have frequently asked the same question."

I grinned at Sarda. "So Vulcans don't joke, huh?"

He cleared his throat slightly. "Obviously Mr. Spock is being truthful."

"Obviously."

Kirk glanced at his ship's doctor then and pretended not to be amused. "Dr. McCoy has full security clearance, Vice-Admiral, and I value his judgement. He has always accompanied me, and has Mr. Spock, when I feel the need for a balance of opinions."

I swore I saw McCoy stick his tongue out at Spock. "Scanner, keep the screen clear."

"I'm doin' m'best. If I make the signal any stronger, their computer'll pick it up as a call and answer it."

"What are they waiting for?" Merete wondered. "Why don't they convene?"

"They are. Look—there's Boma coming in."

Boma came around to the front of the room, closer to our view of Kirk's party. Kirk had moved away from his own men and was talking to Rittenhouse. The rest of the *Enterprise* contingent turned and seemed very surprised once they noticed Boma. I didn't know him, but they evidently did.

"Boma!" Scott exclaimed.

The coal eyes gave him a glare of shadowed indignance. *"Doctor* Boma now, Mr. Scott." He then looked at Mr. Spock, his gaze becoming harder, but even more restrained.

"What are you doing here?" Dr. McCoy asked.

"Investing in what's left of my future."

Spock spoke up boldly. "I am pleased to hear of your success as a civilian astrophysicist, Doctor."

"I had no choice but to succeed as a civilian, Mr. Spock," Boma said. "Court-martial is extremely final."

"I knew it," I blurted. "I *knew* he was fighting with Fleet countermoves!"

"Shhh," Merete cut me off.

". . . necessary," Mr. Scott was saying in that sage, rolling accent of his. "Order has to be maintained, after all. Mr. Spock was entitled to make decisions that were right for his own command techniques at the time."

"I realize your actions were proper regulation course, Mr. Scott. I've learned to live with the outcome, but I still believe rank privilege did us more harm than good."

"You are apparently still ruled by your sentiments, Dr. Boma," Spock said coolly. "I submit your considerable talents have been better applied in the public sector than in the methodical stratification of Star Fleet."

"You made sure I didn't have that choice to make."

Dr. McCoy stepped in without the slightest hesitation. "Spock didn't bring charges against you, Boma. The gross insubordination complaint wasn't registered in his log at all, or have you forgotten that?"

"Believe me, Doctor, I haven't forgotten a single detail about the incident that destroyed my future in the Service. All you mean is that I have Mr. Scott to thank for my dismissal."

"And I'd take the same action again," Scott said. "Spock was your commanding officer. You disagreed with his method and took that as an excuse to be abusive."

"I wasn't the only one," Boma phrased straight at McCoy, with an underlying meaning they both understood.

"The doctor had that prerogative," Scott specified. "You didn't."

"Gentlemen," Spock's strong voice plugged the pump. "Such discussion is profitless. The past is past. Dr. Boma has obviously turned his setbacks into successes, and Star Fleet is now calling upon him in a professional capacity. He deserves—"

"I don't need any help defending myself, Spock," Boma snapped, "least of all from any of you. If you'll excuse me, I have a job to do."

He went away, out of our screen, and the equal and opposite reaction was Kirk moving in. "Trouble?"

McCoy leaned toward him and poked a finger in the direction Boma had gone. "Remember the time a bunch of us got trapped on Taurus II in the *Galileo?*"

"Too well. Why, Bones?"

"Remember the court-martial Scotty pushed for afterward? That's the fella."

Kirk sent a long glance in Boma's direction. "Isn't that interesting . . ."

"Sir?" Scott prodded.

"I'm not sure, Scotty. Don't pin me down yet. But it is curious to find him here, in this particular situation. Spock?"

"Yes . . . curious indeed. . . ."

Scott suddenly looked Boma's way, his sharp eyes gleaming darkly. "Aye—"

"Jim, that's a pretty long reach, isn't it?" Dr. McCoy complained.

"Is it, Bones? We'll see."

"Gentlemen," Rittenhouse called, breaking up our little party and making Scanner fade back the viewer and struggle to refocus on the broader field. Rittenhouse gestured the others to sit down at the conference table, then addressed them. "You've all been briefed about our delicate situation with the dreadnought *Star Empire*. In order for us to efficiently and effectively disable the dreadnought without destroying it, we must act as a unit. Naturally we'll do all we can to keep from harming the occupants, but we must disable them at any cost, and we have an equal responsibility to the wholeness of the galaxy to preserve the ship itself. *Star Empire* is a prototype, produced at great expense, and Federation officials believe it holds the key to ultimate peacekeeping along disputed zones. We must preserve that ship, gentlemen."

"Even if it means sacrificing the people on board her," Dr. McCoy finished for him. The doctor had a full clip of nerve, I had to give him that.

Rittenhouse performed marvelously, skillfully, and I could see how he managed to lure so many intelligent, ambitious people into trusting him. "We'll avoid that unappealing alternative, of course, Doctor, but if the options before us are exhausted, I assure you I will give that order. These are dangerous people. With every moment that passes they're learning more and more about the dreadnought's capabilities and how to use them against us. As implementor and overseer of the dreadnought project, I can tell you that ship is more than capable of disabling and even destroying all five of our ships. Underestimation on our parts would be a fatal error, and I don't intend to sacrifice valuable commanders to a handful of reactionaries. I've invited one of the dreadnought's designers here to explain the ship's primary stress points, targets which will disable the ship, but also preserve it. Dr. Boma? The table is yours."

"Thank you, sir. Gentlemen, if you'll please look at your monitors, the computer will follow my description with appropriate diagrams. The outer hull shell is made of quantobirilium, a material developed by myself. Quantobirilium is a composite alloy, extremely durable, and capable of dissipating energy to all parts of the ship for a limited time. A direct phaser blast would fail to dislodge its molecular cohesion for several seconds, even with shields completely down. It can endure extended phaser fire before it weakens and ruptures. The effect is similar to hitting a rubber wall with a hammer. The energy dissipates rather than shattering the structure. It buys time for the crew to reestablish shield power, maneuver to fire, or other tactics."

"How can we disable a ship like that, even if we do break through the shields?" Commander Scott asked. "Does that beast have any weak points?"

Bubbling with aloof pride, Boma flatly said, "No. It

only has places that are less invulnerable than others."

Mr. Scott frowned. I read "you'll have t'prove it to me" on his face, but he sat back again.

Boma went on. "It has basically the same vulnerable points that a conventional ship has: the nacelle struts, and on the underbelly near the weapons pods. As you can see, the structural skeleton is especially bulky, with extra-heavy supports in a honeycomb pattern, which is, of course, the strongest per-unit design known to our science. Each square unit of strut will support seventy-eight percent more stress than conventional design. Its greatest weakness is the hull-mounted optics of the image projector, which can be easily knocked out. But the ship itself, gentlemen," he said, puffing up, "can take a pounding that would reduce any one of your starships to powder."

"My mother's underdrawers!" Scanner derided.

I looked at Sarda, both of us remembering his statement about one ship's inability to carry out an aggression. We were hanging in space across from one such ship. "That's why Rittenhouse called in his three starships. It'll take combined attack to disable that dinosaur."

Rittenhouse moved his barrel-thick body to the head of the conference table. "It's time for us to make a move, gentlemen. They have a master ship, but we have numbers. Paul Burch is a bureaucrat, not an engineer, and certainly not a commander of starships. We will now take a singular, collective action."

"Ultimatum?" Sarda wondered.

"Sh . . . wait." I leaned at Scanner's shoulder.

Rittenhouse tapped through to the bridge. "Ensign Booth. Open a hailing frequency to *Star Empire*, priority channel."

*"Aye, sir. Hailing frequency on standby."*

*"Commander, Star Empire. This is Vice-Admiral Rittenhouse speaking on behalf of the Federation. You are surrounded and outnumbered. If you attempt to retreat any farther, we will be forced to unify the power of four starships and a destroyer to disable your vessel. If necessary, we will crowd you into the neutral zone and let the Klingon border patrols persuade you. The game is up, Star Empire. Surrender immediately. What is your reply?"*

For many moments their reply was nervous silence, though they were obviously receiving. I spent those moments taking special note of the glances exchanged between Captain Kirk and Mr. Spock. They were expertly subtle communications, unnoticed by anyone else in the briefing room. But I noticed, and I paid attention.

*"Star Empire, we're awaiting your reply,"* Rittenhouse prodded.

*"Pompeii, this is Commander Paul Burch."*

Everyone tensed. His accent was primly English.

*"We understand your message. We refuse to comply and repeat our previous demand for a diplomatic boarding party comprised of Lieutenant Piper and a Vulcan. However, we annex a further stipulation: that Captain James Kirk also accompany them. Those are our conditions, Pompeii. Any aggression against us will result in the destruction of your ships. I'll do this, Vice-Admiral; don't assume I won't. I regret that these actions became necessary. I'm appealing to Captain Kirk to meet privately with us aboard Star Empire, for the sake of the—"*

"Cut transmission."

There was a crackle; then Ensign Booth's voice

from our bridge said, *"Transmission aborted, sir. Star Empire is back on standby at your disposal."*

"Why didn't you hear them out?" Kirk asked.

Surprisingly it was Nash who answered the question. "There's no point in giving them any leverage, Jim. You know the advantage of keeping the psychological upper hand."

"There's also an advantage in knowing the whole story." Kirk turned to Rittenhouse. "I'd like to take them up on their request. Meet with them on their terms."

"Their terms indeed!" Rittenhouse bellowed. "Hand over a starship commander to terrorists? Kirk, you've gone soft."

"We've got to comply if we're going to resolve this problem peacefully."

"That's exactly what Burch wants us to believe. Kirk, don't you see—"

"I see you evading a chance for resolution and I'd like to know why."

"Vice-Admiral," Spock interrupted, "your conclusions are based upon assuming disaster before such an outcome has been implied."

"I'm willing," Kirk said in the forceful wake of Spock's words, "to take the risk."

"But *I'm* not," Rittenhouse said. "You'd just complicate the problem for us. This situation requires drastic action. I'm designating Captain Nash as my second-in-command with the special grade of Commodore for the duration of this incident."

"Vice-Admiral!" McCoy jolted to his feet.

Beside him, Scott also unseated himself. "I protest! That's a direct affront to Captain Kirk!"

Kirk now stood up, never once taking his eyes off

Rittenhouse. Sternly he said, "Sit down, both of you. The Vice-Admiral and I have some definite disagreements on several points, primarily involving the lives of the people on *Star Empire.*"

"You're being insubordinate, Kirk."

"And you're acting vindictive, Vice-Admiral," Kirk shot back, raising his voice until a hot shiver ran down every spine that heard it.

"Jim, be sensible," Captain Leedson began. "You have to admit this situation demands a heavy touch."

"Not before some effort at compromise has been made."

Spock turned on his chair's pivot. "The dreadnought's appropriators have made a request for conference. It is unreasonable to deny their request, since mutual silence is entirely harmful to both sides, Captain Leedson."

Rittenhouse spoke, "Is it unreasonable to deny terrorists a chance to capture elite hostages, Commander? No. I refuse to allow any contact with these people."

"They've requested me," Kirk said, "and I'm willing to go."

"Absolutely forbidden. It would be suicide."

"I agree," offered Captain Tutakai.

"Captain Kirk," Commodore Nash said, "perhaps your well-known courage at leading your men into danger is slightly misplaced here—"

"Don't placate me, Commodore. It's our moral duty to fill in the holes before we fire on *anyone.*" His gaze shot back to Rittenhouse. "Any other suggestion is a violation of Star Fleet emergency action policy, and I, for one, intend to fill in those holes."

In the privacy of our one-way mirror, I pointed at

the screen. "Look," I said to those around me as we watched the argument unfold. "Notice the only dissent comes from the *Enterprise* officers. Everybody else is going along with Rittenhouse."

"Yeah," Scanner drawled, "and he's turnin' cartwheels to keep Captain Kirk from tawkin' to *Star Empire*. Makes his logic kinda thick to swaller."

Sarda pressed his lips together at Scanner's colloquialisms, but that comprised his whole complaint.

"Jim," Rittenhouse was saying, "I don't know you well, but your reputation speaks for you both in nobility and notoriety. I know you have a predilection for defying direct orders and I can't allow that to occur in this case. You give me no choice but to act in the extreme." He punched a com button. "Security." Instantly—and I do mean right away—the room was swarming with behemoths, phasers drawn. "I'm placing you and your officers under special temporary arrest."

"You're joking!" McCoy was on his feet again.

Spock as well. "Vice-Admiral, such an action is highly irregular and against all precedent."

In the same breath Scott volunteered, "There's your formal protest tae Federation Congress!"

Their words, overlapping in an angry chorus, made less sense than the violent indignation on their faces. In the midst of the flurry stood Kirk, an oak of dauntless rebellion, locked in silent war with Rittenhouse.

"Someday you'll all understand why I had to do this," Rittenhouse said, then waved to the security men. "Confine them in my quarters. I want two guards outside and two inside with them at all times. No one countermands their captivity but me. Is that clear?"

Eyes burned at each other as the four from *Enterprise* were herded out of the briefing room while Sarda, Scanner, Merete, and I watched in blank dumbfoundment. On the screen before us, Captains Leedson and Tutakai exchanged a worried sort of in-over-our-heads glance, but they followed Rittenhouse and Nash without protesting these strange turns of protocol.

"Damn . . . damn him . . . he knows all the angles." I stepped back and stared at the black screen.

My head buzzed, warning lights blinking deep in my mind. This couldn't be happening. He had them. He had pressured Kirk down, maneuvered him into helplessness, and pounced. Kirk was the one barrier between Rittenhouse and his military take-over, the one element I'd been counting on to buck the tide with me once I'd convinced him of the Vice-Admiral's plans. And I hadn't even had a chance to talk to Kirk yet! I *had* to talk to him . . .

I flipped my attention to my right, suddenly aware of a funny sensation. Two sets of eyes. Flipped left. Another set.

"What are you all looking at *me* for?"

"Whatcha want to do now?" Scanner voiced for himself and the others.

"How do I know?!"

"It's your party, Piper."

My clothes seemed to be sticking to my body. I closed my eyes and leaned on the half-wall of our access balcony. Couldn't I wake up now? Wasn't there a regulation against nightmares lasting this long?

I shook my head. "I hate this. *Hate*. By the time it's over I'll probably hate you too."

"Nobody hates me," Scanner said, grinning. "I'm too cute."

I paced across the platform. "We've got to break them out of there. Nobody at the Federation is going to listen to us if Rittenhouse succeeds in suppressing Kirk."

"Or discrediting him," Sarda added.

"Kirk and Spock together carry as much credibility as a vice-admiral. Add Scott, McCoy, Burch, and us . . . but it's got to be a combined effort to clean up the corruption before it goes any deeper. We've got to find out where they're taking Kirk and the others."

"You and I are too conspicuous," Sarda pointed out. "Doubtless the ship is being alerted as to our escape."

"I'll go."

The offer came over my shoulder. I turned. "Merete, it's dangerous."

"But they're not looking for me."

"I can go with you," Scanner offered.

"No, better I go alone. I always wanted to try my hand at reconnaissance anyway."

"We can't stay here," I said. "Suggestions?"

Sarda offered, "Perhaps the hangar deck."

"They'll be guarding *Wooden Shoe*, or at least monitoring it. Anything else?"

"You betcha," Scanner said. "Ship's mess. Nobody's gonna be hangin' round down there right now."

"Good idea. Merete, you take care of yourself, you hear me? We'll split up and meet in the galley. Okay? Okay . . . here's to us."

The ship's galley was deserted. Not counting us, of

course. The three of us found a small storage area to hide in and camped out on the floor, out of sight, to wait.

"We shall be able to see the doctor from here if she comes in," Sarda concluded as he lowered himself to the floor beside Scanner and lined up his vision with the entrance to the mess hall.

"You sure she'll be all right?" Scanner directed at me.

"No!" I exploded. "I'm not sure. I'm not sure of anything. I'm not sure I'm *here!* When I'm sure I'll let you know!"

That felt better.

I sat down opposite them and became involved in a serious slump. They watched me, I knew it, but I didn't care. I couldn't care. It wasn't my job to care. This was someone else's responsibility, not mine, and I was getting tired, so tired . . . not fair . . . too much . . . too much for me.

The strength and support from across the tiny area flooded toward me, worked on me, pulled me through, and when I looked up the innate oppositeness between Scanner and Sarda flooded over me. They were nothing alike, even at the first glance. Humanoid both, but that said it all. Even to the positions they sat in—Scanner with legs crossed, arms hanging on his knees, gazing at me through a flop of darkish hair, Sarda at regulation posture, sitting on both knees like a Vulcan at meditation, his bronze hair utterly neat despite all we'd been through. Quite a pair, my fleet. My spectrum of responsibility kept getting wider and deeper, harder to hold on to no matter how I tightened my grip. I had started out in this adventure as dealer of my own destiny and sole victim of my own errors. Now, somehow, three more lives hung on the balance of my next decision. And how could I even count the number beyond that? Star Fleet hung in the same balance, the Federation and all the people it protected, the Klingons and our other "enemies" in a war not yet provoked, all clinging to a lifeline which was the tightrope beneath my feet.

I closed my eyes, drifting away. Through the black velvet of open space, cold and numbing, past binaries and nebulae and all the spectral beauty available among the stars. Into a cool atmosphere and into moisture, a receded warmth, and finally swelter of primordial jungle, the taste of herbaceous growth that echoed Earth's most ancient memories. All around me swarmed the yellow jackets imported to pollinate our Earth-native crops. Beautiful, oh, their sound, their loud buzzing in our glades! The air, thick with the moist scents put off by the cycads and flytraps and sap-jeweled carnivorous plants, filled my senses and clung to my skin like perfume. I wanted to roll in the fronds, dive under the lichen-frosted pads on the salt pond. I could swim all the way from the waterfall to our settlement, to where my parents' laboratory nestled amid dripping skirts of moss, hidden in the swampscape by its medieval architecture, like all the man-made structures on Proxima. We liked it that way. The heavy stone construction stood up to Proxima's moist heat better than anything we might have toted from some other star system, and a growing colony couldn't afford many frills, so we made aesthetic use of practical, available materials.

Over the heavy, grassy scents of wet foliage came aromas of dinner at the settlement. Families gathering over stew or omelets, laughing at the day's mistakes, discussing its problems or its discoveries, joking about our latest mishaps with interplanetary bureaucracies because somebody needed one thing or other for an obscure experiment.

It all smelled and felt so good—why had I ever left? And how long—six years now, counting everything. I wasn't old enough to shrug off that much time.

I put my head in my hands and squeezed Proxima out of it. I wasn't there; I was here, in a chilly galley, in trouble, and about to get into more trouble. That needed to be dealt with.

A movement, very slight, shook me clear of Proxima and I plowed into a new thought. "I wonder what happened between Spock and Boma."

Sarda withdrew the hand that had been reaching toward me. Then he spoke, particularly deliberate, careful. "Spock had a more difficult time acclimating to the Service in the company of humans. In fact, before his request for starship duty among humans, any Vulcans in Star Fleet were quite isolated. Their own ships, their own accommodations, private meal facilities . . . there was not true interaction. Mr. Spock pioneered interaction between our races. I'm sure there were stresses for him to bear which might have crushed a weaker individual."

"Are you trying to answer my question with that?"

"Perhaps indirectly. When the *Enterprise* first began exploring, humans were unaccustomed to Vulcan methods, Vulcan demeanor, Vulcan ways in general. Many humans still tend toward dislike of Vulcans because they do not understand us. In a tense situation, I hypothesize that logic and emotionalism clashed en route to a singular end."

I felt a sympathetic twist on my lips. "Or logic and intuition?"

He thought about it. "Unlikely. Dr. Boma does not impress me as an intuitive individual. Emotion and intuition do not necessarily coexist."

In his way, he had just paid me a compliment.

"Why would things have been so hard on Mr. Spock?" I asked. "Why didn't he just go with the isolated Vulcans in the Fleet if the pressure was so bad?"

A depth crossed Sarda's thought, though impassivity still held on his expression. Only his pause before speaking hinted at any discomfiture, perhaps even a need to guard another Vulcan's reputation. Finally he decided to speak it out. "Mr. Spock is half human."

Immediately Sarda tightened his lips over the echo.

I stared at him.

Scanner stared at him.

"Odious," I said.

"I may retch," Scanner said.

"And I'm on the same ship with him?"

"Y'all can kill me now."

Sarda held his breath and looked from me to Scanner and back again. "I meant no offense—"

"Just watch it next time, Points. Steppin' perty close to the ol' homestead. I bin known to hold grudges nigh onto a day an' a half." He rebuked Sarda with an exaggerated glower, which slowly changed to a grin of surprising familiarity. Only then did I remember that they'd been roommates for a few weeks and probably knew each other better than I realized. Scanner seemed thoroughly comfortable with Sarda, more so than most humans ever got with most Vulcans, and

I wondered if that was because of Scanner's utterly open personality shoving its way through, or if Sarda had, for some unknown reason, opened up to him. The latter was doubtful; Vulcans and humans might be more accustomed to each other, but Vulcans remained scrupulously Vulcan, and they still considered casual display of emotion crude and a sign of weakness. The more I thought about it, the more I felt like a textbook example of that. And Sarda was Vulcan. Trying to squeeze emotion out of him constituted a terrible cruelty, a gross unfairness on my part. All these years I'd respected Vulcans, yet not bothered to respect Sarda.

And he worried about insulting *us?*

I didn't want to laugh at him. So we'd boxed ourselves into a corner again.

Scanner took care of it with another unrefined squeeze on Sarda's arm. "Back home in Cullowhee, we'd take y'all back behind the smokehouse and made you shuck corn. Guess we can let it go this time, though."

If I hadn't been sitting down I'd have fallen down when Sarda firmly responded, "Your generosity is staggering, Judd."

So there was something there. I suddenly got a slap in the face from assuming I alone could break through to Sarda, and lowered my eyes away from petty jealousy.

Sarda said, "I had assumed Spock's mixed parentage to be commonly known."

A mirthless huff carried my thoughts. "No, I didn't know one of his parents was human. But I guessed he had a human half."

"I fail to comprehend your meaning."

His lack of understanding came as no surprise. How could I explain my feelings without insulting him, even hurting him? Lost in a blurred sight of the joint between the wall and the floor beside Sarda, I mumbled, "Kirk is his human half."

Relief flooded over us when we first glimpsed Merete's platinum hair over her blue medical shirt coming into the mess hall. She knelt beside me when we called her into our cubicle.

"Deck two, starboard," she said. "Three guards in the corridor, and there are two inside with Kirk and the others."

"Rittenhouse ain't taking any chances," Scanner said.

"With Kirk," I thought aloud, "I wouldn't either. We've got to disable those guards in the hall."

"Perhaps we might cause a similar disruption of energy as that which freed us," Sarda suggested.

"It'd take us all day to find the circuitry."

"A diversion?" was Scanner's idea.

Merete said, "I might be able to drug them somehow."

"There's a more subtle way." I stood up and stretched my legs. "We can walk down the hall and slug 'em."

"Na-nee na-nee na-na . . . nah nah nah . . . na-nee na-nee na-na . . . *hop! hop! hop!* . . . na-nee na-nee na-na . . . nah nah nah . . . na-nee na-nee na-na . . . *hop! hop! hop!*"

The hard part wasn't thinking of it, or deciding who

would indispose which guard, or keeping in character in spite of the security guards' expressions when they saw four fully commissioned Star Fleet officers doing the bunny hop down the corridor toward them. The hard part was teaching a Vulcan how to do a dance step. Sarda understood music. But not dancing. And not singing.

"Na-nee na-nee na-na . . . *hop! hop! hop!*"

Okay, maybe Scanner, Merete, and me squawking the syllables didn't qualify as much of a vocal lesson, but in a matter of seconds the three security guards outside Rittenhouse's quarters were a tangle of long legs and helmets at our feet.

"Not too bad for four pikers with nuthin' but a communicator between us," Scanner observed, watching Merete put the hypo back in her medikit.

"Get their phasers," I instructed, handing Sarda the phaser from the man he'd taken down with his Vulcan nerve pinch, keeping for myself the weapon from the guard Scanner and I had vanquished, not quite as smoothly. "I don't know why you two couldn't have brought phasers with you when you beamed over."

"You haven't been on a starship long enough," Merete said, a wry smile forming. "Phasers can't be signed out on a duty vessel without proper authorization."

"Which we don't have," Scanner tossed in.

I pressed my lips together. "I don't know what'll make me feel stupider; pretending I didn't know that or admitting I forgot it. Okay . . . let's get that door open. Can you do it, Sarda?"

He fussed gingerly at the panel. "It has been triple-locked. Not difficult from the outside."

"Get ready. Phasers up."

Sarda waited until we were in raid position, then cross-connected the panel. The door slid open.

We lunged in, phasers first, blooming into a perfect triangle, just as we'd been taught. Damn, it felt good to do something right for a change!

*"Hands up everybody against the wall I'm not kidding! Move!"*

Quick headcount—Kirk, check; Spock, yeah; Mc-Coy, okay; Scott, uh-huh; two more security men, check. . . .

Tied up, gagged, and sitting on the floor?

And we were holding our phasers on the people we'd come here to rescue. And they were holding their former guards' phasers on *us*.

What had I said about doing something right?

"Captain . . ." I began, but could think of nothing to say.

"Ah, Lieutenant Piper." Kirk straightened from checking the guards' bonds. "Welcome to the glories of command. You may put your phasers down now."

Unable to keep from stammering, I said, "But . . . we came to break you out . . . we figured you needed help."

Spock, holding his phaser casually, informed, "In fact, Lieutenant, we were on our way to liberate you."

I lowered my phaser. The weapon must have been faulty; it was shaking. "Well . . . we could always go back to our cell . . ."

*You idiot! What are you saying? You're joking with Mr. Spock!*

"That won't be necessary," the Captain said, trying to keep from either laughing or sneering at me. Probably both. He waved Spock out of the quarters, into the corridor where Sarda stood with our three victims, who were groaning back to consciousness. "Scotty, help Spock. Bring those three in here and truss them up."

"Gladly, sir." Mr. Scott gave me a little nod as he stepped by, appropriating Merete's phaser before going out. To me he muttered, "Wha' took you so long, lass?" But he didn't wait for an answer. I dismissed a fleeting image of myself rushing out after and trying to explain to him why we were late for class.

The Captain moved to me, communicating thickly with his eyes. "Bones, take these two with you and check the corridors."

Why was he calling me 'Bones'?

Then Dr. McCoy moved in my line of vision and I remembered. "We'd better get cracking, Jim," he suggested, "or *Star Empire's* crew is going to find themselves up against three starships, and Boma or not, that's too much for one ship to handle. Come on, Lebowitz," he said, gesturing behind me.

"Uh, Sandage, sir," I heard Scanner correct timidly as he and Merete followed McCoy.

Kirk took the time for a deep breath, still absorbing me in that faceted regard. "It seems you're capable of some creative resourcefulness, Lieutenant."

Heat rose in my cheeks, bringing a deep red flush with it. Suddenly I found less confidence in my assumption that he'd wanted me to escape from *Enterprise* and wondered if, instead of playing into his intentions, I'd embarrassed him. After a hard swallow I choked out, "I took a shot, sir. Hope I didn't wing anybody . . ."

"On the contrary, you hit the mark square on the—"

"On your feet, y'grouse." Mr. Scott's firm order preceded a dizzy guard into the quarters, soon followed by two others, then Spock and Sarda. Spock held a phaser on the guards while Scott and Sarda began tying them.

"Captain," Spock said, "it is imperative that you return to the *Enterprise* as soon as possible. Without you on board, the *Enterprise* carries little psychological or military weight against the Vice-Admiral's influence. Commodore Nash seems committed, but Tutakai and Leedson may still be persuaded away."

"My conclusions exactly, Spock. But I can't afford to leave you here either. We're all going back, but not before we arrange an advantage. Opinion, Piper?"

"Oh, I like it, sir." Anything—I liked anything about handing over the rock of responsibility to him, where it belonged.

"Have you got any ideas?" He clearly didn't enjoy having to ask twice.

"Something *better* than the bunny hop, sir?" I didn't think I could do any better than that all in the same month. "Maybe sabotage *Pompeii*'s weapons capability?"

"Say it again, without the question mark."

"We shouldn't leave before sabotaging *Pompeii*'s weapons."

"Why, that's a striking idea, Lieutenant. Congratulations. Scotty—"

"Sir?"

"Do you know enough about destroyer-class vessels to find the auxiliary weapons control on the lower decks?"

"Captain," Scott drawled with a charming gleam in

his eyes, "ye're asking an old pig breeder if he knows his way around a sow."

"Take Piper and Sarda with you and throw some wrenches into their ability to fire phasers. Meet the rest of us in the aft transporter room and don't take your time."

"I'll be able to cripple 'em partially," Scott said, "but I doubt permanently. They'll be able to override from the bridge on a ship with this design, once they pinpoint the damage we do."

"Doesn't matter, Scotty. Just buy us the element of surprise."

"I always did like surprise parties, Captain."

Kirk took Spock's phaser, and Spock stepped over to finish tying up the security guard Scott had started. One more guard, still dazed from the drug Merete had pumped into him, wavered in the line of Kirk's phaser.

"Come on, Piper," Mr. Scott snapped from the corridor.

I turned to follow, but didn't complete my step, my eyes riveted to a man who in some previous life had been my private Aristotle.

"You knew," I murmured.

Kirk blinked, brows lifting in artistic innocence. "How's that?"

"You knew what Rittenhouse planned to do. You had it all figured out." The words ruffled, nearly a whisper, from lips numb with awe. I spoke to myself, not to him.

He suddenly appeared impossibly modest and shrugged, "The signals were there. After all," he added, "you saw them, didn't you?"

I resisted answering, not sure it was a question.

His confidence, both in himself and in me, flowed between us, pumping my limbs, my whole being, full of the strength I needed to go on. I could do it now, continue the fight with Captain James Kirk waving his battle axe at the vanguard. I could go on as long as I didn't have to lead anymore, carry his standard and charge at his flank. My shoulders ached from relief as the rock rolled off, and my feet stumbled beneath the lighter weight.

"Piper!" Mr. Scott called again.

Still looking at Kirk, I found I wasn't ready for petty aggravations when I wheeled around and ran into the third guard's plastishield breastplate. My shoulder rammed the obstruction aside and with new power I growled, "Out of my way, Cyclops."

Mr. Scott was halfway to engineering by the time I caught up with him and Sarda a deck below, at the access door to the chief engineer's direct turbolift. Nothing could stand between us and engineering now. No one else except this ship's own engineer could authorize the engineer's direct lift into use. On *Enterprise,* even the Captain needed Mr. Scott's clearance to use that lift. Assuming it was the same here, I scooted in after them and felt safely cocooned as Mr. Scott keyed in the exclusive access code and rushed us below. He hadn't lied. We hardly stepped off the lift before Mr. Scott was crawling into a circuitry portal in a dismal corner deep in engineering's intestinal tract. He lay on his side in the floor-level hole, working circuit tabs and heads above him. "Eh," he grunted with both effort and chagrin, "thought so."

"What's wrong?" I asked after a glance at Sarda.

"It's the old design. I can't keep it from firing altogether. I can only force it to overload after one or two initial shots. They'll not be able to repair it as quickly, but they do get those first couple of blasts free and clear."

Caught in his disgruntlement, I said, "Who would design a system like that?"

Electricity snapped, making Scott's whole body jump slightly. He swore at whatever he was doing, then shifted position. "Well," he finally explained, "the royalties kept me in scotch and scones for a decade and a half."

I leaned over to Sarda and whispered, "Do me a favor, will you? Just reach down my throat and rip out my vocal chords?"

He would've come back with some stoic witticism if Mr. Scott hadn't asked him about the programming in the computer banks that tied in to this kind of system. Had I paid any attention I probably could've understood what they were doing, but my mind was clouded over with pure relief.

A wizened hand appeared under my eyes, showing me that I'd been drooping my head slightly. I focused on a handful of circuit heads.

"There you are, lass," he said. "We pipers have to stick together."

"Sir?"

"I'm a piper too. Or I was, when I was a lad. Gave it up for engineering, though."

I had no idea what he was talking about, and found myself reluctant to be of no help except to hold a phaser and ask stupid questions, but since he was baiting me I wouldn't disappoint him. "You're a piper?" The inflections told him of my ignorance.

"Bagpipes." Luckily he sensed the next automatic stupid question before I had to ask how he smoked a bagpipe. "A musical instrument," he grunted, wrestling with a stubborn piece of machinery. Sarda climbed in to help, but I could only watch. There wasn't room for three pairs of hands.

"I like music," fell from my lips.

He chuckled, "There are those who'd debate whether pipes qualify as music. Sometimes I doubt it myself. 'Course, t'me, music is a well-engineered piece of machinery. I played pipes when I was a boy in Aberdeen to please my grandmother, but I never really took to it. My grandfather played, and I took the lessons from him. Never could make my fingers move just right. Guess it wasn't in m'blood. I inherited the grandfather's pipes—a fine set . . . staghorn ferrels and silver mounts, a Hardie chanter . . . probably a good three hundred years old. More's the pity I could never commit myself to the art."

"What planet is Aberdeen on, sir?"

He gave me a look that said I'd just asked him where the sun was. "What planet? Aberdeen, Scotland. On Earth."

"Oh—Scotland! Everybody in Scotland has your accent?"

"Or various versions of it."

"Is piping hard to do, Mr. Scott?"

"Was for me. Ah, but my head was in the circuits and conduits that led me to engineering college." He spoke with a slight regret, not for himself, I sensed, but for his grandparents, whose heritage he'd failed to carry on as they dreamed he would, a heritage not his by nature. "I shake 'em out and blow 'em twice a year on the grans' birthdays, but . . ." He shrugged and gave it up.

"You were right to follow your own best talents, Mr.

Scott," I said, aiming my meaning beyond him, to Sarda, perhaps even to myself. "We all have the right to our own aspirations, and to create legacies of our own."

He chuckled again, this time with satisfaction's touch. "Wise girl," he said. Had he set out to teach me something? "That does it. We've done all we can without alerting the bridge. Move out, Mr. Sarda."

I had to shake myself back into a cautious mode for our sojourn through the ship to the transporter room, where the others were waiting for us. They arrived just as we did, making no explanation of where they had been. Of course, Sarda, Scott, and I had only been gone a matter of minutes—perhaps ten. I was losing any natural sense of time; the pressures had squeezed it out of me. Minutes dragged into long, haunting hours, aging me with every endless breath.

The destroyer's transporter would only take four people at a time, so Kirk herded Scott, Spock, and McCoy in there first, washing me with the sudden revulsion of going with them. An irrational need filled me. I had to be the last one here. If I went first and something happened to my friends after I left, the guilt would never leave me. Suddenly, because somehow I had started all this, a terrible unacceptability came over the idea of his keeping me from tying the last knot. I *had* to be the last to leave.

Kirk scanned us, taking only the briefest instant to decide who should be fourth into the chamber, and parted his lips to speak.

I shot forward, ending up at the controls, "I'll operate it, sir."

Whether he heard the silent plea, I couldn't tell, but he understood something in my eyes and nodded ever so slightly. "Very well, Lieutenant. Follow us back to the *Enterprise*, and we'll deliberate on how to get through to *Star Empire* before this annoyance turns into a slaughter. You're in charge. I'll see you in a few minutes."

For the first time in a half century, I smiled. Even so, I was still surprised when he himself stepped onto the fourth transporter disc. Somehow such a move seemed unlikely. *He* wanted to be last too. But he gave it to me.

"I'll watch the corridor," Merete offered, and stepped out the door after Kirk gave her an approving nod. He looked at me then. "Energize."

The *Enterprise* Salvation Committee dissolved in pillars of banded light, then disappeared to the hum of energy. They were gone. Their strength remained.

"Reset," I told Sarda. The transporter clicked and beeped like a trained bird, pulling back on itself as it prepared to send the four of us to *Enterprise*. Beaming would occur automatically once we'd set the controls.

"Ready," Sarda said.

I punched the intercom to the hallway. "Merete, get in here. And you two get on the pads. Where is she? Merete, get—"

She strode in and I motioned her into the chamber.

"Okay, let's get off this ship." I keyed in the preselected coordinates and engaged the automatic signal, giving myself eight seconds to join the others. I closed my eyes and enjoyed the sensation of dissolution as my body buzzed like bees into a billion separate particles of transferable energy, taking my consciousness with it at the last second. Captain Kirk's face, his sober façade gentled by that glimmering blend of calm and lightheartedness, formed first as my mind coagulated and my body, slightly nauseated, formed around me.

But no Captain Kirk waited for us. We transported into an empty room. "Where are they?" Scanner wondered. Then he noticed, as I did, as we all did, that the chamber we had formed into had only four transport pads, not eight as a starship would.

"We're still on *Pompeii!*" Urgency added excitement to Sarda's words in spite of him.

"Stay here!" I leaped straight to the deck and rounded on the control panel. It didn't hold any secrets. "Deactivated!"

"They musta cut us off from the bridge," Scanner said, joining me.

Sarda appeared right behind him. "We must leave this area immediately. They will surely be on their way to us. Doubtless security is already alerted."

They headed for the door, but I got there first and wheeled to face them. "All right, listen to me! If we get separated, meet in the hangar deck. It's our only chance now, damn it all."

"The Arco sled will hold only three at most," Sarda reminded. In that instant I hated him and his Vulcanness for assuming the negative.

"We can't possibly fly out of here—" Merete began.

I shouted her down. "No arguments! We're getting out! Let me worry about how. Phasers on heavy stun."

The door slid open and we were in the corridor, an ominous, empty intestine pulsing with danger, because they were coming and we knew it. But from which direction? And how many? Would Rittenhouse come himself or just send guards? Though guards were more formidable, I found myself having to deal with a surging fear of Rittenhouse. I understood him and because of that I presented the worst kind of threat to his plans. As every moment passed my freedom boxed him deeper into a corner from which he knew he had to break out, no matter the cost. He would give me no more chances. My death would be logged as an unfortunate accident or a strategical necessity. He hadn't missed a beat; I wouldn't be the first. The best I might do would be to force a stand-off—blow his Admiral Santa Claus cover and force Star Fleet to deal with the creeping corruption in its guts. To do that, I had to stay free. Arbitrarily I tossed a mental coin and bolted left, down the corridor toward the center of the ship. At least we wouldn't run into any dead ends.

And run we did, right into a handful of unarmed technicians in white insulated engineering suits. We all skidded to a halt and stared across the corridor at each other, but before anyone had a chance to think I pushed my three on past and said to the technicians, "Up against the wall." They looked at my phaser, so I waved it. "Come on, fellas, it's no joke."

They lined up and I instructed them to face the wall, resetting my phaser for light stun, wide field. Maybe it was a weakness, but I still remembered the pain of heavy stun and couldn't do it to a bunch of techs who happened down the wrong alley. "Sarda, go on ahead. I'll be right there."

Scanner started toward me. "I could stay with you."

"Just do what I say, will you?"

"Yeah . . . okay. I don't have to like it, do I?"

Sarda herded Merete around a corner and sternly called, "Speed is imperative, Judd."

"Right behind ya, Points."

When they were nothing but footsteps, I aimed my phaser and fired. The techs crumpled in a heap. "Sorry, guys." At least they wouldn't be alerting anyone about us for a few minutes. I jogged on down the corridor.

"Phasers down!"

The deep, gruff order came from around the corner, instantly followed by sounds of fighting. Sheer numb panic drove me on faster, and I skidded headlong into a burly security guard Sarda had just thrown aside. I sidestepped and knocked his phaser from his hand, but he scrambled up and dove at my knees. Before going down I caught a horrible glimpse of my team tangled with at least five more guards.

My shoulder slammed to the deck under the guard's weight. Somehow I kept hold of my phaser as he was grabbing for it. With a grunt I flung it hard, and sent it sliding down the corridor. I turned into the fight, grappling with the guard's helmet. I found its edges, clutched, and twisted. Inside the faceplate his features gathered in a grimace of anger and pain, but he kept his arms locked around my shoulders. Behind him flew arms and helmets, shoulders and phasers. I thought I saw two guards go down under Sarda's Vulcan pinch, and I definitely saw Scanner crash into a bulkhead. Merete disappeared behind my opponent's raised visor and drew my attention back to home plate. All I had going for me was leverage, while he had raw muscle and weight. I squeezed my legs up under him, making my body into a knot, then used the floor beneath me as a brace. More fear than power gathered in my legs. Like a coiled spring my body unfolded and the guard's grip broke. He hurtled backward into the corridor wall.

Something leaped over me. Merete.

By the time I rolled to my knees she had reached the guard's phaser, snatched it up, and drew it on him. I stumbled toward her. "Merete, don't fire!"

Red-orange shafts streaked toward the guard, engulfing him in a sickly yellow annihilation. He screamed and writhed, but in seconds only the scream remained. Then it too echoed away.

Horror whitened Merete's face.

The other guards spun around in surprise, and Sarda and Scanner moved in. With phaser stun and Vulcan pinch, they cluttered the deck with security.

Merete stared at the grisly empty air before her, and at the guard's phaser as it lay warm in her hand. Her fingers began trembling. The phaser wobbled and fell. I caught it before it hit the deck.

"Why . . ." she gasped. "Why was it . . . set on kill . . .?"

"Merete, you didn't know. It's all right. It's not your fault."

"I killed him. . . ." She sank to her knees despite my effort to keep her up.

Scanner limped to us and knelt beside her. "They're out to get us, Doc. Like Piper says, it ain't your fault."

"I *killed*." Now her whole body shook, tremors wracking through her, bone-deep.

"Get her up," I said, forcing down empathy. Sharing Merete's pain, a pain that surprised me, could only cripple me now. Both Scanner and Sarda had to help her move down the corridor, where we found a cramped two-person service lift and squeezed into it.

*"Destination?"* the computer requested.

"Hangar deck, emergency priority." I told it as I

lowered my defenses long enough to brush short platinum strands out of Merete's swelling eyes.

*"Thank you."*

I didn't know if it would give us emergency priority without authorization, but the gratifying speed soon proved my guess right. Computers made wonderful monkeys if you asked the right question.

"Merete," I ventured softly, daring to interrupt the torture in her eyes with hope of venting it, "it's all right. You couldn't have known their phasers were set on kill. Do you hear me?"

Scanner nodded. "It scares the curl right outa my hair that they'd break regulations like that."

I took Merete's face in my hands, forcing her to look up. Her eyes were apple green, making a crescent of tear moisture appear verdant. "Do you hear me?"

She shivered. "How can I explain to a mother and father," she began painfully, "that I killed their son? There was no *reason.* . . . How can I tell those he loved? He was only doing his job . . . following orders . . ."

Instead of excellent healing words, I had nothing adequate to say at all. How could I help her? Her feelings were only fair toward the dead security guard, only right awarenesses at the senseless taking of a life. Should I tell her to whoop in victory instead of grieving? How could I tell her the pain was more unjust for her to feel than if we could inflict it on Rittenhouse, who had ordered those phasers set on kill—an unforgivable rupture of Fleet policy.

I wrapped my arms around her and hugged her, and that comprised my whole gift for solace. She murmured, "They won't even have a body to cremate . . .

I'm a doctor . . . a *doctor* . . ." She said it as though her special calling should have prevented the phaser from firing. The guard had felt little pain—only the momentary shock of dissolution, and perhaps a brief searing sensation—but Merete felt all the pain for him. Over and over again as I felt the waves of it pass through her body and into mine. I hoped I could give as much strength as I received of her sorrow. Her pain was difficult to accept through my anger toward Rittenhouse, and for her sake I nulled the urge to slap regret from my friend at her expense. Revulsion for taking life, even one's own life, had to come second to some things—yes . . . I believed that. Today I would begin living it.

The lift door breathed open, dragging us back to the immediate danger, and the four of us piled out at a dead run for the hangar deck. For the first several strides I pulled Merete along, soon to realize she accepted the need to run and was motivating herself. That too could be a kind of therapy. Her tears were dry by the time the hangar deck access doors opened. Luckily Rittenhouse hadn't thought to depressurize the deck. Good—that showed he didn't expect us to escape this way, and right now I'd buy advantages by the ounce from a street vendor if I found one.

*Wooden Shoe* appeared undisturbed. Its two-person capacity scrambled through my mind as we ran toward it to the echo of four pairs of boots. Could we all fit inside? Instantly I knew such cramming was impossible. Three, maybe, but never four. I scanned the hangar bay and spied the closed hangars on the port side, ideas forming. "Scanner! Can you pilot?"

"Twist my arm. I'll take a shot at it."

"He'll never get the chance." A chilling voice, deep and gently sinister, slimed around *Wooden Shoe*. We spun, and faced phasers. That voice would be forever burned into my memory. "Sorry to disappoint you, Miss Piper," Rittenhouse said, charming but serious. No typical sneer accompanied his victory. Only a greyness of complication discolored his confident blue eyes and drew the cottony brows more closely together.

I grabbed Scanner's arm, yanked him hard to me and whispered a fast order into his ear—only a few words before Rittenhouse snapped, "Break it up! Move aside. You, all of you, move off." The two guards behind him kept aim on my friends as we put a few steps of white deck space between us. "You're bright, Piper," the Vice-Admiral said. "I'd prefer to have you on my team. You'd have been a strong asset. As it is, I can't chance letting you go. You're no longer just a hindrance to me. You've become a serious hazard."

"And you're a menace," I told him, still running on the fuel of anathema. As angry at myself as at him, I balled my fists at my own predictability. Kirk wouldn't do something this expected. I would have to learn to be unpredictable too, instead of applauding myself for moving along to the next easiest thing and assuming nobody else would think of it. The intricate blue glare on me now proved what experience could do.

"I don't have time to discuss ideology with you," he said, "though I'll bet you're handy at it."

"I guess we'll never know, sir." I filled my hand with Sarda's communicator and pulled it out of my pocket. "You must be a betting man, Vice-Admiral, or you'd never have tried anything so speculative."

"You have a point, of course. Or are you going to fire on me with a communicator?"

My voice turned hoarse. "Don't bet against it. I'm wondering if you're willing to risk your venture on the bet that you could phaser me down before I could close my thumb on this button. It's keyed into the self-destruct mode of this attack sled. I don't have to describe the explosion to you, or the chain reaction through *Pompeii*, do I?"

A curtain of mild surprise came over him as his gaze dropped to my bone-white hand and the communicator in it. I doubted I could push the button at all, so frozen were my fingers, but I had to convince him otherwise. "We're getting off this ship, sir. I'm sorry, because I think you really believe your system would improve the galaxy for its peoples and you think you can keep the system pure, but—I'm not bluffing, damn it! I see what you're thinking! I'll do this, Vice-Admiral, I'll kill us all right here if I have to. Don't push me. I'm too young and scared and my thumb's shaking on this button."

My tone chilled even me with its finality. Rittenhouse saw it, felt it too. I longed for Vulcan telepathic power as his subdued eyes narrowed and his mind clicked and whirred just beyond reach of my intuitions. Soon the mysterious dam broke and he said, "You would, wouldn't you? Yes. All right, Lieutenant, I won't call your bluff. Go ahead. Get in your little insect and fly away," he said, nearly whispering, "and we'll blow you out of space."

"Scanner," I barked. Behind me footsteps shuffled and faded in a tapping run toward the hangars. In a moment a one-man Tycho fighter taxied into launch position. I never took my eyes off Rittenhouse.

"Merete, get in with Scanner. Tell him to stay on the Arco's tail no matter what."

I felt her nod, though I didn't look, and heard the Tycho fighter creak as she boarded. Sarda, reading my mind—figuratively speaking—had boarded *Wooden Shoe* and powered her up.

"Go on, Piper," Rittenhouse urged in a tone without the taunting I might have expected, free of the smugness I'd always imagined in men with Caesar dreams. This polished mask had hidden his intentions and given him the time he needed for his creeping cancer to appear harmless.

I backed up slowly. Climbing into *Wooden Shoe* proved difficult while keeping a wary eye on Rittenhouse and his men, but once inside I couldn't be hurt by hand phaser through *Wooden Shoe*'s hull. I stumbled into the seat beside Sarda.

"The Vice-Admiral and his men are leaving the hangar bay," he told me while the sled's engine whined behind us.

"Depressurize," I said, but he was already threading that order through to the bay controls.

"Of course, he will fire on us as soon as we clear the destroyer. You recall that Mr. Scott's sabotage still leaves Rittenhouse with a few phaser shots before the system overloads."

"I don't intend to give him the chance to fire on us. There are advantages to being small. I only hope Scanner can stay with me."

"I have plotted and laid-in the most direct trajectory away from the destroyer. It is the most logical escape path."

"Yeah . . . that's why we're not going that way."

"This ship has no shielding. We cannot succeed."

I hit him with a glare as potent as a physical slap. "Don't ever say that to me."

"May I make a suggestion?"

"Please."

"You may pilot with more accuracy if you put the communicator down now."

"Oh . . . right."

The controls were cool beneath my fingers. The sled rose and hovered, rocking slightly on its underbelly thrusters. Behind us the smaller Tycho also floated just to one side, so it wouldn't be scorched by our rear thrusters' exhaust. In my aft viewer buoyed the Tycho's name: *Polliwog*. Scanner was ready.

"Okay," I whispered as I engaged thrusters and the great black funnel of space opened before me. "Here's to us."

# Chapter Eight

ON PROXIMA WE had twelve-gilled sharks with leopard-mottled skins so iridescent they rippled in the water like mother-of-pearl. All the lakes and oceans on Proxima glowed green in the light of our opal sun, and those sharks, echoes of the megalons from Earth's prehistory, roamed our brackish waters in peace and silence. Along their streamlined bodies skimmed remorae, delicate suction fish endlessly vacuuming their hosts' skin, taking nourishment and returning freedom from parasites.

I had no such favors for *Pompeii*. But the remorae provided me with a plan. The instant *Wooden Shoe* cleared the destroyer's hull, I vectored back along the skin of the ship that moments ago had been our prison, and steered a deathly close course along the hull. Behind us, Scanner hadn't expected such a sudden hairpin turn and lost me for a moment, but soon reappeared in my aft viewer.

"Stay with me, Scanner, tightly."

*"I got the idea now,"* squawked the com.

There wasn't time to respond. *Pompeii*'s grey-white hull spread before me, much bigger than I'd expected, yet curved enough to make steering dangerous as I maneuvered at breakneck speed along the engineering hull. Star Fleet code lettering, each letter taller than our entire ship, rolled away beneath us, dizzying me. I blinked dribbling sweat out of my eyes and leaned into my task. Viewports blinked by us, faster and faster. I increased speed.

"Piper!"

Sarda's warning magnified my error. A nacelle strut loomed before us. I cranked the sled hard over, just missing the main wall of the nacelle. *Bamp*—our aft fin grated on exterior fibercoil.

"Too close," I rasped. I fought for control of the rocking sled. Sarda soon gave up trying to help and gripped his arm rests in helpless tension. *Polliwog* swayed and bobbed, careening after us despite the transsonic velocity and the smack we'd taken.

Now *Pompeii*'s hull plates blurred into a single curving grey landscape marked only by flashes of space lights and utility ports. Our engines shrieked as I forced *Wooden Shoe* into impossible twists along the underside of engineering, skimming the sensor dish in a concave arch and surfacing directly on the starboard phaser pod. Without even taking a breath or reducing speed I punched our photon sling control and fired two blue bulbs straight into their weapon pod.

Sparks and light spattered all around us, but we were gone. *Wooden Shoe* shuddered into a somersault, belly-up, and pivoted backward in a mutation of the Ringgold's Pirouette I'd learned from Kirk. The retro-flexion pushed us up against our safety harnesses.

*Polliwog* writhed into a swerve behind us. Somehow Scanner found us through the ion smoke now billowing from the destroyer's phaser pod. Ignoring the piloting computer, I steered *Wooden Shoe* straight out into space, staying inside the cone of space made safe by my destroying that phaser port. By the time Rittenhouse found us and recalibrated another phaser, we'd be out of range. (I hoped.)

"Engage full power," I said, my voice cracking. "Drop the solar wings. We can draw energy from that binary system at zero-mark-seven-four."

A whirring sound followed by a click told me Sarda had done it and our wings were down, replacing the energy we'd lost with that photon shot.

"We have full power," he said.

"Accelerate to point-eighty light speed."

The engines' stridor increased.

"Warp point-eight," Sarda confirmed.

Only after seeing that *Polliwog* still clung to our tail did I breathe freely again. Then I tensed and looked again. "When Scanner stays close, he doesn't fool around. I swear he's not even two meters back! Tell him he can fall off a few lengths."

"Impossible. When we hit the strut our communications packet shook loose."

"Try to pull it in with the service claw. I'll set a course for *Star Empire*."

"We are not returning to *Enterprise* as ordered?"

"Rittenhouse expects us to head for *Enterprise*."

He seemed to understand.

He worked silently with the service claw for several minutes as I watched the energy residue flare and die at *Pompeii*'s starboard pod. They had locked down the leak, but hadn't been able to turn fast enough to fire on us with another pod, and we were away, rocketing toward the dreadnought once again.

Suddenly there was nothing for me to do. I coiled my arms around myself as a shudder ran through me. Nothing to do but cross space.

"Communications reestablished," Sarda informed me as he rebuckled his harness and settled in. "However, our beam is weak enough that Rittenhouse is blocking us from contacting *Enterprise*."

"Can we talk to Scanner?"

"Yes."

"Can we talk to the *Star Empire*?"

"Checking. Negative . . . until we are much nearer."

I punched the com. "Scanner, this is your front end speaking. Wanna back off a centimeter or two?"

*"Hey, when Judd Sandage follers orders, he don't fool around."*

"Fall back. My nerves are shot as it is."

*"Backing off."*

"How's Merete?"

*"Lady Her Honor Specialist First Class Doctor AndrusTaurus is jes' peachy."*

"Good. Thanks, Scanner. Follow and stand by."

*"Standin', sittin', and hangin' by."*

"It sounds like she'll be all right," I murmured to Sarda, or to myself, or to *Wooden Shoe*, or to the stars.

He nodded thoughtfully. "Her reaction would not be unusual for a Vulcan, though a Vulcan would conceal such revulsion from anyone but another Vulcan. It is not my experience that humans or their cultural counterparts react so extravagantly to the fortunes of self-defense."

"Well, I don't know much about the Palkeo Est, but Merete's reaction went beyond culture into something else. It was her own reaction, not a learned habit. At least, I got that feeling."

"The Palkeo culture reflects the human in most ways, though their physiology more closely matches that of native Denevans."

"Too bad we all couldn't reflect your culture instead of each other's. We'd all be better off."

His jeweled eyes flashed, and he visibly tried to contain a deeply personal reaction and succeeded. Instead of rupturing his façade, he drew a stiffer shield over it. "Such a goal is illogical."

Surprising both him and myself, I forced the issue. "Why? Why would it be so illogical if we all acted as disciplined and civilized as the Vulcans, Sarda?"

At first no answer came from my faceted companion, and for many moments it seemed none would. As his jaw tightened I began to regret pushing him. But Sarda rose above my petty pestering once again. "Because such a goal defies the most refined of Vulcan philosophies. The principle of infinite diversity rejoicing in one another, growing and benefiting from their infinite combinations. Vulcan philosophy is for those of Vulcan heritage. There are limited exceptions. Other cultures must remain free to evolve as they will."

Dazedly I nodded. "Sounds familiar," I moaned, but he didn't hear. Or maybe he did, with his Vulcan hearing. "Am I right about Rittenhouse? Reacting on the basis of my own studies? It seems so obvious to me, Sarda."

His Vulcan mind turned on my doubts, changing his face little but greatly variegating something behind the stoic expression. When he spoke again, the depth of tone and meaning moved me in spite of the chill that had been living in me for hours, even though the words were shaded in sobriety. "Your conclusions seem comprised of equal portions of logic and intuition. And . . . I am beginning to trust your intuition."

Warmth filled me from a source which should have carried none. His eyes spread over mine in a soul-completing gaze. Suddenly I understood the whole-ness of Vulcan companionship, a loyalty I didn't de-serve. Through my astonishment I realized Sarda was less crippled by his Vulcanness than he believed. Or, far beneath the shadows, than I believed.

"If I may," he began then with some hesitation, "I have a small gift."

A hand-sized book, bound in silver mesh, appeared between us. I gawked at it several beats longer than necessary.

"Sarda . . . after all I've done to you?"

"Please do not indulge in sentiment. Simply accept it. The words have provided some stimulae for my race and, in that capacity, may deepen your under-standing of Vulcans."

"*Explorations,*" I read, "by Lyras. This looks like poetry."

"It is."

"Vulcans writing poetry?"

"Poetry is an exceedingly measured art, Lieuten-ant, and Lyras a primary Vulcan philosopher. These are not nursery rhymes."

"And I'm not a Vulcan."

"If you recall, I mentioned limited exceptions."

"Oh. I see. Sarda, I don't know what to say."

He put his attention back on the navicomp, and

found refuge in piloting the sled. "Then silence is in order."

I smiled at him and he knew it.

Also more comfortable in silence, I sat back with my book and opened it with a strange decisiveness, not flipping through as I usually did with new books—a bad habit, looking at the middle of a book first. Vulcan poetry . . . anticipation gripped me, and I read the neat, unornamented printing.

> *This is the sixth element,*
> *time crossing time*
> *until all stands still*
> *and we may think.*
> *Study, but touch.*
> *Learn, and later know.*
> *Tame the craggy agonies of toil's time.*
> *Memory and memoring comes late,*
> *comes shattery, scattery.*
> *When all is done, it is not*
> *to die—*
> *It is to die well.*

Power came through those words, though I had no literary training and didn't really understand them. I suspected even Earth litterateurs would have difficulty, since some of the phrases seemed rooted in Vulcan history and Vulcan vernacular. Yet I felt better having read them, for no apparent reason.

I closed the book, held it loosely, leaned back with my knuckles pressed against my lips, and let those words roll in my mind. I ended up with a headache, and . . . new thoughts.

*To die well.*

Even in translation, the Vulcan effect came through. "What makes you uncertain of your deductions?" Sarda asked then.

A very good question, difficult to sort out. "I feel like my awareness of the events leading to World War Three might be making me see things that aren't there, or read things wrong, or . . . he can't be the only deviled egg in the nest. He fits a pattern I recognize—all those underlings in key Fleet posts can't be coincidental."

"Self-doubt is your worry?"

"Not really," I murmured, not sure at all, "but what bothers me is that the pattern seems so obvious to me."

"Such deductive accuracy should not be regarded as unfortunate."

"No . . . but why hasn't anyone else picked up his plans before now?"

The voicing of that nagging doubt, a small cancerous awareness that my being the first to recognize the pattern might be a sign of error on my part, cleared my thoughts and helped organize them. Even more help came when I turned and saw in Sarda's expression that my misgivings had already done time in his thoughts and been dismissed. A peculiar turn of his head guided both our gazes out to the *Star Empire*. It hovered in deep space like a finely sculpted medallion. "Perhaps someone has."

"Calibrating for final approach to *Star Empire*. We may now attempt bypass of the com block."

On the echo of Sarda's suggestion I jolted to life and mashed the com button. *"Star Empire*, this is Arco sled *Wooden Shoe*, emissaries from *Enterprise*. Please come in."

Interspace crackled through the speakers. I winced at the grating noise but still hoped for the semblance of human voice. "We copy, *Wooden Shoe*. Please identify yourselves personally."

"Damn you, Brian Silayna! You drop those goddamned shields or I'll tell everybody about last December at Starbase Three and I'm *not joking!*"

*Ninginginging*. It reverberated through space.

"Their aft shields are dropping. Docking bay doors are opening." Sarda eyed me. A shadowy upturn bothered the corners of his lips.

I avoided meeting his regard as I relaxed my posture and tried to be nonchalant. "I guess they know it's me now."

"Evidently."

We maneuvered along the port side of an impossibly mammoth ship, designed with density in mind. So gigantic it took us several minutes to pass, the dreadnought's size made it seem unmanageably beefy. Its nacelles and hulls were streamlined, for aesthetics, of course, but equally hulking.

"What a bull elephant," I murmured. The thought that its firepower matched its whopping size was frightening.

"An uncomplimentary epithet," Sarda mentioned.

My mind filled with the thundering grace of a charging African elephant, ears flying, tusks gleaming, head tossing, and the great trumpet roar of mastery in its primitive state. "Then you've never seen a bull elephant."

"Have you?"

"On training maneuvers in Kenya, on Earth."

"I shall consider going there."

"You won't regret it."

*Wooden Shoe* and *Polliwog* entered the hangar bay and settled onto the deck with a breathy sound. We waited as the bay doors closed and the area pressurized around us. The four of us climbed out of the fighter and sled and ran for the door, which slid open to reveal a drawn, tense face. He ran toward us. I kept running toward him, toward that special face—and into special arms.

Salvation slammed between us and locked itself in the thudding of our hearts. But this kind of passion felt wholly different from any ever shared before.

"Brian," I choked, clutching him.

His hand pressed my head to his shoulder. "You made it! I didn't think you could possibly get away."

"I couldn't." The desire to bury myself in his warm strength almost overwhelmed me and I almost gave in. Resisting that, I pushed him back a pace. "Will you *please* tell me what's going on?"

"Not me. Burch will." He held my arm as the five of us ran through a corridor ribbed with bulky struts, twice the thickness of any I'd seen on a ship or station anywhere. Everything was structured to take extra stress, built massively, in chunky parcels and fitted together, even to the very walls, which were fibercoil blocks in a herringbone pattern. Everything else, even the struts, went around us in the hexagonal shape of a beehive. From experience with the beekeepers on Proxima, whom we'd brought in to care for the imported bees that pollinated our vegetables, I knew the beehive structure hadn't ever been improved upon for raw bracing strength from outside pressure. The massive structure created an illusion of crampedness in the corridor even though it was actually rather wide for a ship's interior arteries, and I had to consciously avoid crouching as we ran for the turbolift.

"Why me, Brian?" I demanded, using the time as the lift raced for the upper decks. "Was it your idea to put me on the hot seat?"

He glanced subconsciously at the eyes around us— at Scanner, Sarda, and Merete—but I brought him back with a punch on the arm, of respectable force. "Damn it, tell me! How dare you drag me into this without talking to me first! You knew all along!"

"I didn't want to get you involved," he began lamely.

I slugged his arm again, this time in earnest. Anger merged with insult, relief with indignance. "We were lovers, Brian! How could you be involved with terrorists and never slip a word of it to me?" Suddenly I realized what he'd just said. "Did I hear you say you didn't want to get me involved? Is that what I heard you say? Is *that* what you said? Because I'm involved and people are going to die now and I want to know if it's my fault."

"Piper," he soothed, gripping my arms.

I jerked away. "Get your hands off me."

Around us my friends tried to be fascinated with the lift walls, though my least concern was embarrassment.

"Piper, please." That tone. He knew he could get me with that dulcifying tone. "I didn't tell you because I wanted to protect you. We weren't that sure of ourselves. I didn't have the right to risk your career too."

"Then why engage my biocode?"

"Once we left port we realized we didn't know who to trust at Star Fleet. Rittenhouse has cronies all over the service, bought and paid for with commissions and commands and promotions—"

"I know. I figured it out. Keep talking."

"There was no way for us to know where his influence went, who was or wasn't—"

"Brian!"

"Burch trusts me and I trust you, that's all."

"That's it? That's the whole story?"

"We knew our only chance of blowing the corruption open would be to convince Kirk, and Kirk was impressed with you. We figured you'd believe me, and then you could convince him. It was a gut decision. I'm sorry."

*Not sorry enough.*

My voice became suddenly calm, funereal. "You trust me to risk my life," I said, "but not enough to leave my career in my own hands. Not enough to have shared this with me before it turned critical. Don't make any more decisions for me, ever. Do you understand?"

He stepped toward me, saying, "Piper, come on—"

My hand met his chest. "Some things don't mend, Brian."

Mercifully the turbolift slowed and opened. We spilled out onto a wide, anemic bridge, austerely colored and without comforts, built chunkily like the rest of the ship. Only five people turned to look at us, an ethnic assortment that immediately made me think of Rittenhouse, including Terry Broxon at the helm. She turned to me, her face a matt of guilt—carefully absent of any real shame. A fine line indeed.

"Terry!" I blurted. "You too?"

She stood up and moved to the command chair, where the seated man was just turning to face us. Shadows ruled his face, the greyness of fatigue and unaccustomed responsibility, the smudge of an unshaven beard, circles under his pale green eyes, a lock of hair flipped down from a receding hairline. The last emotion I expected to feel suddenly shot through me: pity.

"Lieutenant Piper," Terry introduced, "this is Commander Burch."

Burch seemed to crawl out of the command chair to take my hand in both of his. "Thank God you got here. I'm so glad, Lieutenant." His accent was thickly English, his voice unexpectedly mild.

"You'd better have a talk with your god, sir, before you start thanking him for things, because we're in deep trouble." Okay, so I'd never be begged to join the diplomatic corps. "There are four ships out there thinking some very unsavory thoughts."

He swallowed hard and nodded. "Yes, I . . . I know. I realize this move was rash, stealing the dreadnought, but it had to be kept out of Rittenhouse's hands. He fancies himself a savior, Lieutenant, wants to unify everything, liquidate the sovereignty of the Klingons, Romulans, Orions, Mengenites, Perseans—"

"I know about that, sir."

"Oh . . . good. I'm sorry you had to be used, but I didn't know what else to do . . . there are splinter groups all over Star Fleet who believe the Federation should move in on so-called enemy cultures before they become too strong to control. Rittenhouse has been knitting them together. I figured it out a couple of years ago, but without the dreadnought Rittenhouse's plan lacked a trigger, so he started building it. I

couldn't approach anyone officially, I simply *couldn't*
. . . his influence is too covert. So I started my own
little conspiracy with my own friends and students."
Burch paced around the lower deck, nervous, fa-
tigued, running on a fading second wind and plagued
by obvious helplessness and inexperience. "The only
person I could be reasonably sure of was Kirk. He's
the only person to ever turn down promotion. They've
been pressuring him to accept a position in the Admiralty, but he's been resisting. He's not yet ruled by his
ambitions. And his reputation—" Burch paused, rubbing his knuckles nervously, and seemed to run out of
words. "But even he wouldn't necessarily believe a
tale like this unless we showed him and all of Command we were willing to put our lives on the line."

"And you thought I could convince him?"

"Silayna thought so."

I refused to look at Brian. I stepped down to Burch's
level. "Sir, you underestimated Captain Kirk. He figured it out for himself. None of this was necessary."

"Oh, but it was! Even Kirk's influence at Star Fleet
Command wouldn't outweigh all of Rittenhouse's
voices. We had to draw the galaxy's attention to this
bloody machine and Rittenhouse's plot. The people
who built this menace are hungry to use it. We must
act against them. The integrity of Star Fleet must be
reestablished."

"May I ask what your plan is?"

"Plan? I have no plan! I didn't think he'd actually
pull in three heavy cruisers—I can't fight them all—
I'm a desk pilot."

"You did a good job against the Klingons. . . ."

"Good job?" He chuckled mirthlessly, mocking his

success. "Did you think we were making a Shake-spearean entrance?"

Brian stepped down to me and explained, "When the Klingons showed up we put up the image of *Star Empire* and let it take the beating while we hid in the asteroids, but when *Enterprise* appeared, it took us fifteen minutes just to figure out how to aim the phasers and photons."

I stared at Burch. "You don't know how to work this ship?"

"Very basically. I can make it fly a straight course and I know something about the image projector—Lieutenant Sarda surpasses me there, though."

"Does anyone on board know?"

He shook his head, his chin stiffening pathetically. "Most of these people are my students and advisees from Academy. A few decent technicians, but no specialists. And there are only forty-eight of us on a ship that normally crews five hundred."

I clenched my hands to hide the trembling when it started again. "I'll help if I can," was all I could say.

"And your friends?"

"We're with y'all," Scanner said, not bothering to consult Merete or Sarda. They seemed agreeable.

"Are you specialists in anything?"

Merete remained painfully silent, as though unable to say her profession, but Scanner piped up, "I know a stitch or two about sensors."

"Then get down to the sensory. Sarda, we could use you at the auxiliary weapons turret. Do you remember the layout well enough?"

"Quite well, Commander."

"Go."

The turbolift swallowed those two, leaving the bridge even emptier.

"All right, Piper," Burch sighed, "let's try talking to Captain Kirk."

"We may have to move closer," I said. "Rittenhouse is blocking communications somehow. Scrambling interspace with static."

"Take the helm."

Where had I heard those gruesome little words before?

My body grew cold. The helm chair and console felt like ice around and beneath me. Terry Broxon took the seat at navigations. A glance at her reawakened my amazement that she and Brian, two old friends, could be so close to me, even go through the attempt at the *Kobayashi Maru* test at my side, and still not let me in on Burch's radical plans. True, they both had taken Burch's classes in management and bureaucratic policy-making at Academy and I'd never even met him, but such an excuse waxed flimsy in the light of personal trust. I felt betrayed and was in no mood to shake it off. Self-pity made me angry. I needed anger right now. Anger provided strength.

"Try to close the distance between us and *Enterprise*," Burch said, more a suggestion than an order, "and give those others a wide berth. We have only two advantages and we must use them."

"Which are?" Brian prodded from the engineering station.

"First of all, Rittenhouse doesn't know how poorly we know this ship. Secondly, he *does* know me. I might be a third-rate bureaucrat, but I never give up trying and he knows I won't. He also knows I'm no longer intimidated by him as his captains are. We must employ those things."

*Good for you!* I thought as I urged the massive beast into sublight movement. Even a bureaucrat can wield a sword if he thinks he can! Suddenly I felt surging pride in the Star Fleet that had produced a Paul Burch, and became that much more determined to preserve the good institution that he proved still existed beneath the crust of corruption.

"Three-quarters sublight, sir," I told him as the great ship turned beneath my fingertips and swept forward.

"Maintain." He sat nervously in the command chair, still rubbing his knuckles. Several endless minutes passed as the massive ship moved through space toward the cluster of starships. "Ensign Novelwry, open a hailing frequency."

"Aye, sir. Frequency open."

*"Enterprise,* come in please. This is Commander Burch. Please answer."

But the voice that rasped back at us had none of Kirk's subdued tones. *"Burch, this is Rittenhouse. Give up, right now, or we'll blast you out of the sector."*

Burch winced. "Sorry, Vice-Admiral. I'm quite committed. The only way to stop me now is to make good on your threat."

A very good ploy, I noticed. Burch gave Rittenhouse no choice: cease hostilities and admit defeat, or fire on us and open an official can of worms as wide as the Horsehead Nebula. Threats were one thing, but to actually open fire was something else entirely.

Burch plowed through his own bluff. *"Enterprise—Captain Kirk—do you read us? Please respond."*

*"This is Kirk. Can you boost your gain? We're being blocked. Barely reading you."*

"Boost our signal, Ensign."

"Trying, sir. There's a lot of static."

"It's *Pompeii* blocking our frequency. *Enterprise,* we must confer! Captain Kirk, Star Fleet Command must be made aware—"

*Crrrrrraaaaaack!*

The *Star Empire* shuddered under us as terrible thunderbolts struck her weakest points. Some of the bridge panels started sizzling.

"Good God!" Burch choked, "I didn't think he'd actually do it!"

"Sir, order red alert!" I yelled.

"Yes . . . red alert. Thank you. Go to red alert."

Everything turned red under the emergency system, giving a hellish appearance to a hellish situation.

We took another hit, a long, sustained round of phaser fire, and the dreadnought trembled again.

"A hit in communications, sir!" Novelwry gasped, fanning smoke. "The main couplings at the outlet belowdecks."

"He's not going to let us talk to Kirk," Burch said. "Carr, have you found the full shields yet?"

We only had half shielding? No wonder the hits shook us up!

"Not yet," said one of the ensigns, a thin boy old enough to take charge of any sandbox. "All the controls are tied in to the computer and can't be run manually unless the computer is disengaged."

"Any of you know how to do that?"

200

We were spared answering by another hard, long phaser strike. We hung in sizzling limbo, gripping our flashing panels, until it ceased.

"That can't be *Pompeii*," I said, shouting unnecessarily. "Mr. Scott sabotaged their phaser banks."

Burch turned in the chair. "Hopton?"

"Confirmed," said the stocky ensign at weapons control. "The first shot came from *Pompeii*. After that, they came from *Lincoln*."

"Oh God, oh God . . . Piper . . . go down below. See if you can't patch communications back together. We've got to get Kirk on our side!"

I stumbled toward the turbolift, hoping the dreadnought was as tough as Boma theorized. Merete swung in after me, saying, "I'll go with you. Maybe I can help."

Just before the door hissed shut, we heard Ensign Carr report, "Sir, they took out the outside optical unit of the image projector!"

I slumped against the lift wall and closed my eyes. "What a nightmare."

Merete started to say something, but it drowned in the next endless phaser hit. The lights blinked off, then on again. Big struts roared and moaned like thunder in our heads. Then the ship lurched sideways. Merete and I slammed into the closed door and were pinned there until the artificial gravity could recover and compensate.

I pulled Merete to her feet. "Are you okay?"

"If you hadn't told him to go to red alert, the ship's systems wouldn't be on emergency standby."

"Boma must be directing the attack. Hitting the ship's weakest points. We couldn't have a more formidable enemy than the people who really do know how to use this ship. I don't think Burch even knows how to use the weapons very well."

"You heard them say they're having trouble bypassing the computer."

"I wish I was home."

The lift bumped hard then, but didn't stop. The lights flickered again. "This ship is bent," I decided. "The lift tube is actually twisted a little. Rittenhouse picked the right man when he brought Boma along."

"He won't kill us, Piper."

I stared at her. "Rittenhouse? Are you crazy?"

She hesitated. "He really does think he's doing the right thing. I feel like that, anyway . . . he's just trying to scare us."

Perhaps she couldn't deal with impending death and had to convince herself it wasn't coming. Her inability to handle her mortality frightened me even more than having to face my own. Somehow, Merete had seemed more stable to me than this.

"We'll fight," I assured her. I tried to believe it. "He'll have to face the whole impact of his plans. If we die, at least Rittenhouse will face a shakedown at Fleet Headquarters that might stop him in his tracks. We can only hope."

"Yes," she murmured with false certainty.

Minutes later we were running through the technical stations of the lower decks, trying to find the communications outlet. The hull of the ship hadn't yet been ruptured, but Boma's instruction had blown up countless panels, leaving frayed lines and snapping circuits where working machinery had been. The ship was virtually empty, with only fifty or so people crawling in her thick, endless innards. The feeling of aloneness unsettled me. I tried to ignore it. After several wrong turns we finally found the right room—and a twisted mass of overloaded circuitry, mutilated by blasts on key points outside and blown out by the rush of energy.

I moaned when I saw it.

"That can't be fixed," Merete said.

"What a mess . . . well, it can't hurt to try. Help me clear these panels away. Be careful of the stripped cables. Keep insulated. Don't let that leaking coolant touch your skin."

"I won't. Piper, you shouldn't try it."

"I'm going to try it."

It took a good twenty minutes to sort out everything, but once I'd cleared away the burned debris I discovered the real damage was only to the outermost circuits, those designed for long-distance subspace channels. Every time the circuits sparked Merete begged me to stop trying, especially since Rittenhouse's captains were still firing on us. She had a point. If they hit here again, I would be incinerated. Every few minutes the ship would jolt around us and the lights would flicker. Back-up systems clicked, whirred, and struggled all over the ship. Occasionally Burch would return fire, though I knew he didn't have the grit to fire seriously on other Fleet people. He hadn't come out here to kill, but to prevent killing. Whether he could drum up the necessary mettle to wage a true battle remained to be seen. At least the problem was his and not mine anymore.

And what about Captain Kirk? What would he do now that shots had been fired? He would have to take one side or the other, square off with us or surrender to Rittenhouse. I had a hunch he wouldn't readily do

Rittenhouse any favors, not after what occurred on *Pompeii*. Burch had judged Kirk correctly. The captain of *Enterprise* was a free-thinking maverick who commanded in high style, not easily bluffed, not prone to alarmist apprehensions. He deserved every accolade Star Fleet could shower on him, very much deserved the admiralty he'd been offered. Curiosity rose in me about why he resisted promotion. Could he be unambitious, as Burch guessed? Or did the idea of functioning in the upper echelon of a corrupt fleet repulse him as much as it did me? Had he known about the creeping miscreance even before this incident began? Had Rittenhouse made the mistake of approaching him? It all made sense. But if Kirk had been working on hunches and feelings, this incident had finally forced him to home in on the details, just as Sarda and I did.

"I think I've almost got it, Merete." The instruments scorched my hands as I fought to replace fried fuses and reconnect severed coils. Neither electrical nor mechanical engineering was my specialty, but I did my best to make sense of the puzzle, to give paths to the currents which would carry our voices to *Enterprise* and theirs to us.

"You mean you can really repair this mutilation?" she asked.

"Maybe not repair it, but I think I can rig a skip circuit in the fitting under here. Are there any Jesus clips out there?"

"A *what* clip?"

"It's a little metal clip about the size of your fingernail, with a loop on one end and one of the tines bent sideways. See any?"

There were some scuffling sounds as she sifted

through the debris, while I waited with my fingers cramping around joined scab-triodes. I knew she was doing her best, but I still ended up sweating before her hand poked into the crawl space with two of those wretched little helpers.

"Do you call them that because they're shaped like J's?" she asked.

"Huh? Oh, I guess they are, at that. No, that's not why."

"Then why?"

"Some Earth-native technician named them when they first were standardized about twenty years ago or so. He got annoyed at them. Did you notice how tensile the loop is? They've got a lot of spring for their size. They hold very tightly if—*if*—you can get them in place without having them go *ping!* and fly off somewhere. Once they've sprung, somehow you can never find them. Somewhere in the bowels of every Federation ship, there's a Jesus clip graveyard yet to be discovered."

Merete paused, and I could hear her thought processes trying to make the connection. "But why would you call them that?"

"Because," I explained, "When they go *ping!* you go *Jeeeeeeesus!*"

"I see," she said.

"The absolute truth, I swear. See if you can find a coupling out there that would fit a beta-eight switch. I've got to have something that size or near it to shield the skip circuit."

"Here." She handed in a similar piece. "This is beta-eight sized. What's a skip circuit?"

"It's a circuit that joins other connections, but takes its power from anywhere it finds energy flowing. It'll

205

look through the system till it finds free-flowing electricity and galvanize it into its own system."

"Sounds cannibalistic."

"That's pretty much accurate. Hand me a pincer if you can fine one."

"Come out, Piper."

"What'd you say? Here . . . pull this conduit shell out of my way."

"Piper?"

"Huh?"

"Please come out. I can't let you finish."

Only then did I sort out her meaning. I ducked my head under the panel and looked at my friend. "Oh, Merete."

My friend with a phaser drawn on me.

"Please come out. I don't want to have to hurt you," she said, moving back so I could climb out.

Through my shock I unfolded myself, stood up, and faced her. "Merete, what is this? How can you turn a phaser on me after what happened on *Pompeii?*"

Tears welled in her eyes. Her voice remained steady. "It's set and locked on stun. I'm so sorry, Piper . . . I can't let you restore the com system."

"Would you like to tell me why?"

"I doubt you'd understand."

"Merete . . ."

"Piper, please. Trust me."

"But we've got to talk to Kirk. Surely you understand that."

"I understand what it means to fall prey to unbound pirate cultures. You don't."

"Are you talking about the Klingons?"

"Partly."

"Merete, Rittenhouse is a conqueror-dictator on the

make. He wants to flatten the galaxy into one homogeneous pancake with himself in charge."

The tears flowed on her cheeks now. "They have to be controlled, Piper. We can't negotiate with them . . . they can't be trusted, those kinds of beings. They strike and run, and the Federation is too benevolent to answer acts of war with military retaliation. We've become slaves to our principles. We try to punish them in diplomatic ways. But we don't trade with them so they don't care if we cut them off. We can't hurt them, but they go on hurting us."

"Who, Merete?" I prodded gently.

"The Orions!" She flinched at her own outburst.

"Did they hurt you?"

"Please don't patronize me."

"I won't. At least tell me. I'd like to hear."

Now her voice cracked with effort where before there had been only tears to carry her pain. She inclined her head slightly, as though leaning mentally away. In her pale eyes shone the razor image of memory.

"I was the Palkeo equivalent of six Earth-years old, Piper. Only six. I was a baby, traveling with my parents on the textile freighter *Perceptive,* heading for Deep Space Station K-Seven. We were boarded by Orions. At the last second my mother shoved me into a cabinet and told me not to come out. I waited there in the dark for nine hours, listening to the screams as the crew and passengers were murdered. Brutally. Piper . . ."

"Merete . . ."

"Then I had to listen to the silence for more hours. I was afraid to leave the cabinet. When I finally crawled out, I couldn't walk because my legs had been so cramped. I had to lie on the floor beside the first officer's body. His . . . I sat in his blood. My parents were . . . worse . . . when I found them in the hold. Everybody was dead. And the pirates got a handful of fabric bolts in exchange for all those lives."

"You don't have to go on," I whispered.

She licked her lower lip, catching a tear as it rolled downward. "I stayed on that ship for seventeen days before a Federation border patrol found us. Seventeen days of decomposing corpses. Seventeen days of terror that the pirates would come back and kill me too. Seventeen days wishing I could mend the rotting bodies and make them alive again. Remember, Piper, how a child's mind works? I found a sewing kit during the second week and spent two days . . . I thought if they were hooked together again, they would come alive. But they didn't. My parents didn't . . . the Captain didn't . . . Commodore Nash's son didn't . . ."

Merete's form, her short platinum hair, the medical insignia, the phaser, blurred into a single column of tears and I blinked to clear my eyes.

Beyond shock, I murmured, "Nash's *son?*"

"His son was hitching a ride on the *Perceptive.*"

"And after all these years," I added, "they approached you?"

"I'm the only survivor of any Orion raid. The only one, Piper. I was old enough to understand the crime, but too young to be acceptable as a formal witness to an act of war. The Orions guard their neutrality cagily, so they can go on pirating from all sides and still do business with whom they please. They spit in the face of common decency and racial order, and the Federation is too nice to confront them. Rittenhouse promises to put an end to their raids . . . end the breakages of treaty by both the Klingons and Romulans. It needs to be done . . . the galaxy has to be unified. The aggression won't take long now that we have the dreadnought. You can see that, can't you?"

My eyes drifted shut briefly. Various textbook explanations washed in and out, none adequate. Nothing could erase the mutilation of her parents, of her psyche, during that horrid time. Inadequacy made me nauseous. Tears turned my cheeks into stiff sheets. How could I make her see through the torture, bypass the years? I searched for words both kind and potent.

"Merete," I bridged softly, "Rittenhouse can't be the gentle dictator he imagines. No one can be. The principle doesn't work."

"But it *can*. We all have to cooperate—grow into one strong body—"

"And become pirates like those Orions, except on a galactic scale? Oh, my friend, listen to me. His system is already starting to fall apart. We buck against him and suddenly he tells all his guards to set their phasers on kill. That's not the action of a benevolent father-figure, is it? Burch challenged him, and now he's firing on us. You feel those hits—it's the ship he needs, not us! He's out to kill us! Merete, we're in his way. What happens when a whole race gets in his way? Klingon families, Orions, Romulans—they have the right to be what they are."

Through a sob she choked, "At our expense?"

"No, but the opposite kind of massacre is just as bad, isn't it? Piracy with a banner is still piracy." Another phaser blast bolted *Star Empire*'s outer hull, breaking the half shields easily and chewing away at the fibercoil-quantobirilium skin. It punctuated my words. "Feel that? Full phaser on bare hull, Merete. At least two ships are sustaining fire on us. He means to kill us. And after us, everyone else who balks at his utopia."

Her eyes filled with tears until she could no longer see me. The phaser drooped in her hand. She listened to me over and over again in her mind, felt the phaser bolts, and knew she had been propagandized. Only her trust in me stood between her and Rittenhouse's seduction. I urged quietly, "Think about the Orion children. And give me the phaser, okay?"

She pressed her eyes with one pale, trembling hand. Her finger slid away from the trigger as the phaser dropped into my grip. A sigh passed through me. My shoulders slumped under a new weight just before the phaser fire of three starships cut loose on *Star Empire*'s tough hull, hoping to burn through the special alloy and kill all of us. After us, they would have to kill Kirk and everyone on *Enterprise*. Once it had been only Burch, his people, and me. Now Rittenhouse's prey had scoped out to include anyone on *Enterprise*. He would have to fabricate a great lie about our deaths, a daring battle with insurrectionists, the tragic loss of the legendary officers of *Enterprise* and their nameless crewpeople. As Merete felt the force of the shots, my words rammed home again. I reached out to her.

The chamber exploded into a microgalaxy. Behind Merete an entire panel of electrocoils blew up. The eruption blasted against her spine. She crashed forward into me, plummeting both of us into the com system. I managed to keep hold of her and lower her to the floor, cradling her in my lap.

Her face tightened in shock and pain. Pale purple

blood poured over my legs from her torn back and thighs. She clutched at me and I clutched back. "Merete—damn—I'll take care of you. You're not alone anymore, do you hear? Can you talk?"

She swallowed, but her voice still gurgled. "I thought . . . I believed . . . him. . . ."

Somehow I reached the ship's intercom and engaged it. "Bridge, this is Piper! I need help. I need somebody medical. Hurry!"

Burch's voice came back immediately, in spite of the battle he was waging up there. *"I'll send two nurses. Best I've got, Piper."*

"Please just hurry." I felt the lavender blood suddenly pouring more freely. My agony for her redoubled as I thought back on our time aboard *Pompeii* and realized now the hidden elements—why Merete had insisted on going out into the corridor while we tried to transport back to *Enterprise*. She had warned Rittenhouse that we were escaping. He had made her his pawn, preyed on her sad past.

I held her tightly. "Hurry . . ."

By the time the two nurses arrived with an anti-grav gurney, the pain had gone out of Merete's face, the movement out of her body. We put her on the gurney. Then I leaned over her for a last moment before plunging back into the battle.

"The pain's gone," she whispered. "I can't feel the pain anymore. Please, Piper, make it come back. . . ."

"Your body's just gone numb. It's trying to heal." She was a doctor. Could my lie possibly work on a doctor? I didn't know why the pain had gone, or why she could no longer move. All I could give her was my wish for her to heal. "They'll take you to Sickbay."

She turned her head away. "Better to die," she whispered, "than be so wrong."

"You weren't wrong!" I gripped her hands and squeezed hard. "Look at me. You're just one of billions of good people the galaxy over whose goodness is used against them. You were misguided, that's all. He used your faith and charmed you with platitudes. You're going to learn from this. You're going to live and be a great Federation physician, do you hear me? You're going to *live*. Promise me!" My own tears splashed on the front of her jacket.

"I promise," she whispered.

They took her away. And I was alone again. I turned to finish the job I'd started.

# Chapter Nine

THE EXPLOSION THAT hurt Merete jarred loose some of my repairs, though the fuses held and a few minutes of soldering reestablished connectivity between communications and the ship's mainframe. Working on cinctures to the computer made me think about what Brian said: how it took them a long time to figure out how to aim the weapons. And I recalled one of the bridge ensigns trying to bypass the computer control so the shields could be worked manually. On my way back to the bridge, dabbing Merete's blood from the legs of my jumpsuit, I finally let go of the idea that Burch knew what he was doing. He and his people were looking for ways to override the computer because they didn't know how to work it. They never thought to *ask* the computer for help.

Merete's lavender blood had darkened as it dried to a dull mulberry purple. I managed to stanch enough of it from my pants to keep the fabric from sticking to my legs. Because her blood was on me, I couldn't forget her even long enough to clear my head. I admired her—she hadn't denied the truth once she saw it clearly for the first time in her life. I wondered if I could ever dredge up that much courage, enough to conquer a lifetime of misconceptions. Poor Merete . . . the agony bottled inside her since childhood had never showed in her work. Instead of the bitterness a lesser person might espouse, she vented her pain in a reverence for life. She had to live—she had to.

The bridge billowed. Smoke poured from at least two circuit relay panels. Though it was rapidly clearing, the smoke signaled serious damage. Ordinarily tech crews would immediately pounce on every problem, but with only fifty-two of us on board, we had our hands full just operating whatever *was* working. The broken things, unless critical, had to wait.

Burch was shouting over a grinding record station at one of the ensigns, and on the screen flickered the hideous image of a battle between starships. Phasers incised the blackness of space, biting at the ships as they maneuvered around us and each other, and I immediately understood from the way they moved that *Enterprise* had looped in to draw their fire away from us. So Kirk had made his choice.

I found my way to Brian at the engineering station and hastily asked, "Fill me in."

He wiped the sweat from his forehead, fighting to stabilize his panel. "Kirk moved in just after you left the bridge. He fired on *Pompeii,* and Rittenhouse ordered the three others to retaliate. Captain Tutakai resisted, but Nash moved right in and cut into *Enterprise*'s shields with photons at short range. You can see the damage for yourself. Then Leedson moved *Hornet* in on us and Tutakai followed in *Potempkin.*

They haven't broken this ship's tough skin in more than three places yet, but we can't hope for much more with only half shielding."

"Commander!" I left Brian without a glance and headed for Burch, but had to follow him as he scurried from station to station, giving his inexperienced crew moral support and trying to learn as much as he could in an impossibly short time.

"Commander, I think we can get full deflectors."

"What? How?"

"Quit trying to bypass the computer for control. Ask it to help."

"Do you know how to talk to it?"

"Sir, it can't be that different."

"This way." He grabbed my wrist and pulled me up toward the science officer's station. "You do it."

My disgusted look did more for me than him. He had all the good intentions in the galaxy but no experience. I certainly couldn't do any worse at this than he could. I pushed two key toggles. "Computer." Nothing happened. So I punched more buttons, guessing entirely about the tie-in pattern. "Computer."

*"Working."*

"Engage defense/offense mode."

*"Specify."*

"Engage deflection systems and implement. Also bring forward all the indices regarding aiming the weapons and pinpoint firing, and free it up to the helm."

*"Affirmative,"* the pleasant voice said, then paused as it worked. *"Primary shielding engaged. Access to weapons tied in to helm and weapons control panels, available through voice command with manual confirmation and dual override."*

Ensign Hopton stared into his viewer and shouted, "We've got shields! All over the ship!"

Burch's pale face flushed with the delight of respite. Suddenly we had a chance to survive another two minutes.

A short-lived chance. It soured immediately as Terry Broxon's smile withered into shock, then despair. She touched the com link in her ear. "No . . . Commander, *Enterprise* has dropped her shields!" She switched on the bridge-wide com system, flooding the area with voices.

Spock's voice, garbled.

Rittenhouse responding.

Spock again. "*. . . serious damage . . . Captain Kirk is being taken . . . main bridge links . . . to phaser control . . .*"

We held our breaths, every one of us. The bridge of *Star Empire* became as quiet as a mausoleum. We listened. Terry Broxon and Ensign Carr battled to clear the static interrupting Spock's words. Finally they succeeded. And I soon wished the static could return.

"*You have sliced through several levels of our engineering hull, including the flow-tract casing of our coolant neutralizing solution.*"

"Oh, my God," Burch breathed, slumping.

"*A restricted leak would be no problem. However, with the flow released on several decks, the solution will fail to keep the induction coolant inert. I have estimated seventeen-point-three-nine minutes before the coolant eats through the subflooring and contaminates the entire ship with Wade-Gauberg trichloride ammonia. Of course, the gas will not harm the ship, but personnel are in immediate danger until repairs*" *can be made. Since Captain Kirk is unconscious, I am forced to make a decision. The Enterprise is surrendered to you, on the condition that you effect immediate evacuation of all crew people on board the vessel. Please reply."*

Kirk unconscious?

Paul Burch withered into the command chair. The light left his eyes. With the dullness of rain striking mud, he groaned, "That's it. We're finished."

My whole body tingled, an electrode of conflicting emotions as Rittenhouse slowly and thoughtfully responded. *"Mr. Spock,"* he began, *"Captain Kirk is totally incapacitated?"*

*"Sir,"* Spock answered with a razor-edge of controlled impatience, *"Captain Kirk is dying. We have nineteen percent casualties among the crew. Dr. McCoy is fighting for the Captain's life even as the trichloride threatens it. Speed is essential, Vice-Admiral. You must clear personnel from this ship. We now have fifteen-point-eight minutes. I am ordering my crew to the transporter rooms."* Urgency pushed through his forced coolness, and came out in a raised voice and a get-your-stupid-ass-moving stab in each word.

"It's all over," Brian murmured behind me. "Without *Enterprise*, we're helpless."

Burch stared at nothing, his mouth buried behind whitened fingers. He didn't respond at all.

*"Very well, Spock."* Rittenhouse's tone carried abject triumph, a definite salt of condescension. *"I've ordered Potempkin and Lincoln to move in to close-transport range so that you can transport independently of each others' pads. Have the excess of your crew meet at a central point."*

*"Acknowledged. All persons not beaming out from our transporter rooms will meet in sickbay."*

*"Mr. Spock, I think it's very curious that the flow tract insulation system failed coincidentally with a one-in-a-million rupture by phaser fire from outside. Would you care to explain that while Potempkin and Lincoln move into position?"*

So Rittenhouse suspected a trick. He did, however, move the two starships into *Enterprise*'s immediate space, probably figuring the deaths of the whole crew, no matter how circumstantial, would be impossible to explain to Command. And he needed friends at Command.

Working even Vulcan patience to the bone, Spock's voice, clear and resonant, flowed through subspace. *"Your phaser fire, Vice-Admiral, cut laterally across the neck of the ship, where, as you know, the flow tract's main plumbing is closest to the outer skin of the ship. It also happens to be the location of a starship's insulation system battery core. The chances of such a hit weakening both systems are eight thousand—"*

*"Potempkin and Lincoln are almost in position, Spock. Give us the coordinates of your sickbay."* Rittenhouse spoke with a triumphant drawl, insulting Spock by cutting him off. He knew he had us.

Burch knew it too. All this time he had been sitting there absorbing it. "Brian," he rasped, "inform the crew. I'm going to surrender the dreadnought before more lives are lost."

Bells went off in my head. Finished. Over. No more Kirk to lean on, to draw from.

Yet I still felt his strength. He was still with me, even in defeat. My heart didn't skip the beat I expected to lose once I didn't have Kirk's presence to buffet me. The scaffolding hadn't collapsed. A true hero would know—take defeat with dignity. Die well.

Burch touched the com button on the arm of his chair. *"Pompeii, this is Paul Burch. I hereby relinquish—"*

"Wait!"

I found myself beside him, both hands stinging, palms cupped over the com. Burch gawked at me. So did everyone else. So did I, in a way. What was I doing?

The scaffolding held. I *knew*.

"Just wait."

We watched the forward viewscreen as *Potempkin* and *Lincoln* pulled up to a limp *Enterprise* and dropped their shields to accept transporter beams.

Brian came down to me. "Piper, don't prolong it. The fight's over. Believe me, it hurts me more—"

"Shut up."

Paul Burch cupped his hand over mine in a wholly patronizing way and cleared his knotted throat to gently say, "Lieutenant, we shan't give up entirely . . . we'll carry our fight on to Command. Perhaps we've done enough. But for now, the time has come to end it."

I heard none of it. Still watching the two enemy starships pull up to *Enterprise*, I let only his defeatism seep through if not the actual words, and then only deep enough to nudge a response. I turned my eyes slowly to his, and narrowed them, trying to osmose the truth to him since he couldn't figure it out for himself.

My whisper nailed down the implications, syllable by syllable. "You don't understand. Kirk knows what he's doing."

He frowned. "But Kirk is a casualty." Then he shook his head. "You don't think—"

Phaser beams from *Enterprise* incised the blackness of space.

*Potempkin* writhed like a choking animal and veered away from *Enterprise,* her unshielded hulls ablaze with blue lightning and molten shell matter.

*Enterprise* fired on *Lincoln* an instant later, not waiting to assess the damage on Tutakai's ship. Red knives of light scored her primary hull, jumped space and ate at the port nacelle until *Lincoln* also vectored away. Subspace filled with panicked orders and responses between them and Rittenhouse. But before *Pompeii* could move in, *Enterprise*'s shields popped back up and she rose upward, away from her victims.

Burch pushed himself half out of the command chair, only to drop back into it. "How—"

"Kirk's not hurt," I said, hoping it wasn't just a guess. A vision plagued me—him standing just off the viewer while Mr. Spock sang the sad dirge of surrender.

"But how did you know?"

Several answers popped into my head, but they all seemed a little too pompous. No matter how I said it, I would somehow be taking credit for Kirk's artistic bluff. So I shrugged.

"Don't drop our shields!" Burch snapped, enthused. "Magnificent! Kirk is a brilliant rogue! I'd never have possessed the . . . the . . ."

"Moxie?" I suggested.

"Broxon, what's the damage on those two?" Terry shook herself out of a trance created by Kirk's bold deception. "Damage? Oh . . . oh. *Potempkin* is moving in again, but she's keeping her starboard side protected. *Lincoln* got hit harder. Nash'll be out of it for a few minutes. Their warp drive is out completely . . . navigation bank is ruptured . . . port impulse thrusters are badly damaged. She's still maneuverable, but she'll have to come about in a big circle. My scanner shows—"

"Sir!" Ensign Hopton interrupted. "Rittenhouse is ordering *Hornet* in. He also said something I didn't understand about getting their phasers operable again. Doesn't make sense. *Pompeii* hasn't been fired on."

Burch looked at me. "Didn't you say Chief Engineer Scott had sabotaged their phasers?"

"Yes," I said. "They must have found it."

"It's all right. It bought us time. Take the helm again, Lieutenant. And—thank you."

Color rose in my cheeks; I felt its heat as I took the helm, with little time to rest in his lauding. *Pompeii* had found our tampering and bypassed it, able now to use, not phasers, but photon torps. Before we could breathe again, *Star Empire* took two salvos at short range. The ship rattled hard. Not a person on the bridge remained standing when the impact dissolved. A second later came sustained phaser fire from Captain Leedson's *Hornet,* tipping the dreadnought hard to starboard. Out of sheer empathy I felt our shields weaken as I clutched the deck brace of my chair to keep from rolling. Sparks flew everywhere. Relays snapped, circuits overloaded and burned, filling the bridge with an electrical stench. Somewhere near me I heard feet scrape the deck and people coughing.

"Li Wang!" Burch choked. "Try to lock down the grav compensator! Engage the damage control computers like Piper showed you!"

When the gravity stabilized I pulled my battered,

aching limbs back into the helm chair and tried to keep the dreadnought a moving target. It couldn't be any more dangerous than hovering still in space. At least they would have to work to aim at us.

"Sir, I think we should return fire, okay?" I suggested.

"What?" Burch corporealized through an acrid cloud of green chemical smoke and choked, "Can you make the computer do it, so we don't waste energy?"

"Well, I can't speak for the computer, but it should—"

The ceiling exploded over us. A hammer blow of raw force pounded my head and shoulders, flinging me sideways from my seat onto the lower deck level. Electrical eruptions sparkled all around me as panicking circuits searched for power relays and tapped each other, then dueled for supremacy. Each system thought its duty more valuable than the others, and fought to survive, to preserve and implement its programming. In order to get back on my feet, I had to do the same thing. Remember my programming—trained reflexes—survival instincts Star Fleet had drilled into me. How boring they had become on the thousandth-odd training drill, yet today, recalled, they were buoys. I clung to them. *Captain, did you ever run on pure training reflex like this? Did you ever have to fight for lucid thought? Tell me you did so I can deal with my human fallibility—tell me anything. Let me hear your voice. Let me know I didn't guess wrong.*

Knees . . . where were mine? I crawled forward through green fog and hot stench, careful to avoid bare electrical burnouts after almost putting my hand down on open circuits. The bridge sizzled. The fans clicked on and the smoke looped toward the vents. I pulled myself onto tingling feet and blinked my stinging eyes clear.

On the upper walkway, Brian Silayna and Ensign Li Wang bent over another form.

My heart thudded in my throat. Burch.

We needed him. We needed his rank on our side. We needed his familiarity with Rittenhouse. We needed a command authority, even a semicompetent one, to hold onto.

And there he lay.

I moved through a kaleidoscope toward them. Bile rose in my throat.

His entire left side was a matt of scorched fabric, fused with skin. Blood and flesh, a black and red panorama of gore, bubbled up through melted threads. The smell turned my stomach.

"Dead?" I hoped.

Brian shook his head. "Not yet." He punched a com botton. "We need somebody from Sickbay on the bridge right away with a burn unit and an anti-grav."

A trembling male voice answered, *"Coming. How many injuries?"*

"Just one."

The most important one.

Mercifully Burch remained unconscious. We lived his agony for him.

We were alone.

# Chapter Ten

THE BRIDGE OF Star Fleet's ultimate war machine was a barren place as Brian, Terry Broxon, the ensigns, and I watched helplessly as two midshipmen carried our salvation to the turbolift. Burch was the only person on board who knew anything about the *Star Empire*, and even he hadn't known all that much. The ship was in the hands of ignorance.

"We're as good as dead," Ensign Novelwry said, and nearly choked on his words. Behind us on the viewscreen, two more of Rittenhouse's henchmen-run starships powered around us ominously, glowing like the bands of violet light of a faraway sun: Captain Leedson on *Hornet*, Captain Tutakai on *Potempkin*. Cronies bringing their twisted dreams with them, bought with the very starships they commanded, promised admiralties in the "new" Fleet, with the Klingon Empire dismantled and its planets in Federation conservatorship. A soiled vision at best.

How deeply into Star Fleet Command did this corruption run?

"What do you think we should do?" I whispered to Brian.

The faces around me were solemn, afraid, seeking strength in each other that hadn't fermented yet. It wasn't there to be tapped.

*"Brian . . ."*

He glanced around. Surrender clutched him; I could see it happening, see his mind give over to the crutch of his abilities, taking refuge in the numerological sense of engineering. He withdrew from decision-making before my very eyes, collected his equipment, paused, and stared at me. "Take it, Piper."

Panic seized me. "The hell I will, damn it! A ship like this? Are you crazy?"

"It's your place. Look. *They* can't."

*"I* can't. Sorry." I dropped into the helm seat. If he was pushed hard enough, Brian could command. But the hand I played was a bad one, I realized as I heard the lift doors open and swallow my only ace, taking most of me with him. The ensigns looked blankly around, waiting for someone to take charge. Behind me there was a faint clicking.

*"Enterprise,* this is *Star Empire."* Terry Broxon's voice. "Commander Burch has become a casualty. We have no command-level officers above the rank of lieutenant, and no one at all trained for this dread-nought. Can you supply us with an alternate commander?" Her voice shivered. The fear was surfacing. In the hands of children, the dreadnought was powerless and foundering.

Through the terror a firm, warm voice cut, it's timbre alone assuaging the horrible isolation. *"Kirk here,* Star Empire. *Damage report."*

Terry cleared her throat. "Main shields seven and

twelve down completely, port flank shields sixteen through twenty severely weakened. Parts of the bridge are destroyed, but we're still operational. Engineering reports impulse power damaged but under repair, estimating twenty standard minutes to eighty percent power. Auxiliary control and—"

*"Enough. Ship's status?"*

"Running on a skeleton crew. Burch never expected battle. Most of us have never been on a starship. The ship seems stable at the moment . . . but . . . God, I don't want to die in space. . . ."

*"Belay that, mister. Man your post. You're at red alert."* Kirk's voice was a buoy. A moment later, as if providentially, the viewscreen cleared and we got a roomful of the face we very much needed to draw upon.

I flinched. Behind the Captain, Mr. Spock was batting smoke from a shattered computer console, and Engineer Scott had taken the helm. What had happened to Sulu? Where was Uhura? Were things that bad on *Enterprise* too?

Terry had recovered herself. Kirk must have known training would prevail if, like a computer, it received the right code. And he knew the code.

*"Star Empire,"* he began carefully, "we can't beam anyone aboard your vessel with shields up." It sounded like lesson number one in tactics at Academy. I wondered why he couldn't direct transporter beams to the places on our ship where the shields were down; then I remembered those places were in the warp nacelles, where it wouldn't do any good to beam a living organism. Fried matter couldn't pilot a starship. I gripped the console in front of me, sinking into the

sturdy face, beaded with sweat—*Enterprise*'s bridge looked hot—and wondered how he could remain so unfazed. We were under attack by three starships and a destroyer, and he looked like a housecat in a window. "Give me a rundown of bridge personnel."

Terry nodded, though Kirk couldn't see her. "Ensign Li Wang at navigations, Ensign Novelwry at weapons control, Ensigns Carr and Hopton standing by at engineering, Lieutenant J. G. Broxon at communications, Lieutenant Piper at helm."

"Put Piper on."

*Damn, I knew it, I knew it!* "Pi—" My throat closed up.

*"Star Empire,* do you read?"

"P-Piper here."

"Can you handle that helm?"

"Hell if I know, sir."

"I can command you from h—"

The ship shuddered and lurched to starboard, pushed by a photon blast on the underside of the primary hull. I clung desperately to my position, hoping against hope the ship's shields were still up on our impulse drive. Ensign Carr was knocked insensible on the upper walkway, and for too long Hopton stood there and stared at her. Before us, the viewscreen smoked and crackled, distorting the Captain's comforting face until it wasn't comforting anymore. There was a maroon flash as his shoulder seemed to swing toward me and he turned to issue orders on *Enterprise,* but we heard only the mockery of his voice translated into static.

"Captain!" I shouted. "Sensors . . . We've been hit in the sensory." Mashing my intercom, I called, "Sensory, anybody down there? Scanner, you down there?"

*"(Cough) bet we are . . . took a salvo in our frickin' angular light retrieval unit. Whatchall doin' up there, Piper, playin' poker?"*

"Can you put that thing back together? We've got to keep contact with *Enterprise*. Kirk's commanding us from there."

*"You tellin' me communications went with us? How do I get a transfer off this shuttle?"*

"Come on, Scanner, quit screwing around! We're going to die here and I'm not done with myself yet!"

*"Yeah, yeah, 'knowledged, workin' on it."*

"Terry, is that channel open?"

Broxon turned to me, her pale features curled in effort. "It's open. But I'm getting intraship distortion."

"Clear it."

"What do you think I'm trying to do!"

"Okay . . . okay . . . okay. . . ." My hands spread out across the helm as though I could hold it all together if it just knew I was here. I glared into the bubbling form of Captain Kirk, who was talking to me, doing everything I could to acquire by osmosis some talent at Vulcan mind melding. "Getting any of that, Terry?"

"Mark . . . six. . . . Course . . . two-zero . . . one. . . . Mark six. . . . Course two-zero . . . eight . . . one. . . ."

"Mark six. Got it. Plot that, Li."

"P-p-lotted."

"Take it easy. We're still here."

I touched the helm controls. A simulation . . . a game. Not real. Mistakes wouldn't hurt.

The ship swayed into motion, pivoting on its primary hull. The movement was innately graceful, not like the crawl of the injured dinosaur we were. It was a brilliant maneuver, putting *Enterprise* and us at each other's oblique backs, presenting full shields to the attacking fleet. "Captain, you're something." I hit the intercom again. "Sarda, where are you?"

Buzz, crackle, fizz . . .

*"I am presently in auxiliary control."*

"We need you on the bridge."

*"Acknowledged. On my way."*

Well, that felt better.

We took another phaser shot from *Lincoln* that crippled our port flank shield, and as the blue lightning skittered across space near enough to rattle our teeth, *Enterprise* returned fire at one-half-power phasers. Kirk evidently wasn't ready to strike with full force. Surprisingly the strike was just enough and well enough aimed to force *Lincoln* to veer off us. "Nerve," I muttered, "and integrity."

Everyone on the bridge jumped at the sudden parting of the lift doors. Sarda appeared behind me.

I rose slowly from my chair, our gazes matched in mutual tension. Vulcan training bisqued his fear, but it was certainly there.

Gripping the rail, I looked up. "You have to assume command."

His hands tightened at his sides. The amber eyes flooded with thoughts. "I am . . ." he began, "unqualified to command."

"You're a Vulcan. That alone qualifies you. Look at these ensigns. They can't do it alone. Your abilities—

this ship is nothing but a giant weapon. That's *your* speciality."

"Then I will assume weapons control."

"There's nobody commanding, Sarda! Nobody to tell you when to fire, or where or how much, or what potency. You've got to do it!"

His lips pressed together. Clouds gathered in his eyes, heavying them, but they were glittering with something intensely new. He stepped down to my level. We were very alone in the universe.

Sarda spoke quietly, firmly. "You will command," he said. It was a mystically soft urging, one that knew me. "It is your *Kolinahr*."

> *Tame the craggy agonies of toil's time.*
> *Memory and memoring comes late,*
> *comes shattery, scattery.*
> *When all is done, it is not*
> *to die—*
> *It is to die well.*

Memory . . .

Something unconventional.

Sarda's eyes, his taciturn expression pushing to me a ripe emotion—confidence—crystallized into sharp focus before me. I swayed slightly, and recovered.

"Lieutenant Broxon," I called, "take the helm!"

Sarda moved to the weapons control position. The command chair exhaled under my thigh.

"Raise secondary shields," I said.

Terry turned to me, as did Li Wang. "Secondary? What's that?"

"This ship has triple shielding. Find them and put them up. We're taking this hammering for nothing. We should be protecting *Enterprise,* not the other way around."

"Us? We're a bunch of midshipmen in diapers!" Her voice was chattering with incredulity.

I waved my hand suicidally. "Ah, what've they got that we haven't got? A few years and some laurels to sit on. Sarda, can you pinpoint optimum humanitarian targets on those starships?"

"Will attempt to do so. Sensors are failing."

"Scanner, what's the buzz?"

*"We're all having a nice quilting bee down here. 'Fore long we'll have y'all a fine blanket."*

"I need forward scanning."

*"I can give you forward port."*

"I'll take it. Terry, lean us starboard, point-three-three. Put our sensors between us and them." I leaned forward, feeling my eyes snug up until I was manufacturing a prime squint, and tired to make sense of the misting shapes on the viewscreen. "Hopton . . ."

"Yeah. Huh?"

"See if you can plug into the library computer's gateway node."

"This stupid bull doesn't have a library computer," he spat.

"It has a ship's mainframe system, doesn't it?"

"Yeah, but—"

"Then plug me in, mister!"

He stared for a moment. Then: "Aye-aye."

Shields didn't keep the ship from rocking under Rittenhouse's battery. No doubt, he was out to kill us. Surely he knew by now his career was dust. He had

nothing to lose. No creature could be more dangerous.

"Where are those secondary shields?" I demanded.

"I'm looking for them," Broxton reported, playing
monitor against console in a relay of jump codes and
indices.

"Good enough," I murmured. She didn't hear me,
and I was glad that she didn't because it certainly
wasn't good enough. I slouched back into the command chair as though it was a lump of gorsy moss on
my home planet, with one calf pulled up onto the other
knee. I must have looked absurd. Realizing that,
though not mending it, I forgave the ensigns for not
handing their fealty over to me at the outset. They
didn't know me, after all; I was only a lieutenant, and I
wasn't even in uniform.

My eyes narrowed. I started thinking. What was it
Spock had said about this ship? Big . . . massive . . .
like a chubby *Enterprise*, streamlined, with extra limbs
and invisible teeth. Transwarp drive in experimental
stages . . . if it worked, they were going to mount it on
a new design of heavy cruiser sometime in the military
future.

"See, moose," I muttered. "Brand-new, and already you're obsolete." I sighed. Warp or transwarp,
it didn't matter here and now. We had to stay sublight
to hash this out. And damned if I was going to take this
ship into warp.

A slight breeze, very soft, whiffed my hair at the
side of my face. "May I ask what you're thinking?"
His voice almost made me faint. What was it about
Vulcans? Where did they learn that controlled baritone
warble?

For a long moment I just gazed at Sarda, as though trying to inflict an emotion on him. My hand moved away from my mouth. "I'm thinking about the phaser banks. What good is it to have five phaser banks if you can't use them all at once?"

He nodded thoughtfully. "Logical."

I sneered. Didn't he realize I was *asking* him? Since I got approval for my "logic," I forged on. "Can two or more banks fire at once with any accuracy?"

If a Vulcan could shrug, he did. "Unknown. I presume you mean at different targets."

"Of course."

"Perhaps . . . with the assistance of the computer system—"

I vaulted out of my slouch. "Hopton, link the mainframe to weapons control and free it over to Sarda."

"Yes, ma'am." He quivered over the console. "Connectivity established."

"Systemwide?"

"I . . . think so. It should be."

"Go for it, Sarda."

"I cannot guarantee that such a procedure will work, or even that I am capable of engineering it."

"I don't give a flying—I don't care what the guarantees are. Just do it. Terry, can you make this moose move?"

"Moving the moose, ma'am. Where to?" Were those good spirits I heard?

"Pivot on our latitudinal axis seven-point-two-five degrees. No! I mean *thirty*-seven-point-two-five. Sorry."

"Thirty-seven-twenty-five, aye. Executing."

"Full impulse power."

*"Seventy-four percent impulse available, Piper,"* Brian filtered up to me from somewhere deep in the engineering decks. *"That's all."*

"It'll do. Best speed sublight, Terry."

We left *Enterprise* behind, and I sent a silent thought to Captain Kirk. I hoped he would understand.

"To die well."

My maneuver, with a little adjusting for clumsiness and lack of visibility, lowered *Star Empire* into the core of the gauntlet. Starships all around were shifting, or so our nominal sensors said, vying with me for position. Apparently I surprised them by moving at all, much less taking an initiative. I intended to use that surprise.

*"Christmastime,"* Scanner's voice blurted from below decks.

"Oh! Great!" I stood up, looking into an almost-clear star field with ships resolving into form. The screen flickered twice, then stabilized. "Scanner, I love you forever."

*"I'll take a full lieutenancy instead."* He sounded satisfied. I could imagine his impish smile, and I smiled too.

"Sarda?" I prodded.

"There has been some memory erosion. . . ."

"From the damage?"

"Negative. . . . I believe it is from tampering by inexperienced personnel. It seems they were attempting to set up a domino contagion or a logic bomb, perhaps to prevent override by prefix code."

"Hmmm . . . preventative medicine."

"Essentially."

"Not a bad idea. Can you finish what they started?"

He straightened and half turned. "I am not Mr. Spock," he said with un-Vulcan emphasis.

"That's all right," I soothed, holding my hand out to him. "That's . . . fine. Whatever you're doing, keep on doing it."

"I will," he said. Uncharacteristically this followed: "And thank you, Piper."

I smiled, though he couldn't. "Anytime. Terry, don't stop our movement. Use all the innerspace you've got. Li, plot a full arc that swings us around and continually presents our bow to the fleet."

"Okay . . . trying. Lieutenant! *Enterprise* is matching our move, except in mirror form. She's coming about!"

My feet actually left the deck. "That's my Captain! Get me circular scanners. I want circumference of the ship on these monitors so I can see what's going on."

"Scanners operational."

Just then, the destroyer *Pompeii* fell into our forward viewscreen and an equally clear picture of Rittenhouse jammed into my brain. How smug he was. How self-righteous. How did he dare profess policy for the entire galaxy? His evangelizing had been an irritant in my mind since I left *Pompeii,* injecting me with a desire to smack him down and read him the UFP Articles of Federation, presupposing universal respect for intelligent life-form rights and fundamental freedoms, the right to self-determination, even for the Klingons.

"Terry, where are those secondary screens?"

"Almost . . . got 'em! You want them up?"

"No!"

She looked at me.

235

"No," I repeated, stretching out my fingers, sculpting events as best I could. "Hold on that . . . keep your finger on it . . . let them think we're broken. Hold . . . good . . . good . . ."

I sensed more than saw the other ships gathering themselves to fire on us. There was an infinitesimal glow on *Pompeii*'s bow . . . or was there?

"Shields!"

"Shields up."

The ships fired. Lids drifted over my eyes. I waited.

The next sound, breaking out during the rocking of the *Star Empire* beneath us, was the voices of Broxon, Hopton, and Li raised in a hat-throwing victory shout.

"Look at that!"

"It's bouncing off!"

It was. Phaser fire was dancing in a corona of electrical jag-tooths around us, but our doubled shields held, and we still had trinary shields to go to if we needed them.

What a ship. "Rittenhouse," my teeth vibrated, "take this. Fire!"

The auxiliary monitors and the main viewscreen flashed with blue lances spidering out from several points on *Star Empire*. I felt like they were coming out of my very eyes. Each made good strikes on vulnerable points on *Pompeii*, *Lincoln*, *Hornet*, and *Potempkin*, although the beams that hit *Potempkin* were glancing.

"Again!"

The spider shots branched a second time.

"Lieutenant!" Li called. "*Enterprise* is firing. She's looping in and out like a fly, distracting the two ascent-plane ships!"

More cheers rose from us as *Enterprise* swooped

past our bow at full sublight, potshotting until *Hornet* and *Lincoln* veered away from us.

"Damn, he's good," I muttered. "Cease fire. Take it easy, Sarda. I don't want to kill anybody. I want to discourage a fight, not insist on one."

"Agreed. Most wise, Lieutenant."

"That's the hard part, isn't it?" Terry asked. "They want to blast us, but we don't want to blast them."

"Well . . . I don't know about Captains Leedson and Tutakai or Commodore Nash, but Rittenhouse had blood in his eyes. He wants the Klingons, but Burch arranged it so he has to get us first. Damn political upheavals . . . wasting lives, resources . . ."

"It's real big, isn't it, Piper?"

I looked at her, absorbing the uneasy awe in her face, and suddenly I realized how young she was . . . how young we all were. I felt like an older sister.

"It's a major shakedown." I couldn't lie to her. "There'll be plenty of courts-martial. Star Fleet against Star Fleet . . . things won't be the same."

She shivered, and quit asking questions.

Distraction. I inhaled slowly. "Status?"

"Secondary shields two through sixteen are pretty mucked up."

"That doesn't tell me anything, Broxon."

"Drained sixty-five percent. Also, flank shields and shield twelve amidships down forty percent."

"What do we do now?" Hopton grumbled, staring into the screen. "How do you handle a standoff? I mean, what if they don't give up?"

Frowning, I hunched my shoulders and hoped for direction. If only I could get communications back. *Kirk, I need your voice right now. I need to know what to do. What would you do?*

"I know. . . ." My throat was dry. "You tip the odds, that's what."

That in itself was a question. Out in the star-rutted fabric of space, parts of the *Lincoln* were fading from white-hot to Antares red, metal flowing like lava where we had made our most direct hits.

"Let's surround them," I said.

Everyone looked at me as though I'd grown a third ear.

"Surround them?" Terry repeated, incredulous.

"Sure. We've got them outnumbered two to four."

"They'll laugh in our faces," Li Wang decided.

I wrinkled by nose. "Hell, they're eighty percent water, just like the rest of us. Move us to the outer perimeter, opposite *Enterprise*. Box them in between us and Kirk."

Wondering if I had slipped out of sanity's questionable noose, Terry and the ensigns doubtfully obeyed. Soon we had *Lincoln*, *Pompeii*, *Hornet*, and *Potempkin* hovering in space between ourselves and *Enterprise*. Now to salt the clouds.

"Arm photon torpedoes."

Once again, many eyes touched me. This time they were filled with apprehension. They didn't want to kill any more than I did.

Sarda carefully said, "Piper . . . may I point out that photon salvos the strength of *Star Empire*'s, fired at so close a range, would disintegrate ships as damaged as *Lincoln* and *Hornet* presently are.

*Disappointed in me, my friend? Do you think you're the only one who is forced to take life with your personal gifts?*

"I know," I told him. "Arm photons anyway. Their

sensors will pick up the energy flux and they'll *think* we're crazy or desperate enough to fire on them, even to the death. I want the upper hand, Sarda. I want them scared of me."

The respect that mellowed his face was empowering. He murmured his approval. "An inspired tactic."

Deeply honored, I whispered, "Thanks." My voice cracked, though.

It worked. As we watched, *Hornet* and *Potempkin* retreated, trying to put distance between us. *Lincoln* couldn't move as fast, but limped slowly away. Even in crippled condition, slipping away to tend their wounds, the starships, any starship, were cathedrals of lights and beauty, given character by their battle wounds. Too bad the wounds hadn't been won honorably.

"Honor's everything."

"I'm sorry?" Sarda queried. "You said something?"

"Who, me?" I responded, savoring the image of those ships' bridges and the panic I was causing. "I never say anything. Terry, keep us moving. Follow them. Let them be the prey for a change."

With catlike smoothness, *Star Empire* surged through space in pursuit of the retreating ships.

Sarda appeared at my side. "I must advise caution," he said in a low voice. "It may be unwise to push too far."

"But they should know we *will* push." The tapestry of starships was breaking up before us, disbanding or regrouping, questioning their motives, I hoped, and getting a taste of the rank corruption they had taken part in. "Taste it, you slugs, you captains . . . look what you're wasting. Analysis, Sarda . . . are they giving up?"

"My response could only be an assumption, and I prefer not to do that," my Vulcan colleague said as casually as if we were discussing cultures in a petri dish. "It does seem that we have put them into a degree of disarray."

"Does it seem satisfying to you?"

He couldn't keep a nibble of honest pride from seeping into his response. Between us and *Potempkin,* two bits of flotsam collided and blitzed into a flores-cent arm, then died. "I admit to a sense of success. Still, it would be premature of me to—" He froze, staring.

Broxon jumped to her feet. "Piper! Look!"

From well below our viewscreen swung the battered sleekness of *Pompeii,* coming about bow to bow with us, gathering herself for—what?

Was Sarda right? Had I pushed Rittenhouse too far? Pushed victory headlong into menace, with us as the menace? I understood now about winning with dig-nity—this might've been Kirk's lesson to me when he refused to pursue that Klingon vessel once he'd dam-aged it. Lose with dignity, but win with dignity too.

I stared in horror as *Pompeii* wheeled up on her rim, leveled off at an angry slant, and leaned through space toward us.

"He's on collision course!" Terry's voice cracked.

Hopton gasped; Novelwry stumbled to the turbolift and fled the bridge entirely.

"Sarda—"

"Confirmed. Collision course."

"Lunatic!" I gasped as *Pompeii* increased speed. "Quick, Terry, how does transwarp work?"

"How do I know?" Her face screwed up in agony of desperation.

"Find out!"

"I can't . . ." She started crying, fingers tumbling hopelessly over a board now inert with complication. "I can't find it! Oh, God!"

*Pompeii* angled straight in at full sublight. Suddenly the truth dawned; I could fight, but I couldn't kill. Not yet. *He* could. . . . Rittenhouse had chosen and kept *Pompeii* as his flagship, now I knew, because that was the ultimate purpose of destroyers—suicide when necessary. Triple shielding . . . miracles . . . nothing would deflect the force of a thundering destroyer.

"Not now. . . ." It was a dead whisper. A small sound, maybe a sob, caught in my throat as I put my hand on Terry's console keyboard and tapped out an emergency automatic comsync.

*TO . . .*

*Pompeii* veered in, damage crackling.

*DIE . . .*

My eyes squeezed shut as *Pompeii* swelled in our screens.

*WELL.*

I forced my eyes open, refusing to be snuffed out without facing my enemy, presenting every semblance of honor left in me. To my left, there was a soft clicking as Sarda searched for a weapon that might save us, but he couldn't find one, nor could he find it in himself to use it even if it was there. His thoughts reached to mine even over the few steps that separated us. We stood in a unity of souls, and waited to die.

The screen went ice-white with brilliant destruction, then glassy with needles of blue-green energy and phosphorous gases. I braced for impact. Spine straight. Legs locked. *Star Empire* lolled beneath us as the main screen cauliflowered with mercury-rich fireworks.

My hand closed around the arm of the command chair. Death wasn't too bad after all.

*Look. This is a strange poetry. I begin to understand.*

"What?" I asked aloud. Sarda's thoughts washed in my head, but he didn't speak.

"It wasn't us . . . ." Broxon whispered.

It was *Pompeii*. Had been *Pompeii*. Now it was bloom upon bloom of matter-antimatter freed to destroy itself. Waves of aftershock rocked us.

I stumbled forward, gaping. "Yeeeeoow!"

When I landed on the deck again, the screen was clearing, decorated with flotsam as it sizzled and bumped our deflectors. Then, from low to starboard came the opalescent cream flanks of the starship *Enterprise* bursting through the eruption's violent glitter.

At the last second, the starship arced away, narrowly avoiding collision with us, and for a blessed few seconds our screen was filled with her passing service lights and insignia. She rolled away, vectoring to a gentle distance, and completed the roll for victory.

"They did it!" I cried, pounding Terry's shoulder.

*"Son of a gun,"* Scanner buzzed from the bowels of the com system. *"Captain Enterprise kicked his butt!"*

Within minutes, *Hornet*, *Lincoln*, and *Potempkin* were surrendering to James Kirk.

All my bridge people but Sarda had slipped below decks to collect themselves. The two of us waited for more capable officers to take over. Evidently Sulu and

Uhura had been launched in another Arco attack sled; they'd been waiting for a break in our shields, hoping to dock with us and come aboard. If only I'd had communications, it all would've been so simple.

*"Transporter room to Lieutenant Piper."*

"Piper . . . here."

*"Captain Kirk is on board with Mr. Spock, ma'am."*

"Kill the 'ma'am,' will you? I'm really tired of it."

*"Yes, ma'am."*

"I'll be right there."

*"Piper, this is Kirk."*

I bit my lip. "Yes, sir."

*"That was a very impressive display of resourcefulness and altruism, Lieutenant. I haven't seen such a successful improvisation since . . . well, it's been a while."*

"Thank you, Captain. Do you want me to join you there, sir?"

*"No need,"* he said softly, and his face formed in my mind. *"Remain on your bridge. This time, we'll come to you. Kirk out."*

The com clicked off. I slumped, covered my face with clammy hands that felt detached from my body, and collapsed against the arm of the command chair. They could *give* me the goddamned ship before I'd crawl back into that chair.

Shivers wracked my body, but I couldn't cry. I tried, knowing I needed the release, but the episode wasn't real yet. I couldn't entirely give in. Not here, not on the bridge. Later, though, in the privacy of my quarters . . .

There was a hand on my arm, and with it came a gentle wave of telepathic support.

Sarda was standing with me, holding my elbow. His other hand was tucked behind his back, as though he dared make only half a commitment. My shivering abated, nerve by nerve. I put both feet on the floor.

"Congratulations, Piper," he said quietly.

We shook hands solemnly.

"And to you," I said.

# Chapter Eleven

". . . FOR CONSPICUOUS BRAVERY under fire, for loyalty and adherence to Star Fleet and its humanitarian code, and for innovative reasoning in a situation which defied standard policy. As Chief-of-Staff for Military Forces, I am honored to present you with the Federation of Planetary Systems Congressional Medal of Valor with star cluster, and confer upon you the rank of Lieutenant Commander. Congratulations. You've displayed the rare gift of uniqueness within the system. Star Fleet takes pride in your strength of individuality."

The image of Rittenhouse's cottony hair and blue eyes dissolved before me and rematerialized into the leathery, dark-eyed, grey-framed face of Rear Admiral Baldridge.

Applause rose behind him, rippling through the hangar bay of what was now my home ship. An honor, they said, to have the ceremony on board *Enterprise* instead of in the Academy Colosseum. I swear I felt "the honor" stick right through my uniform's fabric and into my skin. A sea of dignitaries, both civilian and military, spread before me, flanking Baldridge's crooked smile. They, in turn, were framed by a colorful line of government banners, seals, shields, standards, coats-of-arms, and signets from all the member-systems and trusteeships within the Federation. The air-conditioning breeze fluttered them, but I didn't feel it at all. Behind me and to the right stood Sarda, Scanner, Brian, and Terry, each wearing a glittering Silver Palm and Star for Conspicuous Heroism. Behind them, Burch's forty-odd crewpeople stood with their Bronze Clusters for Bravery.

But the gazes I felt most strongly came not from them, but from the line of *Enterprise* officers directly in front of the podium. Somehow I had yet to summon the grit to thank them for this travesty. For the hundredth time I wished they'd told me their plans, instead of surprising me by recommending me to become the youngest recipient of the Federation's second-highest award. Thanks, guys. Thanks a lot.

My legs knotted. Baldridge's cool, dry grip squished over my clammy palm and pumped my arm.

Hardly audible, I rasped, "Thank you."

He cupped his other ancient hand over the broadcast link and confided, "You helped save Star Fleet as we know it, Commander, with your ingenuity."

"I . . . had help, sir."

He nodded, let go of my hand, and turned to the crowd. "I believe the caterers have finished setting up the buffet, so on this heroic note, let's by all means indulge. There are two buffets, so if you'll line up either on the port or starboard decks . . ."

His instructions blurred to a senseless hum in my head. I remained at attention behind him, mostly because my legs wouldn't unlock. At least I was in uniform this time. One particular face surged strength from the first row. Merete winked at me and smiled. A Silver Palm sat unused on the table. Her service log would read that she'd been recommended for the medal, but had refused it. Her decision was right for her. I'd asked them not to do this to me either, but they pushed me into it. Star Fleet needed it, they said. Something about morale. The fortitude to get through all the arrests and courts-martial about to happen. Solidify the fabric of the Fleet, they said. Okay, I said.

As I meandered through the crowd, my only real satisfaction came when I saw Sarda talking to Mr. Spock, speaking with a restrained Vulcan intensity as they headed for the tiered buffet tables. At least I'd accomplished that connection. The rest would be in Sarda's hands.

But my friend had taken one step, however nominal, toward home.

The hangar deck became a cacophony of social congratulations for me, and I thank-you'ed my way along, feeling conspicuous. Everybody paused to admire the dazzling gold-and-platinum medallion hanging from its tricolored ribbon around my neck. Funny . . . there hadn't been any pin after all.

I endured the handshakes and shoulder thumps with surface grace. Enthusiasm was beyond me. They would have to live without it and be happy that I hadn't retired my commission and hopped the first transport back to Proxima.

"Tedious duty, Commander?"

I turned, but Captain Kirk was already walking at my side.

"Sorry, sir. I didn't think you were talking to me."

He nodded, repressing a grin. "A change in rank takes a little getting used to."

"I'm not in any rush," I grumbled, not meaning to convey my displacement to him. "Tedious? No, not at all."

His forefinger and thumb made a small sign between us. "Maybe just a little bit?"

He caught my straying gaze and I felt a sheepish smile break across my lips. "Maybe a little."

Satisfied, he turned his light brown eyes away and scanned the well-dressed crowd of interracial representatives. Ambassadors, officials, bureaucrats, politicians, officers, each with his, her, or its own reason for making an appearance at the honors ceremony. Kirk watched them casually, and I would forever be grateful that he averted his gaze from me at that uncomfortable moment.

"Captain," I began, "I never thanked you for offering me the honor of piloting *Star Empire* into space dock."

He pursed his lips in a tiny shrug. "No call for embarrassment. After all, it's no shame that you didn't know how."

My cheeks reddened again. "What's going to happen to the dreadnought, sir?"

"No decision yet, but the rumors lean toward its being decommissioned and dismantled. The Special Review Board may decide its existence was contrary to the principles of the Federation."

"And do you happen to be serving on that review board, by any chance?"

"By a certain chance."

"Hmm . . . good."

"Why, thank you." This time he did grin, warming the space around us. Captain Kirk's presence provided a shield from well-meaning congratulators. They seemed to leave me alone now that he and I were together. "Are you regretting your actions?" he asked. "If so, it's normal aftershock."

"Not regret, exactly. I do feel sad that all those people on *Pompeii* had to die because of Rittenhouse's misguidance. They were only following orders. His errors got them killed and got me a Medal of Valor."

"You'll find any honor has its cost, usually paid by someone else. The cost would've been much higher if we hadn't moved against them."

"I'm glad Dr. Boma slipped away from *Pompeii* in the Tycho. I never really felt he was the kind to be taken in by Rittenhouse."

"Boma was," he said, then paused, looking for accuracy, "a racist. He thought humans should prevail. But even above that he respected life. Once he realized Rittenhouse's plans to slaughter the dreadnought's crew, he engineered the power failure so you could escape from the brig, then slipped away. It takes a courageous man to admit he's wrong in midstream."

I sighed thoughtfully. "Yet, in a way, he's right. Humans do make the best commanders. But it's *because* of our flaws. I didn't understand that. I . . . had misconceptions too."

"We all do. Life is an ongoing classroom."

After we'd gone a few steps in companionable silence, I asked, "Any news on Commander Burch?"

"Dr. McCoy says he should be able to stand for the Medal of Honor presentation in another week or so."

"I'm glad he's getting it. He's the one who really

had courage. Command isn't his field, but he took it on anyway for the sake of galactic diversity."

"Plus it takes some of the sting out of your having to endure the Medal of Valor."

"Oh, *no*, sir—"

"Just a little?"

"Maybe just a little."

We shared a chuckle and a long mutual glance, relaxing that much more in each other's company.

Cagily I began, "I hear, what with the upset at Command, there are going to be some openings in the Admiralty."

He eyed me again, this time with a different edge. "So . . . ?"

We both knew exactly what I meant, and strode slowly through the crowd looking at each other, both waiting for the other to speak first. Finally I broke.

"So . . ." I parroted—and couldn't do it. I took refuge elsewhere. "Think they've got a place for me?" The last of it dissolved into lighter laughter, no matter how I fought for a straight face.

Kirk's chuckle eased the string of tension I'd run between us. "I wouldn't be at all surprised," he said. "Commander, have you ever been sailing? On the sea, I mean."

My turn to shrug. "There's not much wind on my home planet, sir."

His eyebrows bounced once. "I'd like to introduce you to it. I have a very old, very comfortable vintage schooner moored on San Francisco Bay. I think you'd appreciate her."

"Captain," I answered, "I'd relish that."

"We have . . . things to talk about. And I think we're both entitled to a weekend's shore leave, don't you? I could offer a few thoughts on what command is like, and even a tip or two on what it means to be close friends with a Vulcan."

Once again our gazes meshed, understanding flowing like a deep, cool wine between us. We knew each other, but not too much, not too deeply to smother the mystery.

"Yes, sir," I said with new strength.

That food was beginning to smell incredibly good.

# TYCHO CLASS LIGHT INTERCEPT

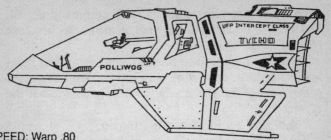

SPEED: Warp .80
CREW: One
ARMAMENTS: Two Forward Phasers
Rear Grapple with minor
capacity tractor beam

Design: Brian Thomas
Art: C. Paul

---

# ARCO CLASS ATTACK SLED

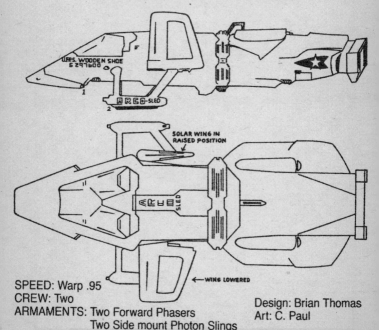

SPEED: Warp .95
CREW: Two
ARMAMENTS: Two Forward Phasers
Two Side mount Photon Slings

Design: Brian Thomas
Art: C. Paul